THE
SILENT
FOREST

Also by David Kummer

The Misery House: The House on the Hill (Book #1)
My Abigail: A Psychological Thriller
Until We Burn: A Psychological Thriller
Home: A Dystopian Journey

THE SILENT FOREST

BOOK 2

THE HOUSE ON THE HILL SERIES

DAVID KUMMER

Published by David Kummer

Edited by Marni Macrae
Cover design by Aspire Book Covers
Interior design by Jordon Greene

Printed in the United States of America

FIRST EDITION

Hardcover ISBN 979-8-8693-2985-1
Paperback ISBN 979-8-8693-2983-7

Fiction: Psychological Thrillers
Fiction: Ghosts
Fiction: Small Towns & Rural

This book is dedicated to
my mom, my grandma, and my wife,
who all taught me perseverance and how to overcome.
And, of course, to my cats for never leading me
into the silent forest.

PART 1
THE FIREWORKS

CHAPTER 1
NEW HAVEN (EDGE OF TOWN)

When her cat went missing, Mallory Clark lived in a single-story, clapboard house. It was her worst fear — losing Luna — and at first she blamed Roland, her husband. Her day would only get worse.

She'd always hoped, secretly, that Roland and she would die together. Two soft hospital beds, side-by-side. Apart from him, Mallory only had her sister. They'd all lived here forever, and they always would.

But on the day when her cat went missing — taken — Mallory was distracted. She'd been in the garden for a couple hours. With soft, warm dirt against her shins, she cradled a basket of tomatoes and peppers. The pressure in her knees was getting worse, and the sharp pain in her lower back had returned.

"Lord almighty." Mallory stood up and groaned with a hand on her spine. "Break time, I think."

She lifted the basket and crossed the backyard toward the small patio. It was a beautiful late afternoon, heat starting to cool off as the sun drifted toward its bed.

Their little blue house — *home* for thirty-five years — was about two miles outside of New Haven. When they were younger, she and Roland could walk to town, passing by the old railroad station, which hadn't been in use since the 40s. She knew everybody in town, knew all the stories, and she'd come to understand their town was a lie. But a nice one.

On warm, summer evenings, back in the early 70s, Roland and Mallory would meet with George Davis and whatever girlfriend he had at the time. George had always been a flirt. Later on, they attended his wedding at the Methodist church on 1st Street and stopped by his store weekly.

Until it burned down.

And now, in less than a week, they'd be attending his funeral in the same, high-steepled sanctuary where they'd clapped for him and his bride. In the dark, Mallory could still hear those church bells, and with every passing year they sounded more grim.

Every time she and Roland drove into town, they passed the spot where George's shop had been. As young adults in New Haven, they had been regular customers, and George's dad had always offered a friendly smile.

"People don't smile like that nowadays," Roland said to her one evening. "This town ain't the same."

"Things don't stay the same forever, Roland."

"Sure, but why's it gotta change for the worse?"

She heard those bells, and she had to agree.

When George took over the Davis family store, it'd felt right. And now, ever since his tragic death, everything felt very, very wrong.

When Mallory trudged to the house, she was thinking about dinner and Roland's doctor appointment that weekend. But to her shock, there was a long-haired, orange cat sitting at the back door, huddled against the wall.

"Cleo!" She rushed over and bent down for him. Her knees

were shaky, but she grabbed onto her cat. "How'd you get out here?"

Mallory looked around with a worried expression. She twisted the door handle, Cleo clutched to her breast like an infant, and nearly tripped as she hurried inside.

"Roland!"

She slammed the door behind her and set Cleo on the floor. He meowed and slunk away through the kitchen, toward the bedroom. She saw Roland straight ahead in his recliner, leaning all the way back, eyes half-closed.

Mallory rushed down the hallway and into their bedroom. She flicked on the light, checked under the bed, behind the curtains. Cleo sat on the carpet, watching with his ears back. When she didn't find anything, she hurried back into the living room. Roland was still half-asleep in his chair, an old *Wheel of Fortune* playing on the TV.

"Roland!" she yelled again, stomping on the carpet. It rattled the walls and the boxy television.

He peered up at her, squinting. "What, hun? I'm—" He yawned loudly.

"Cleo was outside, and I don't see Luna anywhere! She's—"

"She's probably under the bed." Roland stretched his arms out straight like a mummy rising from a sarcophagus.

"She's not! I checked!" Mallory clutched at her chest with both hands. "Why'd you open the door?"

"I didn't open anything," he protested.

"Well, the cats sure didn't do it!"

"Honey, I've been in this chair the whole time you were outside." He lowered the footrest and sat up straight now. "And you know how loud that damn door is. I would've... heard if it..." He scratched at his stubble. "They must've..."

"You were *asleep*, Roland. It's not like your memory's all that sharp, either. *Luna isn't here.*"

Roland frowned as soon as she mentioned his memory. He huffed, eyes on the carpet.

"I'm sorry, I wasn't trying…" Mallory groaned and ran both hands over her face. "I don't know how they got out. But we gotta find her. I should call my sister. I bet… I bet that farmer's dog would kill her if he —!"

"No, no he wouldn't." Roland rose from his chair, pressing against the armrests for support. "Come on, hun. Let's check around the house. Maybe she… crawled up under something. We'll find her. We can call your sister later. You know she's probably busy."

"Beth could… I don't… I just don't know how Luna got out…" Mallory shook her head, and they stepped into the kitchen together. Her sister, Beth Turner, was married to the man who owned the pizza shop. He'd always give them discounts, and her sister was always reliable in a crisis like this. "Maybe she could —"

At that moment, their landline rang. Mallory and Roland exchanged a look. He moved across the room and answered it, leaning against the counter.

"Hello, Roland Clark here." He pressed the phone harder against his ear, and his eyes widened. "What? *Where?*"

He glanced over at Mallory, and she mouthed, "What is it?"

Still speaking into the phone, he said, "Okay. Right. I understand. Yes, we're coming. We're coming right away. Thank you, sir."

He hung up the phone and breathed a sigh of relief. "Well… good news. Someone's got Luna. They found her up the road. By the old Campbell's Soup billboard."

"That's like a mile away." Mallory furrowed her eyebrows.

"He said we gotta come quick. He's got somewhere urgent

to get to. Not… sure who it is. Do you know anyone with the last name Hemlock?" Roland opened two drawers as he spoke and looked through them.

"No. What are you looking for?"

"Keys."

Mallory reached over to the counter beside her and jingled them. "We don't keep them in there, honey."

"Right." He straightened up with a red face and extended his hand. "Well, anyway, I don't know any Hemlocks, and I know everyone in this town. So, I'll go meet him—"

"I'm clearly coming with you," she said. Mallory handed him the keys and walked over to the table.

"Okay, *we'll* meet him. I can drive us over."

She grabbed her purse from the kitchen table and pulled out a dark, plastic pepper spray canister.

"It's not far, so—uh, why do you need that?"

"Just in case." Mallory walked to the oven and shuffled through the same drawer he'd been digging in. "I don't think Luna would run all the way over there. I don't think she'd even leave the porch. She's scared of everything!"

"But the guy—"

"Right." Mallory straightened up, holding Roland's hunting knife and pocketing the pepper spray. "We have to go. But I'm taking these in the truck at least. What about your shotgun?"

"My shotgun?"

"Can you bring it, too?" she asked. "If it's… If everything's fine, we'll leave it in the truck. But just in case."

"Okay, Mallory." He paused. "This seems like… No, you're right. Let's be safe about it."

Neither of them said it, but Mallory knew they were both thinking about George Davis and his son. She knew the gossip going around town, and she trusted her gut. They needed to be careful.

<> <> <>

Nearly ten minutes later, they were finally leaving. It had taken Roland some time to dig his shotgun out of storage and then go pee before they left. Mallory grew more anxious with each minute. She found herself waiting by the truck, staring at the hillside across the road.

I hope he doesn't just let her go, she thought. *Hurry up, Roland…*

Every day seemed shorter, and every task took more time — struggling out of bed, hobbling to the kitchen, even walking to the car. The days slipped through her fingers, more liquid every morning. Two thick curtains were closing on their final act.

Luckily, it would only be a few minutes to the Campbell's Soup billboard. It was faded now and barely legible, but even after sixty years, she could never forget it. They'd never taken it down, and no one wanted to redo a billboard nobody would ever see. Nobody except her.

North of New Haven, there was a whole range of hills, and their house was so far around the back they couldn't see any of Main Street. Just the huge hillside covered in towering trees. And behind their house, endless fields eternally farmed, like all the others. But when the sun set in the evening, those hills came alive with color and shadows.

The west side of the hills was the most forgotten and the quietest. But Mallory loved being so close.

Roland finally emerged, and they started off, his beat-up truck following the winding road, as dense woods towered over their right. The truck was caked in dirt, wore multiple scratches and dents, and Mallory had gotten tired of seeing it in the driveway.

The engine rumbled and shook like it didn't want to make this trip ever again.

"Why don't you buy a new truck?" she'd asked him after they sold all their fields. It was too much to keep up with, even after she retired from nursing. A younger farmer bought the fields and let them keep the blue house. "All that extra money, since we sold —"

"Now I don't need a new one," he'd said, avoiding her eyes. "This one can get me by 'til…"

Til the end, he didn't say.

But she knew.

Most people didn't. Roland hid it well, but his months were numbered. They had been for a couple years. Each visit to the specialist — fifty minutes away — was just an update. *How many months now? Is he ahead of schedule? Yes, we have our affairs in order. Yes, we've talked to the insurance people. No, they won't cover it.*

George had known. *His family brought us lasagna until I had to ask them to stop. His boy helped Roland fix and clean the truck last summer.*

They finally saw the billboard in the distance. A faded mess, it had once shown a Campbell's soup can with a dark-haired lady beside it. She wore a bow and a blue-and-white dress. Now, the yellowing soup can was the only thing recognizable.

As they pulled close, they noticed an older man standing beside the billboard. He wore a loose-fitting, camouflage outfit and smiled behind his patchy, gray beard. In his arms, Mallory saw a jet-black cat.

"Luna!" she cried out.

Roland pulled over to the side of the road. The old stranger approached their car, holding Luna in his arms. She kicked with her back legs for a moment and then stopped fighting.

Mallory cranked her window down. "Thank you so much! I can't believe you found her out here."

Silas Hemlock came closer, still smiling. He had bright eyes below his wild, bushy eyebrows. There were more wrinkles on his face than both the Clarks put together, and his hair was solid gray.

"Well, here you go," he said, sticking Luna through the window. "I found it walking by the road. I've always had a soft spot for cats, so of course I couldn't just let it go once I saw the collar."

"I never thought that collar with our telephone number might actually have a use," Roland laughed.

Silas smiled. Then he stepped back from the truck. "I apologize for being so rushed, but I must get back. My friend and I were hunting, see, and he injured his ankle. Nasty business, really."

"Oh, wow..." Mallory saw the concern on his face. Luna, walking in circles on her lap, rubbed against her chin.

"Yeah. Fell out of the deer stand. Not too high, but enough. I need to take him in, I think. Get it x-rayed." Silas exhaled and rubbed his head. "We have to get to our truck somehow. Not sure if he can walk..."

"Where's your... gun?" Roland asked, leaning forward slightly. "Your hunting rifle?"

"Left it back with him." Silas narrowed his eyes. "So I could meet you over here."

Roland nodded. "And he's hurt?"

"Can't hardly walk."

"You know..." Mallory paused. She glanced over at Roland and then down at Luna. "Sir, I used to be a nurse. If you... I could help wrap it up, at least."

His eyebrows rose. "Really? I mean, I don't want—"

"I owe you one. For Luna. Maybe we can give you a ride, too. Back to your truck."

Silas Hemlock smiled. "Thank you both. Really."

<> <> <>

Leaving Luna in the truck with the windows cracked, Roland and Mallory followed Silas past the billboard. She glanced up at it one final time and plunged into the tree line.

A noisy choir of birds overhead and the gentle leaves rustling filled Mallory with something she hadn't felt in a while. The forest smelled fresh and youthful, all shades of green and yellow exploding around her. She forgot about the pepper spray in her pocket and started to smile.

"We should hike together, Roland," she suggested, taking his hand. "It's so nice out here."

He grunted with a nod. His head was on a swivel, snapping in every direction as he stared far away.

"This forest is always alive," Silas said without looking back. "There's nowhere else like it."

"Oh, we live close by, but we don't hike much." Mallory noticed a small bush to the left. "Wow, look at that. It's so red."

Silas chuckled. "Have you lived in New Haven long?"

"Oh, yes." She smiled. "Our whole lives. Graduated from… well, the local school. We were high school sweethearts. They changed the school name, but we were class of 1959." She squeezed Roland's hand. "Our fiftieth wedding anniversary is actually this winter."

"Well, congratulations. That's quite an achievement."

Mallory grinned. She saw a squirrel climbing a tree. This hunter was surprisingly friendly. Easy to talk to. And what a beautiful place. Roland didn't seem into it, but she thought he might just be overwhelmed with the forest like she was.

Why haven't we come out here more? Instead of watching from the house.

Silas led them deeper in, and she looked back, noticing the road wasn't visible anymore and neither was the billboard.

"What about you?" she asked him. "Local?"

"Oh, yes." Silas chuckled. "I've actually lived here longer than you, I believe."

"Really?" Mallory tried to do some quick math. This guy couldn't be *that* old? He didn't seem any older than seventy-something. He did have an intense, aging strength about him, though, like a seventy-year-old firefighter.

"How much farther?" Roland asked out of nowhere.

"Not too much."

Mallory looked over. Roland's face had turned a greenish color. He was gripping her hand so hard it ached.

"You okay?" she asked quietly, letting go of his hand for a moment to squeeze his bicep. "Are we walking too fast?"

Roland shook his head and swallowed hard.

"I think my husband might need to go back," Mallory spoke up. "He seems ill."

Silas kept walking forward without stopping. They were on steeper ground now, and he moved with long, lunging steps.

"Hey, did you hear me?"

Roland stopped walking and bent over, hands on his knees. Mallory looked at him, hurried away, and tapped on the hunter's shoulder.

"Listen, sir—"

Silas Hemlock spun around, raising a handgun. He held it with both shaking hands, pointed at Mallory. "We have to keep going, ma'am."

Mallory froze and raised her hands. She took a few steps back, closer to Roland. "Wait, listen…" She could hear the *thud-thud* of her heart growing quicker. Her knee pain returned. Her sick gut-feeling. "We… wait—"

"Stop talking." Silas stepped closer. He was slightly taller than them on the steep hillside. "*Stop. Talking.*" He jerked the gun toward Roland. "Hands."

Roland straightened up, moaning, and raised his hands.

"I am not a hunter." The old man's grip on the gun was shaking worse now. "I won't kill your cat. But I will kill you. I'm taking you up there. Dead or alive."

"Please," Mallory begged, hands still raised. "We just wanna go home. We won't tell anybody. I can't walk much more. I'm not—"

"Stop talking," he said, gritting his teeth, "or I will shoot you."

"I—"

"*Mallory,*" Roland spoke weakly. "He's serious. Listen, please. Just think."

"I wasn't *even* supposed to do this today!" Silas waved his gun in the air for a moment. "The other guy… He isn't so forgiving. He's the brawn, and I'm the brains. So, consider yourselves lucky. Now, come on."

"Why?" Roland asked before Mallory could speak. "Why is it better for us—?" He clutched at his stomach again, taking deep, shaky breaths.

Silas cocked his head. "What?"

"Why's it better for us to go… there and not die here?" Roland huffed for a minute and spat on the ground. "All the same, right?"

Silas looked disgusted. "You get a month together—eh, month or so—if you'll stop talking and walk. Limited time offer."

"I'm not going up there!" Mallory screamed. She collapsed to the earth, sinking to her knees. The pain got worse as they crunched against the ground. She screamed again, "We'll give you money. Please, just let… let us…"

As her voice faded, Silas stepped forward. He lowered the gun partially and stared at her.

"I am sorry," he said without much emotion. "I am every time."

From the corner of her eye, Mallory saw Roland curl his fists. And then he moved.

He jumped toward Silas, hollering. Roland swung his arms down and connected. Silas stumbled back, barely holding the gun. He reset his feet, regripped the weapon, and brought it crashing down on Roland's head.

Mallory heard a terrible crunch. Her husband of forty-nine years landed face-down in the leaves and twigs. There was blood trickling from the back of his head down his neck. She saw him writhing, pressing into the dirt, legs twitching.

"Please stop!" Mallory cried. "We have money. However much you want. Please, please, please."

Silas turned to her, frowning, and pointed the gun down at her husband.

"Please…" Roland moaned from the ground. "Let her go. You can have me."

"I need you both. Hungry mouths to feed. Well, *a* hungry mouth."

"I'll… I can help—"

Silas closed his eyes when he did it.

The world flashed and the air split.

Mallory's ears rang. She fell on top of her husband, clutching at his hands, his hips. Trying to turn him over. He wasn't twitching anymore. "You bastard!" she screamed. "No, Roland… Roland!"

The world flashed again.

<> <> <>

Silas Hemlock trudged past the Campbells billboard, hunched over. In one hand, he gripped a keychain. A small locket jingled against the keys, showing a picture of Mallory and Roland, much younger.

He approached the truck without a word and opened the side door. The black cat was on the seat, sleeping. In the fading sun, it rolled onto its back and stretched out, showing all its sharp teeth as it yawned.

Silas grabbed the animal with both hands and tossed it onto the grass. He pulled his gun out of its holster, pointed down, and held it for a moment. Then he placed it on the passenger seat. Finally, he shut the door, walked around, and climbed in the driver's side.

As he pulled onto the road and drove away, the black cat watched.

CHAPTER 2
NATE WOODS

In the three weeks after Malaki was arrested, I grew up a lot. Summer was running out, eighth grade coming quick.

It had been a pretty big summer for me overall, but especially the end. Everything moved so fast. By the end, I was a lot older but wishing things would stay still.

—Change. It's a bad word. But sometimes, change can be good.

My room, for example. It was different. Rhys had been staying with us ever since we picked him up on the way back from Dairy Queen. Three weeks. He had climbed into my dad's truck, out of the storm and soaking wet, sat right next to me. After that, he never left my side.

I liked Rhys. But he didn't seem exactly normal. Mom said I needed to be nice to him, so I… tried. Sometimes, though, it felt like he was lying.

Those three weeks were pretty calm. For me, anyway. I was looking forward to the Fourth of July. The whole town got together every year to watch fireworks. After that, I could count the weekends until school on one hand. Only a few baseball games left, and we still hadn't lost that summer. I was looking forward to the eighth grade season more and more.

I never asked Rhys about school. I didn't know if he was going or how long he might stay with us. He had a sleeping bag on my floor and a seat at the dinner table—although our family ate together less and less. We were friends, I guess. But after three weeks, you kinda have to be. Even if he scared me sometimes.

Another big, good change: I'd been working random jobs since school ended—a whole month ago!—and saving up money. Mowing lawns, feeding people's dogs when they went on vacation, watering Coach Bagg's girlfriend's flowers. Everyone paid me in cash.

Course, I was doing all this on top of my chores for Dad. Even after Rhys came around, my chores never got easier or smaller.

My sister Kaia took me into town whenever I needed to go. She never complained, because Kaia spent a lot of time in town after that night at the house. She'd drop me and Rhys off, and we'd visit all the shops while she went the other direction. I didn't know what she was doing, and I didn't have time to worry about it. I was busy making money and saving up.

A couple times, she couldn't take me, so I rode my bike. I'd never used it much besides biking with Mom, but when Rhys moved in, my parents got him one from Mr. Turner—he owns the pizza shop and had tons of old, dusty bikes in his barn. They were kinda gross, but Dad bought one, cleaned it up, and gave it to Rhys.

What was I saving up for? Pretty simple.

First, I wanted some walking-around money now that Rhys could go into town with me. I liked buying stuff for myself but also him. It made me feel like a good person. Rhys *really* liked Mr. Turner's pizza shop and the skeeball machines at the antique mall. He seemed amazed, which amazed me. New Haven is *not* a very cool place.

Mostly, though, I was saving up for a PlayStation. I know, I'd always been an Xbox guy, but all the kids at my school — the ones you're supposed to watch and copy — had PlayStations now. Mike — his dad was Coach Baggs — had one. I stayed the night at his house a few times, and it was *amazing* and yeah.

So, Rhys and I had a lot of fun playing on that. I didn't have enough money for many games yet, but we got *Spider-Man 3* and *MLB,* and he picked out one I didn't really like. It looked like a game for little kids. I bought it for him anyway.

Like I said, big summer, big changes. Those were the obvious ones. But there were smaller ones, too. My body changed — not always fun. Plus, I was doing pushups and sprints and anything I could to get better at baseball.

I started noticing things. The awkward silence between my parents. Dad barely smiled anymore. They made mistakes, and for the first time, I saw them. I really saw them. So, I kept my focus on baseball, because that was so uncomfortable to think about, and I really wanted the other guys on the baseball team to think I was… a good fit, I guess.

I just… got older. I realized it all of a sudden. When I stayed at Mike's house, he stole his dad's beer, and I'd never tried that stuff before. I drank a whole can. I felt really weird and older and smart. I didn't tell anyone.

Except for Kaia. I told her everything.

We'd been closer ever since that night when terrible things almost happened. Her life had changed, too. She didn't have Allison anymore, and we tried not to talk about it, but you run out of things to say. We spent a lot of time talking — in the woods, on our bikes, or in the yard — so it came up once or twice.

And Rhys… he had a way of bringing up what you wanted to avoid.

The three of us spent a lot of time together. Dad was always in the barn or driving his tractor, so Kaia, myself, and Rhys explored. Sometimes we'd go straight across the road and through the no-man's field. Out in the woods, we had our little space. Rhys liked it—the hut Kaia made beyond the creek.

—I was too embarrassed to tell Rhys we called it the "Wolf Cave." For some reason, the name embarrassed me now. I'd been trying to think of a better one ever since.

One day, we wandered back from it. The no-man's field had grown to our knees. Across the road, we saw our house in the distance and the red barn to one side. Past that, Dad's tractor moved back and forth in the bean fields, kicking up dust clouds.

As we approached the road, Rhys stared at our house, wide-eyed.

"Have you always lived here?"

I said, "Yeah."

Kaia added, "It's been in our family for years."

"I had a house like that... before. A family house." Rhys smiled, but there was something missing from it. "We had it for years, until..."

—He would do this often. A piece of information, a memory. And then he'd go silent. At first, it creeped me out, even scared me. Eventually, I just got annoyed.

Finish the story, I thought each time. *Have a complete thought for once.*

Without another word, we met the road. Kaia looked left and right, but not the way a kid does when they're scared of a car. She looked like she was waiting for something to come.

"What if..."

Rhys and I focused on her.

"What if we took our bikes up that way?" she said, pointing

to the left. "Followed the road a while?"

I turned and stared. Not at the road but in the distance. To our left and a few miles north, the abandoned house sat on the tallest of many hills. Miles away. I'd biked all the way once, with Mom. And I still had nightmares about it.

But much closer, only a couple miles away, smaller hills rose out of the flat land. We could bike along the winding, country road for a while and then turn right, just before Jeremy Adams' house. That road led to the base of the hills, where they were all soft grass and wildflowers and warm wind. On the other side, far away, the hills were covered in a dark forest.

"Yeah… I'd go that way," I said. "Just to where the hills start."

Rhys nodded.

"Alright, you two. Then let's do it."

And we all went. We strolled back to the house, said bye to Mom, and rolled our bikes out from the dusty barn. Mom didn't ask where we'd go, and nobody said.

We didn't tell ourselves the true reason for biking that way. I'm not sure Rhys knew. And I knew Kaia didn't want to admit it.

Only a month before, Kaia had lost her best friend. Allison went missing, her husband Malaki too, and all the signs pointed up there. When Kaia went searching for her — inside the house, all alone — Malaki had attacked her. He'd been arrested. The sheriff's department was holding him now. But for three weeks, Kaia hadn't talked about it much. Not to me or our parents.

That night, things in our family turned weird. The worst change of the summer. We rarely ever ate dinner together. We hid things and didn't say stuff, even if we wanted to. Everyone was worried about breaking the silence.

"Do you think she's up there?" I wanted to ask Kaia. "Are you going to try again?"

But I didn't. I was too afraid of the answers.

We had buried everything, and nobody wanted to dig it up.

The first time we biked to the hills it had been pretty tiring. For them, anyway. I'm an athlete. We followed the twisty, country road until Jeremy Adams' house came into view, the bike wheels humming underneath me. I'd pedal real hard, legs burning, the handles vibrating, and wind gusts smacking against me. I'd get ahead by a lot, then I'd basically wait for them to catch up.

Ahead of us, there were flat fields until the edge of the world. New Haven mixed in somewhere. So, we turned right and went until the hills rose on our left. Ahead of us, the road bounced over the hills, and another one went around the back.

We pulled off next to a dead tree and left our bikes resting against it.

They must not have been too tired, because we started making the trip almost daily. The forest hut—the shameful "Wolf Cave"—was alone in the forest. We'd left it for wide, open hills and wildflowers around our ankles.

Now, there were things I didn't want to do with Rhys, like chores because he slowed me down. Sometimes, he got really annoying, so I liked going to Mike's house and getting away for a night. Mike Baggs always had a new idea for something we shouldn't be doing, and it made my heart race.

But I always wanted to bike with Rhys.

In those hills, Rhys had more color in his cheeks. He didn't look so pale or stiff, sitting there in the flowers. This one time, there was a random cat in the hills. It stayed away from me, but it went toward Rhys. With a meow and arching its back, the jet-black cat moved toward him.

"I think she wants you to pet her," I said.

Rhys put out a shaking hand. The cat forced her head against his palm and then her back.

"I wonder why there's a cat out here."

Rhys didn't answer. He continued to pet the cat. The shock on his face made me feel something strange.

We never saw the black cat again.

Every time we went, his eyes would get red after a while. He'd sneeze a lot, really loud. But Rhys never wanted to leave. Whenever his allergies got too bad, we'd head home, but he always said he could stay a bit longer.

"Why do you have bad allergies?" I asked him one day on the way back, rolling our bikes beside us, walking home under a red and yellow sky.

Rhys shrugged. "I never went outside much as a kid. We had a big house, so I just stayed inside."

"Hmm. Gotcha."

Out there, Kaia was the opposite of Rhys. Even though it was her idea to explore those hills and she asked us to go along, Kaia was the first to suggest leaving. She usually looked spaced out, staring into the distance. She frowned and squinted, eyes locked on the tallest hill and the old house.

It was far in the distance and looked tiny unless we walked about a mile. Then it grew and grew. From those first couple hills, the smallest ones, I could see Jeremy Adams' house and farm directly to our left. A little farther away, New Haven spread out. The buildings were so small — even the huge church steeple — they could've been playthings. A little town, a few streets, set up by some innocent kid.

While I sat there and watched the ant-sized people move around Main Street with their ant-sized cars, Kaia would stay in her trance. Watching the house. Then she would shake it off and lay in the flowers for a while. She rarely spoke, deep in thought.

I stayed beside her. If you didn't mind picking off ticks, those hills had the best view in New Haven. On really clear days, I could see the end of the world—coming closer.

"You ever notice how that big tree by the church looks like a piece of broccoli from here?" Kaia asked, sitting up.

I laughed. "Yeah, it does."

"And the school looks… Well, it is pretty small. But up here even more."

"Yeah."

"Less than a month 'til you go back." Kaia stretched out her arms and sighed like someone who was done with high school and didn't have to worry about their summer ending.

"Yeah. Right, yeah." I cleared my throat and turned away for a moment.

"How are you feeling about it?"

"Sorta excited. But summer went by really quick."

"It's not over," she said.

"Right, yeah. It just feels like it is."

Squatting down, she studied something on the ground for a moment. Then Kaia looked up.

"One more year of middle school. Before you know it, you'll be graduating high school."

"You sound like Mom," I laughed.

She smiled. "Mom's right sometimes."

—Kaia stumbling toward us, leaning heavily on Mom. Rain falling from the sky. The blue-and-red lights flashing behind her. The outline of the house. Dead windows and a dark sky.

"Is she okay?"

Dad jumps out of his truck and bolts toward them.

I'm in the passenger's seat, and my ice cream cone is dripping onto my hand. Rhys is beside me, drenching the leather bench seat with all the rain his clothes soaked up. We haven't said a word yet.

Dad wraps his arms around them both. I can hear Kaia sobbing and her messy words. My parents are standing there, tight around her.

Rhys speaks. "She will be okay."

Those police lights blind me for an hour, and then we head home —

"Nate?"

I refocused, rubbed my eyes. "Sorry. Uh… daydreaming."

Kaia stared at me like she knew, but I doubted it.

With a late smile, I said, "We should head home, I think."

"Okay. Let's start back." She kept her eyes on me for another second and then shuffled away through the tall grass.

I used to ignore the house. It had always been a dumb Halloween story kids told at school. But ever since that night, I couldn't block it out. And the harder I tried, the harder it gripped me.

"Are we coming back here tomorrow?" Rhys asked as we moved away, back over the first two hills.

Our bikes were waiting by the road, resting against the dead tree. A cool breeze washed over us and the sun painted everything, every blade of grass, in gold. The lower it sank, the less I could see his expression.

"No," I answered before Kaia had a chance. "I've got a baseball game."

"Oh. Okay." Rhys frowned. "What's that like?"

"You can come tomorrow," I said. "You'll see."

He nodded and looked over his shoulder one time.

<> <> <>

Dad dropped me off at the baseball field at nine in the morning. Our game was an hour away, but I wanted to get some batting practice in before my team arrived. After I stretched, Coach Baggs pitched me about thirty balls. Even Mike wasn't there yet. Then the opposing team's bus rolled up, my own team trickled in, and we started going through our normal warmup routine.

It's crazy that we won any games over summer break, honestly. Our school was so much smaller than most we faced. Our middle school team only had twenty kids, spread out over three grades. The second-best kid on the team left in May, so I had to really carry us. I guess it was kinda nice, though, to have everyone depend on me.

I'd been really working on my swings, because I had the speed to be a threat, but I needed to hit consistently. Especially for our team. Those other kids had a hard time getting on base, so I needed to get some RBI's. That's where I'd hit it and they'd score.

I really wanted to hit a home run before summer ended, because then I could get another one during the school season. Nobody hits home runs in middle school, not even eighth graders. It would be pretty badass — that's what Mike Baggs said when I told him.

Nobody in New Haven was the homerun type of person. Coach Baggs won sectional in high school, but that was the best team we'd ever had. Not even state champs. Sectional.

People from New Haven didn't win. They just did okay. They didn't leave or get famous or do anything special. They just stayed. I didn't want to be like them. I knew making the Major League was basically impossible, but even college baseball... Nobody from my town ever did that — Well, it used to be my town.

The game arrived. Before I knew it, we were standing in a line, listening to the national anthem blare through the cheap speakers.

I glanced over to the bleachers where my parents were standing, with Rhys next to Dad and Kaia beside Mom. I could tell Rhys was overwhelmed. He looked around at everyone, standing with hands over hearts, and fidgeted a lot. As soon as the song ended, he was jabbering about something. Dad chuckled. We made eye contact, and he smiled a little wider.

The first inning was a drag. I didn't get to bat—I'm telling you, these kids *suck* at getting on base—and I didn't make any plays on defense. Still, I was sweating terribly. Those ten a.m. games were the worst. By the middle, everybody was drenched, dying, and it was over ninety degrees.

Second inning. Our team at bat.

"You're up, kid." Coach Baggs stuck up his thumb and jerked it toward the diamond field.

Gripping the warm, rubber handle, I got ready outside the dugout. A few stretches, a couple swings of the bat. *Process. Focus on the process. Not the result.*

Other kids on the team kept catching my eye. I would glance over through the dugout fence, see them sitting, talking. I thought, *Maybe they're talking about me.*

Mike was in front of me in the batting order. He was the clean-up hitter, but there was nobody on base to "clean up." Our offense was dead. Had been all week. Mike struck out, like usual, and I realized the team needed *me* to kickstart the offense.

"I've got this," I muttered.

I stepped up to the plate and shook my head, beads of sweat falling to the ground. I gripped the bat, shifting my weight back and forth. The pitcher was staring at me with dead eyes.

He wound up and threw a fast one to the outside. It curved a little and slowed down. Umpire called, "Ball."

Weak throw, I thought. "Do it again."

He did. A faster one but losing speed just as quickly. Drifted outside.

I stepped forward, timed it perfectly, and ripped through with the bat.

The ball exploded off its surface, rocketing through the gap and rolling into center field. I sprinted to first and they didn't have a chance. Maybe I could've gone to second, but I knew I was about to steal on the next pitch.

These kids. Way too slow.

Everybody was cheering. My team, my family, the crowd. Not a cloud in the sky. A terribly hot sun against an endless sheet of blue.

"Coach, I've got you this game," I called over toward the dugout. All those admiring faces.

He gave me a thumbs up.

It's gonna be a good day.

CHAPTER 3
NAOMI WOODS

"I'm watching all these guys I grew up with sell these… huge farms." Cliff leaned against the kitchen counter, pressing both hands flat. The kind that've been in the family for generations. Two hundred years, Naomi!"

I was standing at the kitchen sink, peeling a cucumber and staring out the window. Rhys and Kaia were upstairs getting ready. Cliff had just gotten back from dropping off Nate at the game. We were rehearsing this script we'd done a dozen times.

"That's a long time, honey."

He nodded. "Yeah, sure is. Way damn longer than us. And they're… selling them. Don't have a choice. No profit. No sons that wanna take over."

"Girls can be farmers, too, if they want."

"I'm not talking about that. You know what I mean." Cliff grunted. He crossed his arms and walked over to the back door.

I shrugged and didn't stop peeling. "But I'm right."

"Yeah. You are. Boys, girls, anyone can be a farmer. But they don't *want* to, any of them. And that's the issue."

He observed his bean fields through the window with a wistful, lost expression on his face.

"It's hard on everyone," I offered. "Especially right now."

"Not getting any easier," he huffed and reached for the door handle. "Holler when you're all ready. I'll be in the barn."

I watched him go, through the kitchen window, and I knew he was thinking about Nate. All these farmers Cliff had grown up with were selling their fields. Left and right, family farms, dropping like flies. And his time would come. This house, these fields—we'd lose it all. Nate would never be a farmer, not here anyway. Lord, I didn't blame him for it, either.

But maybe Cliff did. Or maybe he would.

When we got married, it had been enough that we had each other. We knew all this would never last, and eventually we'd move on, but we *still* had each other. I was starting to wonder if he still thought the same. Things got older and we got different. Out of nowhere, it seemed.

I rushed into the bedroom and changed into something for the game. Jean shorts, a loose top, and ten swipes of deodorant. It was going to be a blazing hot morning and afternoon, so I wasn't taking any chances.

When I came back into the kitchen, the back door was still shut, and our large fridge was wide open.

Wow, Rhys is up first today.

I moved around the island counter in the middle of the room.

"Good morning," I said. "You want something to eat?"

The doors swung shut, and it wasn't Rhys standing there like I'd expected. Instead, Kaia was facing me. She had dark bags under her puffy eyes and a look of deep embarrassment.

"Oh..." She cleared her throat. "Hi."

"Are you still coming with us to the game?" I asked slowly, watching my tone. I didn't want to set her off or push her away from coming. "I can... make you some breakfast real quick—"

"I'll come," she said. Then Kaia wrapped both arms around her stomach.

I couldn't help but notice how scrawny her arms looked at the moment, and my heart stuttered. "Breakfast, maybe?"

She shook her head. "I'm not hungry."

"Oh, okay. Well, um… we're leaving in about ten minutes, but if you need longer—"

"I'm fine." She nodded sharply and stepped toward the kitchen door. "I'll go get ready." She walked away briskly, head down.

Before I could stop myself, I said, "Kaia."

She stopped on a dime and turned. "Yeah, Mom?"

I cleared my throat. "Just… I love you, honey."

"Love you more, Mom."

Then she vanished up the stairs. I was left with the unspoken wall. Every day for three weeks, it had pushed us apart.

A few minutes later, I found myself alone with Rhys. He was standing at the back door, staring outside. We were waiting on Kaia, and then we'd walk outside, yell toward the barn, head into town. But for those few, calm minutes, I stood by the kitchen counter, putting away the dishes, and I was just a mom. We weren't in danger.

"What's it like?" Rhys asked quietly.

I glanced over at him. "What'd you say?"

"What's it like to be alone?"

"Um… Well, we have family, of course. We aren't really alone."

"But sometimes."

"Sure, sometimes, but—"

"Everyone's alone up there, you know."

A shiver ran up my arm. "Up where… Rhys?"

He turned to me, his eyebrows drawn together, lips pressed shut. "How did you survive?"

"I don't..." I took a deep breath. "Go see if your sis—See if Kaia's ready. Will you?"

He smiled a little bit as he walked back toward the staircase. "I will."

<> <> <>

When we got to Nate's baseball game, that was the first time we'd all been together in over a week. Just a month before, it would've been unthinkable to go so long without seeing each other. Back then, we always ate dinner together. Talked about our days, our plans. Now we walked on eggshells.

Things had changed so quickly, throwing in new stressors and unbelievable tension. It was everybody, too, not just me and Kaia. There was stuff with Cliff. With Nate and of course Rhys. Everything was different.

Sure, things weren't changing so fast anymore. After three weeks of "normal," a lot of busy afternoons, we'd settled down. But this wasn't truly normal. We just didn't acknowledge it.

At the baseball game, the first few innings dragged on. An unforgiving sun hovered right over the stands. Today's game wasn't crowded. The bleachers were two-thirds empty and scorching hot to the touch. Everything felt like a hot sidewalk.

I couldn't blame the folks who stayed home, inside. I've never minded the heat, but these country folks love to play it up. White men with sunburns and freckles. Women with little handheld fans. I didn't mind standing out from these people, and over that summer, we were more different than ever.

—Honest, I was counting down the games left before school started. Then we'd get a nice break from sports and all the hassle.

I loved watching Nate play, but I was still counting.

Looking around the crowd, I couldn't help basking in the popcorn smell and noticing all the empty chip bags baking on the ground. New Haven was home to a lot of things: White men with bright-red necks. Overworked, stressed-out farmers. Sons and daughters who would have to sell their generational, family farm.

All of us, empty buildings and wind-swept chip bags.

Cliff felt the pressure. He was spending more time than ever in his fields, on his tractors. Everything needed cut and raked and bundled. I'd see his silhouette in the mornings, standing out of bed before dawn. Then in the afternoon, I'd get one hour with him, during the worst heat of the day—if I was even home. Finally, evenings; he'd take off his dirty boots, lock the kitchen door behind him, peel off his drenched shirt, lock the bathroom door too, and shower.

It hurt me to think how isolated we'd become. I knew he had good reasons and intentions, but those only carried a person so far.

All of this was somewhat normal. But it wasn't normal that we never kissed anymore. We fought over little things. We couldn't seem to get along quite right.

He wanted to vent endlessly about all his friends who were having terrible luck, and I felt bad, honest. But whenever I told him about my stuff in town—I was organizing a church meal drive for Allison's parents, putting up missing posters, trying to keep our town connected and calm—he didn't seem to care.

"That's nice," was all I ever got.

"Okay."

Especially when the kids weren't around, things were different between us. And it unsettled me. I couldn't put a name to it, but something had shifted under us.

He was on my right side at the baseball game. Rhys one over from him. On my left, Kaia was silent, but I'd almost gotten used to it.

Ever since the incident—I didn't know what to call it when my daughter ran headfirst into that godforsaken house and nearly died at the hands of a psychotic white boy who confessed to murdering her friend but—things had changed. At home, she didn't want to talk about anything. At baseball games, she didn't jabber about Nate's teammates or his talent. She watched, but she wasn't invested.

Rhys asked, "Why do they have one player squatting?"

Cliff turned to him. "What do you mean?"

"The one there." Rhys pointed. "Behind the kid with a bat."

"Oh, the catcher. Well, he… catches the pitches."

"Oh." Rhys paused and leaned forward. "That's a weird job."

"I guess so." Cliff looked over at me and chuckled. "I could use a few quick innings here. This damn heat is unbearable."

Rhys raised his eyebrows when Cliff cursed. I scowled at my husband.

"Sorry."

I sighed. "Thought you farmers were heat resistant."

"Well, I must be getting old, 'cause it's been getting to me these last few weeks." Cliff wiped a hand across his forehead.

"I've always said the perfect game is A) Nate gets on base every time and B) Nobody else gets a hit. Either team. Nate wins and we're home by two."

Kaia added, "That'd be a tie, Mom. Zero-zero."

"Oh. Well…" I smiled at her. Was that a little bit of snark in her voice? "Nate can get a homerun or something."

"He's always talking about that," Rhys said. "He said he's

going to. What… what is a homerun?"

Cliff started explaining what the term meant, while I watched Nate warming up his swing outside of the dugout. Something had changed about him, just like Kaia. He held his shoulders back and stood taller. It showed in his expression and the way he talked. Nate was starting to see himself as a young man, not a "kid."

At home, he and Kaia were busy, too. They'd spend chunks of time away from the house. Kaia had started going into town more than ever, and Nate had baseball practice and games constantly. Still, he'd play tons of catch in the yard with Rhys and let him swing the bat. I would chat with them on their way inside the house and back out.

In public, through appearance, our family put on a good show. "Everything is normal. We are *not* undergoing a traumatic month from hell." But underneath our calm cornfield, in the thickest, densest rows, there were animals fighting to the death, blood stains on the ground.

It wasn't normal to have Rhys with us. To lie about him. Cliff worried the townspeople and the sheriff would come after him, so we lied. Said he was Cliff's nephew from out-of-town, just staying with us.

"I'm gonna call somebody," he told me a couple weeks ago. "I'll find his parents or his old school or something. Don't worry about it."

But I did worry, because it had been two weeks. No updates from Cliff.

"I'm sure we could foster him," I suggested. "We just need to contact CPS and get everything cleared away."

"Right. Yeah. I'll do that, yeah."

And still no updates.

I grew to love Rhys. It wasn't hard. Every child needed somebody, so I was more than happy to care for him. In some ways, he reminded me of Nate last summer. Curious and quiet. But now Nate was growing up, and every day he seemed less like a kid.

Everybody was finding new stress and new walls. Kaia more than anyone. Still grieving Allison, needing space. I hated to watch her suffer. I wanted to ask her about Allison and the house and what she'd seen, but ever since that night, for three long weeks, she'd kept to herself. We talked a lot about the weather and when the famous "July in New Haven" storm might hit.

At least she'd agreed to come to the game today. She had hints of her old self: snarky, wise, at peace. Maybe things were getting better.

Nate stepped to the plate confidently, and I refocused on him.

"Was his first hit a single?" I asked Kaia.

"Mmhm."

He stood waiting on the pitch. I tried to think of something else to ask her. Our conversations were forced these days.

Four more pitches without saying a word. I couldn't keep track of the ball-strike count without even trying like Kaia and Cliff. He was busy talking to Rhys, who now asked about the bats and why they were so heavy. Cliff answered all his questions, trying his best to explain.

A week ago, he'd said, "He just doesn't know things, Naomi," and rubbed his forehead with a fist. "Things that every kid knows. I don't understand it."

"And nobody's come looking for him," I'd pointed out.

"I don't understand at all. But I'm working on it. I've called a couple people."

Nate struck the ball, smashed it out past third base. It hopped twice and rolled another foot. Cliff clapped and whooped as Nate rounded first and headed to second. The kid in the outfield threw in, but Nate was already standing on second, breathing heavy.

"Two for two," Cliff noted. "He's on fire today."

"So, what is that called?" Rhys asked energetically. "If he goes to the base number two?"

"A double, buddy."

"Oh."

The game carried on. I found myself people-watching during the middle innings, checking out the familiar and not-familiar faces around us. Quite a few were missing, and none of the ladies from church had come. Except for Susan, a few seats away from us. I meant to catch up with her after the game and make sure she could lead the prayer meeting this week, because I was going to be late.

I realized one family in particular was absent, and it got me thinking.

"The Dawes family isn't here today," I mentioned to Kaia.

"I think Smith quit the team," she said. Her gaze stuck to the game. "Haven't seen him at practice when I drop Nate off."

"Have you seen him around town at all?" I asked.

"No, I haven't."

"Have you… heard anything?"

I hoped it didn't sound like an interrogation, but truthfully I wanted to know what she did in town all day. Nate's practices were about two hours. She'd spend all that time in New Haven, plus other days. Sometimes taking the boys with her to "shop," but mostly by herself. Those two could probably waste a whole afternoon with the skeeball machines or coming here, to the baseball field. But Kaia had to be doing something with all that time. I had no clue what.

Whatever the case, she'd never spent so much time in town. Not even during high school with Allison and — *When did I become a helicopter parent?*

Maybe it's fair. She just went through hell. I'm worried about her —

On the darkest nights, when I glanced at the house on the hill, the lights still turned on. Just for a second, but I saw.

"No," she said in a flat tone. "I don't know anything."

"Oh. Well, I've been meaning to talk to Smith's mom, anyway."

Kaia studied me, now interested. "Anne? Why?"

"Well, the other people at church… They seem afraid of them. Or something," I carried on. Keeping my voice casual. Keep her talking. "They've really isolated the Dawes."

"I don't think anyone at that church has a heart," Kaia said. "I don't think they care about… they're just some stuck-up…"

"They can be, sure. Anyone can."

Kaia didn't respond.

"Is it weird for you that Nate is growing up so quick?" I asked. I felt like pressing my luck with these questions, since we were stuck together in the bleachers. "Like… he'll be in high school in just a year. But he seems older already."

"I guess so," she said. Kaia raised her eyebrows. "Is it weird for you?"

"Yeah. It is. But it's weirder that you're leaving soon."

Her shoulders tightened. I knew she didn't want to talk about it, but Kaia hadn't brought up her college search in weeks, and there was only two months until most universities started. Plus, she'd be a freshman, meaning that whole extensive move-in process. We were running out of time.

"Can I be honest, Mom?"

I nodded. "Please."

"Well, I…" Kaia frowned. She rubbed at her jaw. "I'm thinking about taking a gap year."

"Staying here for a year, you mean?"

"Yeah. I just… don't know where I wanna go. And I feel like I'm not ready to leave New Haven. It's sort of…"

She hesitated and her eyes started to drop.

"Go on, honey. I'm listening." I added, "And I think that might be a great idea, really. The best thing for you, maybe."

"Yeah, I have like…" She shook her head. "Roots here, and I can't pull them up yet." In a much lower voice, she said, "It hurts too much."

"I think that's okay. It's okay to wait a year. You know your father and I love having you around. You're a huge help. And I'm gonna miss you no matter when you leave."

She looked away. "I thought you might be mad."

"I know we both went, but college isn't for everyone. And for some people, it's about timing. Do whatever you need to. We're here for you, however you need us." I grabbed her hand and squeezed it. "Your dad feels the same. He's just busy with his 'crops' and stuff." I added finger quotes, and she laughed. "You know how it is in the summer."

"I definitely do." She sighed and closed her eyes for a moment. "I might try to help him out more. I need… something to do. Take my mind off things."

"Of course, honey. I think he would really appreciate that."

She glanced at me. That face, so much like mine. Kaia got more from me than from her dad. Her almond-colored eyes. Her lips and curly hair. She was way beyond either of us.

I'd suspected this for two weeks. She couldn't leave yet, because she couldn't leave Allison. Somewhere, deep down, she couldn't let go.

Do you call it grieving if you believe the person might still be alive? I couldn't imagine the feelings she grappled with. Allison's parents had given up. They'd stopped putting up missing posters. The cops had charged Malaki with her murder, since he'd confessed, and yet… for some reason, Kaia held on. It was naive or it was the most love I'd ever seen. She was the only one who believed anymore.

—Nobody took down those white sheets of paper with Allison's face. She was plastered all over town, and we couldn't simply rip her down. Out of respect, of course. And maybe out of fear. In case things weren't…

The game ended. Nate won easily and hit another double before it was all done. Cliff left Rhys with us and went to talk to Coach Baggs while the crowd trickled away.

"Naomi! Hi!" Susan moved over to us, smiling wide. She had on a nice dress, fit for church more than a ballgame, and wore deep red lipstick. "Oh, Kaia. You're looking great, girl. And —" Her eyes flicked to Rhys and widened. "Oh?"

"This is… Cliff's nephew," I said before she could get any ideas. "He's staying with us for a few weeks."

"Well… hello." Susan stuck out a hand slowly, as if she was afraid.

Rhys shook her hand without looking up. "Hi, miss."

After we verified the prayer meeting plan, Susan left a moment later, casting one more strange look at Rhys. When she'd gone, the three of us made our way to the bottom of the bleachers.

"Why… why do you lie about me?" Rhys asked, staring down at some popcorn spilled onto the ground. He crushed one puff with his heel.

"Some people wouldn't leave you alone until… they knew all about you. We don't want them to bother you."

He accepted this with a nod and changed the subject. "How

is Nate so good at this?" He was staring ahead now, through the back fence behind home plate. "Does he ever mess up?"

"He's been practicing for a long time," I explained. "Ever since he was a little kid."

"I wish I did."

CHAPTER 4
KAIA WOOD

I'd gotten into the habit of driving my mom's car a lot, which wasn't exactly new. I never had a car of my own, and I didn't have any reason to. When I had my permit, I did all my practice driving with her in that green Chevy Malibu, older than I was. Once I had my license, she let me borrow it almost whenever I wanted.

So, whenever I needed to go into town — put on my detective hat — she let me take the Malibu. I felt bad about lying to her. Honestly, I did. But there were some things I had to keep to myself, no matter how much I wanted to tell.

"Mom, I love her. Mom, I haven't given up. Mom, I'm still searching, I'll never stop, I'll search forever, and I'm pretty sure I want to love her forever in whatever way she'll let me."

But I couldn't say those words to Mom or anybody else.

I found a coloring sheet in the glove compartment one day. At some point, I must've torn it out from the coloring book Allison gave me at our graduation party. This was the first sheet. A picture of a farmhouse. The red and white crayon image was perfectly colored. And underneath, in scratchy handwriting, she'd written, *I think I could be a farmer but only with you teaching me.*

I remembered — the most painful memories are always crystal clear — when she'd done it. The coloring book was in my room, hidden away in my sock drawer. I hid it, and I don't know why. There was nothing obviously romantic about it, and yet… to me, it was breathtaking, electric, and it said, over and over again, "I love you too."

Allison colored it at the library. During high school, they used to let us go over to the library for study hall. One perk of living in such a stupidly small town and graduating with thirty people. The teachers didn't care what we did over there, and the librarian was "monitoring" us, but truthfully they just didn't have extra rooms in the tiny ass building they called a school.

I remember browsing the books with her. I would run my hands along the leather spines, and then our fingers brushed over each other's, and I laughed quietly.

"Do you think the librarian would get mad if I brought a coloring book?" Allison whispered with a clever smile.

"Girl, why?"

"I'll leave it here, on the shelves nobody reads, and then we can come during study hall and color when we're supposed to be 'researching.' Great idea, right?"

"You're doing too much."

She did what she said. Left a coloring book there. We'd take some crayons from Mrs. Houchin's room, since she always had craft supplies like that. Allison and I would sit with a coloring book, tucked away in the back corner. She'd color like her life depended on it, tongue between her teeth, and I'd watch her.

"You get so intense like that," I said, leaning my head on her shoulder.

"I'm gonna color this entire damn book by the time we graduate, and it'll be perfect." She paused for a moment to crack her knuckles. "Just wait and see."

She did. The entire damn thing. Not a single mistake, as far as I could tell. And at my graduation party—after sharing a moment I would never, ever forget—she left the coloring book for me with a note.

Thanks for being my study buddy. ~Alley Cat

There was a little drawing of a man beside it, but his head was replaced with a heart, and in one stick-figure hand he held a yellow flower.

<> <> <>

I'd never felt that way before.

I've missed people, of course. My school friends. My parents and Nate. When I'd stayed the night at a friend's house for the first time, I cried. Mom had to come pick me up.

And I've lost people, too. My grandparents were all dead before I graduated high school. Friends moved away or just stopped talking to me. It hurt.

But nothing hurt like losing Allison.

I couldn't think about anything else. I couldn't eat. I couldn't sleep. When you've known somebody for so many years, they're attached to everything. Like bits of them are stuck on every surface. There was no escaping. Nothing would distract me. No amount of sad music or movies.

Like… I'd been really feeling the new Bruno Mars she forced me to listen to. Allison and I, that had been *our* album for a month. But I hadn't listened to it since. It made me nauseous to think about. All those happy songs sounded fake now.

And even my favorite songs—like *Fast Car* by Tracy Chapman—didn't hit the same way. That song used to be the most relatable. It was perfect—about escaping the generational cycle of trauma like substance abuse and poverty. A song from the perspective of a queer black woman. And ever since Allison went missing, I couldn't stand even the opening chords.

It wasn't me anymore. I didn't know what was. I'd become an entirely new person, in a bad way, and I wanted to go back to being someone.

Strangely, though, when I saw Allison's face on the missing posters all over town, it didn't feel the same. First, her picture was grainy and unfocused. Barely recognizable. And second, I could imagine it was somebody else's unsolved case. A third-person view of some tragedy, not my own.

Searching for her was the same way.

I only felt better—or at least distracted—when I searched. Working, thinking, putting in hours. I could dissociate, and I imagined I was investigating a random mystery. Someone else's pain. It didn't hurt quite as bad, and I channeled all my energy into solving it.

—But in my memories and at night, her picture was crystal clear. The pain was sharp and wedged into my ribs.

How did I try to find her? When everyone else had given up, how did I keep going?

First, to start looking, I started listening. I would hang around town and eavesdrop *everywhere*. Whenever I could get into the bar, I'd sit there for a couple hours. I was over eighteen, and nobody here would tell me no. Eavesdropping was so easy…

Ask people what they knew. Be friendly to all the waitresses and bartenders.

Hear all *sorts* of stuff. Most of it garbage, but some helpful shit too.

I talked to everyone. Waiters. Store cashiers. Mailmen and people crossing the street.

I needed the whole town to recognize me.

And the best thing about being a tragic little girl in their minds? They felt bad, and they would talk. Oh Lord, would they talk.

When I got braver and I had some info—everyone had given up. Her *parents* had given up—I started asking questions. Introducing myself to new folks. I'd ask them about easy things. Did you go to school here? Did you know George? Have you heard about the house? The conversations always came back to the house. Or about Malaki and Allison. I just needed information. Truckloads of it.

I needed them to know my name.

Somebody will talk. Somebody knows something.

I learned a little bit. Wearing a smile is like camouflage, and people will say anything. The family who used to own the house—the Donnellys—had died off decades ago. They ran out of money and sold their land, but it wasn't enough. The house fell apart. The family clung to it until they died. And now it was abandoned.

But that's not it. There's something else. I know there is.

The library was useful, too. I found out a long time ago—before the world wars—there'd been some kind of human trafficking ring based out of the Donnelly house. The family took a pretty huge hit after the gruesome details came out. Dozens of women had passed through, most of them heading east, never heard from again. The news reports were dry, but it gave me chills. What they described... No wonder I couldn't sleep at night.

None of the townsfolk wanted to talk about it. Local secrets, best left in the past. They changed the topic to "those hills give me the creeps" or "so tragic, but everyone knew that boy was bad news."

During these informal interviews, I didn't mention my own experiences, of course. I was there to learn, not give away what I knew. Most people knew pieces of my story from local gossip, but I didn't fill them in.

I'd never kept a secret like this from my parents before. Not just the "steal some whiskey from your dad's liquor cabinet" kind. This was serious. This was a job. I was really looking, and I was really hiding it from them.

My parents would probably find out soon. Some loud-mouth man would tell some church-going white woman and she'd snitch to Mom. But so far, so good. And my parents were outcasts now anyway—right there with the Dawes. They didn't know it yet, but I did.

I kept searching. I kept holding onto hope. I didn't have anything else. I didn't want to sit in my room, drowning in depression. I was *seriously* losing my grip.

But they hadn't found a body, so I knew she wasn't dead. She couldn't be. Even if Malaki confessed. Even if our town was moving on.

I wandered around New Haven, annoyed the old people, and I never stopped.

After a while, it paid off. Asking around. Putting my name out there. It worked.

Somebody got in touch with me.

I can admit, I was terrified. It could've been anyone. I could've been in serious danger. But I never thought about stopping.

This is for you, Allison. I'm gonna save us.

<> <> <>

After Nate's game, everyone else went home, but I stayed in town for a while. I told my parents I was going to the library, which wasn't a total lie. They didn't know the rest. They hopefully never would.

I traced the familiar path to the post office. I'd been making this trip every chance I got. I would drop Nate at practice or make an excuse to go into town. Straight to the post office. As soon as I stepped into the room—warm and stuffy, lined with a hundred PO boxes—I'd move toward it. The small key fit perfectly into the lock. I'd twist, peer inside…

If I got a new letter, I'd rush to the library and read it. Write a response. Put that shit back in the PO box. If I didn't have a new letter, I'd visit a shop, waste time in town, and check once again later before I went home.

After the first one, the letters always came in PO box #32. And I put my answer in the same one. With each letter, there was a smaller, dirty-yellow envelope inside and a reminder: *Please write your response on the back of this paper. Do not keep this writing. Return to the box. I will answer within three days.*

On the day of the baseball game, I didn't get lucky. Not at first.

I walked inside, eagerly. Across the tile floors and the room that smelled like sanitizer and paper. But I found an empty PO box.

People swirled around me—that post office could be strangely busy at times—but I lost myself for a moment. Without thinking, without speaking, I left the post office. Shoulders slumped. Staring at the ground.

I had to waste an hour or two, then I'd check back. But I hated doing it.

If *I* could choose, I'd drive up the hill right now. I'd barge inside. Let all hell break loose. I didn't care anymore. I couldn't wait any longer.

But the letters told me to wait. To be patient. They promised answers, and those answers would give me a better shot at surviving. Both of us surviving.

Suffer a little longer. You can do this.

<> <> <>

I walked along Main Street, heading for the crystal shop. The First Street church bells rang out, solemn and deep, echoing across our small town. It carried on for a minute. Gave me a feeling like somebody had died.

New Haven had settled in for its afternoon nap. I was the only one outside. A few cars rolled by, but then everything fell silent. So quiet I could hear the wind passing. I shivered, despite the heat.

On the other side of Main Street, there was a small building with four long clothing racks on the sidewalk outside, the discount section. Our only vintage clothing spot. Allison and I always went there together. It was a staple on our shopping trips.

My throat squeezed tight as I remembered a sweater she'd almost bought. Burnt orange and gray. I had a crazy idea to go buy it, unless it'd been taken, but decided not to. Every good thing had been taken, and I didn't need the reminder.

A little farther on—passing her black-and-white image on almost every traffic light post—there was a huge antique store. It stretched out over a whole block. Didn't look open. The doors were closed. No older folks were sitting outside on the wooden benches, talking in murmurs. No teenagers ran inside, holding quarters and making a beeline for the skeeball machines in the back.

Even for a sleepy mid-week afternoon, New Haven seemed more dead than usual.

Don't get all weepy and sentimental, I reminded myself. *One day, we're both gonna leave this fucking place.*

All the buildings towered over me. It felt like the whole town was staring. Closing in. When I passed the local grocer, all the people inside stopped and turned. Through the glass, I saw their eyes.

That's one downside of putting my name out there. Everybody knew me, and they all had a reason to watch.

I pressed on and reached the crystal shop. With deep breaths, I collected myself and got ready to face the inside.

Maybe it was dumb, but I wanted to prove something to myself. I wanted to spend a few minutes in here without freaking out. Put on a mask and act okay. The whole world did it. I could, too. I needed to.

It was a small test, in some ways. Just like the search for Allison. Little tests to prove I could. And then, someday soon, I'd face the big test, and I'd see her face-to-face.

Allison used to be the one who hated going in here. I smiled despite myself. *And* she *would run out without warning.*

But I pushed those memories away as I pressed into the glass door and stepped through. Ms. Hargrave had a missing person sign plastered on the window. Half the shops on Main Street did, but it stung worse in the places we'd gone so often.

Bells tinkled above me, and Ms. Hargrave looked over from behind the glass counter. There were necklaces and crystals and jewelry in the display cases. More of the same scattered on top.

"Hello, Kaia."

The shop was freezing. She must've had the AC blasting. My heart started to pound faster.

"Hi."

With a forced, failing smile, I moved past.

Everything rushed at me. The shelves, the stones, the smell

of this store. I took deep breaths and moved unsteadily to the back, shuffling my feet. I could feel Ms. Hargrave's eyes on me, so I found the magazine shelf and pretended to browse for a few minutes.

"Beautiful day outside," she said from behind the counter.

Without turning around, I said, "Yeah, it's alright." I pictured her wrinkled face and exact expression: a sad smile, pitying eyes.

I counted to ten once. Then again. *Can't avoid things forever.*

I faced Ms. Hargrave and forced myself to make eye contact. Then I swiped through their Baja hoodies, the different colors schemes, and tried to focus on the rough fabric as I moved each one aside.

Don't spiral. Stay grounded.

"I saw you in town the other day," Ms. Hargrave went on, still staring.

"Yeah." My voice cracked. I cleared my throat. "I've been… staying busy. Trying to."

"That's good, sweetheart." Without blinking, she added, "You're an inspiration, Kaia."

"I… Thanks, um…" I threaded my fingers together. "I'm gonna… head out." Squeezing both hands tight, I shuffled to the front of the store. "I've gotta… I'm hungry, so, you know…"

Ms. Hargrave watched me go.

"Have a good day," I squeaked, opening the door and feeling the heat rush over me.

"You have my condolences, Kaia," she said as I left. "I'm sorry."

I spent the next hour down the road at the pizza and wings restaurant. I texted Mom first and promised to bring her breadsticks. The other New Haven food option — an old-fashioned diner with the permanent smell of burger grease — didn't appeal to me on such a hot day, and I decided on pizza because it was closer to the post office, and I needed to check one more time before I went home.

I was studying the menu when the waitress came up.

"Hello, my name is Cassy. I'll be your…" She stopped talking, so I looked up.

"Oh. Hey, Cassy."

"Hi, Kaia."

Cassy smiled at me. We went to high school together. She had long, blonde hair, a skinny white girl, and wore cut-off jeans all the time. Today, she was wearing her work uniform — black shorts and a tight, red top. Her eyes were focused on me.

"I'll be your server today." She cleared her throat. "Can I get you something to drink?"

"Just water."

"If you wanna look at our cocktail menu," she said, leaning across the table and reaching for the menu at the far side, "we actually have a new —"

"No. Just water."

"Alright." She frowned at me and then said in a cheerful, uppity tone, "Well, just let me know if you need anything else, honey."

Honey? We're the same age.

She didn't bother me too much after that, but I saw in her eyes she *wanted* to. And she kept calling me honey. Kept using a fake-ass, cheer-up smile. It made me wanna take my pizza to go.

I ordered a personal — pepperoni with green olives — and a side salad. Plus breadsticks to go. Cassy left me alone after that.

Sipping on my water, I looked around at the restaurant. It had a few booths, all wooden and uncomfortable. Some beer signs hung on the walls, and a couple flat-screens played ESPN. The waitresses all wore black shorts and red tops like Cassy. The other customers were all men, lots of them having lengthy chats with their own servers. Something about middle-aged men talking to these young girls real flirty always gave me pervert vibes.

The amount of empty booths wasn't lost on me. Or the small number of staff working.

How much longer 'til this place closes? I wondered, because you couldn't *not* wonder. They were never busy. Their food wasn't amazing. And like everything in New Haven, things turned over with the seasons. A fresh start also brought death.

I stared at one sign, a neon beer can with a brand name I didn't recognize.

If I come back twenty years from now, will the whole town be dead? What about ten?

Did I always think about death this much?

Am I already out of time?

My food came right before I spiraled into panic-mode. Cassy stood by awkwardly until I told her I was fine. She left. I chewed my pizza quickly and stared into the swirling wood pattern. I only ate about half of it plus the salad, hoping Mom wouldn't press too hard about why I stayed in town. She probably didn't like me skipping out on her dinner plans, but I wasn't *doing* this for the dinner. She just couldn't know that.

Tired of hiding shit. I groaned and rubbed my forehead. *I need this to be over.*

When I looked up from my salad, everyone in the restaurant was staring at me. They all quickly looked away—except for Cassy—but it twisted my stomach into a knot.

I couldn't eat any more food. The salad wasn't as good as Mom's, the pizza was a let-down, and everyone else kept staring an awful lot. Whenever somebody left, they watched me on their way out. I couldn't read their expressions. These faces I'd seen my whole life, but they were blank. They were strangers.

"Here's your check," Cassy said, handing me the leather book.

I handed her my credit card. "Thanks."

"Are you doing okay, honey?" she asked, our hands meeting on the card.

I crossed my arms and nodded. "I'm fine."

"Are you sure?"

"I need to hurry, thanks."

She cleared her throat and went to the register, returned a moment later, and handed me the receipt. I shakily signed my name and left a good tip.

"You know, if you need anything… I know how it is. I lost my sister, you know." Cassy bit her lip. "It's really hard to move on after—"

"Thanks. Here." I slapped the receipt onto the table and stood up, feeling unsteady.

"Kaia—"

"Thanks. Bye."

I shuffled out of the booth and Cassy moved aside. The restaurant's bright TVs and neon signs were shifting around like a fun-house mirror. Cassy frowned at me—I hated the pitying expression on her pretty, innocent face—and left toward the register.

I tipped you ten bucks. Leave me alone, girl.

Am I that easy to read? Am I so obviously fucked up?

For two weeks, I'd been watching this hourglass in my mind. The pale sand trickling to the bottom. Obviously, if I didn't do something, if nobody saved her, Allison would die. But now, I started to think the hourglass was mine, too.

If I didn't do something, I was going to go crazy. I would never forgive myself. I could never move on.

We were both gonna end up here. Buried in New Haven graves. She was meant for so much more than this backwards, backwater town. We were meant to go places. Together.

<> <> <>

Ten minutes later, I left the post office holding a plain, manilla envelope in my hand, the color like paper sitting in the sun for ten years. I turned off Main Street, heading for the library on Second. The school was over there, too. One building for K through eight and one for high school. Crammed together. Our town library — a converted one-room schoolhouse — was tucked away beside the brick school buildings.

Ever since she went missing, I'd been avoiding the school. High school and Allison went hand-in-hand. That's when people figure out who they like, hate, love. It's when I knew I loved Allison. We did everything together. We became ourselves together.

I'd avoided the whole block of memories. Until the letters started coming.

When I responded to these letters, I usually wrote about Allison. It seemed healthy. It felt good, at least, until the memories turned into gruesome nightmares. But she kept floating to the surface of my thoughts. I needed to keep writing about her.

And I had strategy behind it, too. I figured the more I told this mysterious writer about us — the more I made them *feel* for me — the sooner they'd give me all the info I needed. Give me their trust.

So they said, anyway.

I used to hurry down this road with Allison, trying not to be late for first period. Now, I hurried alone, and I carried this envelope that might hold her life.

Am I already out of time?

<> <> <>

When the library and school came into closer review, I felt those crystal-clear memories resurfacing, and I pictured Allison... holding a crayon, sticking out her tongue and concentrating so hard.

"Damn it."

I reached up with my one free hand to wipe my eyes. In my other, I held the envelope, wanting to shove the thing in my pocket and hug myself all the way to the library. But I guess *women's* pants don't get pockets.

"Stupid ass letters and coloring books," I muttered, hunching my shoulders. I spat a string of expletives as I carried on down the road.

I didn't *want* to think about Allison. I could barely sleep most nights, imagining her somewhere chained up. In the dark. Horrible images. The kind that made me raid my parents' liquor cabinet or find somewhere to...

Deep breaths. Look around. What do you see?

Out loud and quietly, I said, "There's a dude running up there. Looks kinda gross. I don't mess with that. A blue car. The church with death-bells and that huge tree. I'd sit there again... some shade..."

I saw on the internet about ways to stop a panic attack, and that one worked the best for me. I thought about asking my parents to get a therapist. I thought about it every day. But I told myself I didn't *need* one because we were gonna save Allison, and then I'd be happier than ever. Happier like months ago.

It still didn't make sense how quickly everything had turned. One day, we were running together in the rain. I could still imagine her drenched top sticking to her chest. If I focused on that version of her — the one who could never die — then I felt better. We shared a meal and laughed about the future, how crazy it all felt. Then she was gone.

"Not forever," I grumbled. I turned onto Second Street and spotted the library ahead. "Red car up there. Ugly car. And some mom chasing their toddler around the yard. Library. The school."

Maybe I should've seen it coming. But everyone had high-school friends who got hitched and it felt like *one* of them might literally go insane if the other one left. I felt that way about Malaki. But I didn't expect… I never thought he was actually evil. And I didn't use that word lightly, but it absolutely fit and nobody could argue.

He was evil. And because of him, I'd lost my best friend.

I couldn't imagine facing him ever again. I wanted nothing to do with that bastard. And yet, I had a feeling our paths would cross. He had answers I needed. Maybe he was the key.

Day to day, it was getting harder and harder to cope. If these letters ended up being a hoax or a joke, I'd lose my shit. I couldn't take it anymore. I wasn't even scared of the house now. I had its image burned in my head. I lived in its shadow. Those sharp-angled roofs and the penetrating windows. The cold exterior, rotting porch. I could see — or remember — the vines clinging to every surface and the fountain filled with mold and weeds. From Main Street or the hills, anywhere I stood, the house towered over me. It blocked out the sky. It cut through the clouds and begged me to come closer.

I knew I would go back. The sooner the better. But even still… I couldn't imagine actually *stepping* through the doorway again. Making that choice. And I couldn't imagine stopping, either.

It had a grip, and I was done trying to fight it.

"Hey there."

I jerked up to find Jeremy. He was blocking the sidewalk that led to the library front door. His bulky arms were crossed, holding no books. It wasn't the first time I'd seen him here. I ran into him at the library twice last week alone.

"Oh. Hi." I lowered my eyes.

"How are you doing, Kaia?"

Don't look away, I told myself. So, I refocused on his face—eerily like my dad's but with a bigger beard—and held eye contact. I didn't blink. I didn't cry. I cleared my throat and said, "Doing fine. Thanks."

He nodded and shifted on his feet.

"You much of a reader?" I said, gesturing behind him. I also crossed my arms, hiding the envelope against my chest.

"Oh, no..." Jeremy cleared his throat. "I was just... um... checking out some old newspapers."

"Mm. Gotcha. Anything specific?"

"Well, you know." He smiled, fake as hell. "Nothing too specific."

"Cool."

He studied me for another moment, but I kept my walls up. Jeremy glanced around us and then stepped closer to me.

"I'm actually... looking into Wheeler," he said, lowering his voice. "I think... Well, I can explain it to you if—"

"Oh?" I frowned. "The sheriff? Sounds like something my dad would want to hear about."

Jeremy gave another fake smile and narrowed his eyes. I knew they hadn't been talking for a couple weeks, but he probably didn't expect that.

When he didn't say anything, I quickly said, "Gonna head

inside, then."

"Yeah… Let me know if you need anything, okay?"

"Will do." I moved ahead on the sidewalk, making Jeremy step aside into the dead grass. "Have a good one."

"You too."

Moments later, at my regular library table, I ripped open the envelope and ate up the words. They were written in neat, tight writing. Black ink on a yellowed page. It looked different from a pen, somehow, but I didn't know anybody who wrote using one of those… fancy things. Fountain pens.

Dear Kaia from New Haven,

I'm sorry to hear about your friend, Allison. She sounds lovely. I find it amusing our town still has a library, in fact. I expected it to shutter many years ago. Thank you for your descriptions. It has been too long since I walked those roads.

As well, thank you for your continued responses. You are beginning to gain my trust. I have lots of things I can tell you. I'm sorry for being so vague in my previous writing, but one never knows who to trust in this current climate.

Dear Kaia, there is much going on at that house, things beyond your wildest ideas. Indeed, I fear Allison has been caught up in some terrible wrong. But all hope is not lost. I know some of the wrongs, and I knew the boy, Malaki. I know what he has and hasn't done.

Before I can trust you further, please outline for me what you saw or heard in the house. I believe there is more beneath the surface than you may expect.

I implore you to not give up hope. We must find a time to talk in person.

Until then,

Stay safe.

<> <> <>

Things were always worse at night.

Even when I tried not to, my thoughts wandered back to her. I'd seen her almost every day for six years. I'd give anything to see her again.

One night — it doesn't matter when; they were all the same — I was sitting on my bed, watching television (they finally let me have one in my room after all the shit I went through). The show turned blurry, and I zoned out. Before I knew it, a happy memory rushed in, and then it fell apart. Puzzle pieces scattered on the carpet. Glass shards in my feet.

Last school year, Allison and I were here. On my bed. During the winter, Christmas Break, we'd spend hours in my room and watch the light dying through the window. We wore long, wool socks and shivered under a blanket. My laptop sat at the foot of the bed. A mind-numbing Christmas movie played loudly through the speakers.

"Smells like your mom's baking," Allison said.

She was leaning against my chest, watching the screen. This time, though, when I looked down, she was staring up at me. I had my arm around her shoulders. She smiled, showing all her teeth, and I didn't know why.

"Cookies, probably," I said. "Mom's always baking cookies."

"Is Nate in his room?"

"Probably downstairs." I laughed. "Eating the cookies."

"Oh, right." Allison reached up and brushed a strand of hair from my face. There was some kind of tension I couldn't name.

She studied me, batting her eyelashes.

"What are you thinking about?" I asked.

"I... Nothing. I don't know."

The sun sank lower. Her smile grew wider. The night went by too quickly. Christmas Break passed in a hurry. Back to school. Sprinting headfirst into graduation. And before I knew it, she was gone.

I came back to reality, laying on my carpet. I crawled over to kneel by the window. There was an incense holder and a pack from the crystal store. I placed a stick of incense and held a lighter to it. There was a small pile of pale ash on the windowsill.

Everyone was happy then. Nobody knew how things would fall apart.

Smoke tendrils reached into the air, and I settled on the carpet again. This scent would calm me. It had before. I leaned against the bed sheets and buried my face, waiting for some relief.

You'll never get it back. That feeling. That moment. Even if she's alive, she'll never be the same. And neither will you.

I started to spiral, so I sat up and looked around the room, noting different colors and objects. But memories clung to everything, and it all turned blurry again. There was a tearstain on the bed sheet where I'd been laying.

I tried taking deep breaths, thinking about nothing, but nothing—the concept—was so overwhelming. This wasn't a calm anxiety. I was suffocating in here. I couldn't go outside. I couldn't answer questions or explain.

Vividly, I saw Allison by the window. She was standing in her underwear, hands on the windowsill, back to me. It was nearly dark outside. She pulled off her shirt. I watched from the floor. I think I'd been talking. And then she turned.

This time, scars marked her whole body. Her face was half-melted and missing. With a terrible crack, her legs bent inward, and her bones started popping.

"Allison!" I screamed. "Allison, stop!"

It kept happening in my mind. Over and over. Her knees crumpling. Her body collapsed, wearing scars and gaping wounds.

"Allison!"

I pulled the covers off the bed and hid under them on the floor. Pressing both fists into my eyes. Trying to forget the image.

What's happening to her? Is she alive?

You'll never get it back. That feeling.

There's nothing I can do.

You haven't even tried.

I started crying, scratching at the floor. I crawled over to my dresser, blankets wrapped around my shoulders. I could smell her perfume as if she'd been here. Visualize her big, toothy grin and her cute elbows pressed into me.

I reached into the bottom drawer and pulled out the bottle of whiskey I'd taken from Dad's cabinet. He didn't know, and he didn't need to.

I sank to the floor with it, choking.

Please, just let me sleep.

CHAPTER 5
BENJAMIN "CLIFF" WOODS

"Baggs is really excited," I said to Naomi. "He was going on and on."

She nodded, staring ahead.

"I mean, he's been coaching Nate for… what, six years now?" I laughed and thought about how quickly childhoods were gone. "He said their eighth-grade team is gonna be the best one in years. Should be a lot of fun once those two are back in school."

We were on the back porch, like always. Naomi and I each had our spots, two chairs beside a circle table. From here, we could see our backyard with the huge oak tree, the distant forest, and my soybean fields in between. Most evenings, it was the perfect spot to cool down after a hard day. But today had been easy, and the record heat meant I could never cool off.

"Well, that's good."

We were silent for a minute. The type of silence born from almost twenty-five married years.

It had been a lazy day for me, which I didn't often get. There was a big storm rolling in soon, so I couldn't mess with the hay field much 'til it passed. I'd done some minor upkeep on the tractor that morning — I would finish it tomorrow — and then went to Nate's game. I had picked up a couple parts in town and tried not to look at the empty spot where George's shop had been.

There was a lot going on right now, and I was falling behind on my never-ending to-do list. But I tried not to worry about it. There were more important things.

"Baggs did say if Nate wants to play in college — like seriously play — then he's gonna have to find a bigger high school. Better competition and all that. New Haven won't cut it."

Naomi turned to me. "Like what? The only school besides New Haven is almost an hour away."

"I know."

"We chose *this* home." She ground her teeth. "Are *you* gonna drive him an hour to school and back? That's four hours a day, Ben. That school's never gonna send buses out here. Too stuck up their own —"

"I mean, I could," I interrupted her. "I'll… find some podcasts. Do all my work here while he's at school."

"Oh, okay." She forced a dry laugh. "Funny how you never offered for Kaia to go there, now all of a sudden —"

"She didn't want to!" I protested.

"Says who?" With her eyes, Naomi pushed me against the back of my chair. "You never asked her. Never offered anything like this. 'Too busy,' you would've said. *Did* say."

"I know, Naomi, I'm sorry." I threw up my hands in surrender. "You're right. I'm just trying to do what's best for Nate."

"Yeah…" She exhaled and her shoulders slumped. "I know. Sorry. Just frustrated." She reached for her water. The sweating glass left a ring on the table. "And scared."

"It's all fine, honey. I was just telling you what his coach said."

She nodded, but her expression didn't change.

"What are you scared of?"

"There's a lot going on. You know that. Rhys is a… big change, obviously. Nate seems older now. And Kaia's…"

"Well, Nate has to get older sometime."

Naomi huffed. "You know what I'm saying. Ever since that night, he's more serious. Less like a kid. I don't like it."

"I don't like it either, really. But I think he's gonna be okay. He's growing up and… Yeah."

There was a pregnant pause as I waited for her to speak. I knew from her expression she had more to say. We'd been arguing a lot more than usual lately, and I was trying to do better at this part. Listening.

"I get worried about the two boys. You know? Like… do you think Nate likes him?" Naomi asked me. "Is Nate okay with him staying here? Is he gonna resent us for it?"

She was watching the two boys in the yard. Nate and Rhys were playing two-man baseball. One pitcher, the other batter. Then they would switch. Rhys barely ever hit the ball, even when Nate pitched real slow. On the other hand, Nate kept trying to blast it over the huge oak tree. He would sprint to retrieve the ball, and Rhys would wait awkwardly in the shade.

"I think he likes him. Not sure, really. He's nice to him. They get along."

"Right. But it's got to be weird for Nate…" Naomi rubbed the back of her hand.

"What? Having Rhys here?"

"Having him *live* here. Having to lie about him. And it's not like we have a plan. You think Nate can't tell? He's smart, Ben."

I frowned. "I mean… what's there to plan for?"

"He can't just live here forever. He has a family. He has people. Somewhere."

"Yeah, I guess you're right."

Naomi shook her head. "It's fine for now. And I know we needed to give him a place. But I'm just saying. We gotta figure out where he came from. Or become his foster parents or something."

"Yeah. True."

"And you're really busy right now. I know you said you'll call someone, and it's not the best—"

"Just give it time," I said. I leaned over and placed a hand on her knee. "I haven't been able to find anything out yet. But if nothing works, I'll call… the government or something."

She laughed a little. "The government?"

"I don't know. Who do you call for a thing like this?"

"Social services. Or the school."

"Oh, alright. I'll call them, then. Alright? We've… we've got bigger things to worry about right now. But I'll call someone."

"Okay. CPS, that's who you call. Just do it soon. Please, Ben? Even if we're just going to foster him, that's… paperwork and stuff. You know?"

"Yeah, because I *love* paperwork and stuff."

"But still. We have to."

Even though the sun had fallen below the tree line, it was a sticky evening. Just sitting on the porch, my armpits were soaked through. The boys had sunk to the grass and were sitting under the oak tree, tossing the ball back and forth, talking about God-knows-what.

In a way, having Rhys around made it easier for me. I didn't feel as guilty for not practicing baseball with Nate. He still wanted to hit a homerun, but he had Rhys to throw him easy pitches. I had a ton of work to do anyway. I was *constantly* working. Drinking water by the gallons, sweating it right out. This was the filthy, drenched part of summer. This whole month of July, and it had only started.

"How many people you think will be there?" Naomi asked. "George's funeral, I mean."

She looked at me for a second and then focused on the distant forest. The sky around it was turning red. The leaves were crowded, whispering. Wind rushed against my cheek like a cold drink of water.

"Most of the town, I'd guess." I exhaled and ran both hands over my face. "I know it's not until Monday, but I can't stop thinking about it. I'm not ready."

"For the funeral or the people?"

"Both. It's just hard thinking about George."

"I'm sorry, hun."

"I know we weren't super close. But… we grew up together." I took a deep breath. "And he was always nice. Always in town. Things are so different… Getting different. Everybody leaving, selling, dying… You know. With everything that's happened, people don't act the same."

"To you?"

I nodded and wished I had a glass of whiskey. I needed to buy more, because apparently I'd finished off a bottle and not realized it.

"Talk to me, honey," Naomi pressed. She leaned over and put a hand on my knee.

"Well, you know about Jerem. Still won't talk to me. Still mad. And in town… it's just hard, Naomi."

She grabbed my hand. "What's going on?"

"People there… aren't the same. When I go into town, I can feel 'em looking at me. They whisper. They avoid me. At the hardware store, the guys don't chat with me anymore. Used to talk about the fields, at least, but now… nothing. They're cold businessmen. And I've… I've known them for forty years! Hell, I—"

"Maybe they were just busy, you know?"

"Yeah, maybe. But it's never been like this. Not ever."

She shook her head. "And Jeremy's still mad?"

"*Still*. It's Sheriff Wheeler, too," I went on. It felt good to open up like this and complain about everything. "I never told you, but… you know he actually follows me sometimes when I'm in town? I'll see his little cop car in my mirror, trailing. Then he'll stop at the edge of Main Street as I go."

"That's weird." Naomi scratched at her scalp. "What about…"

I went on, "At least Jeremy's coming around, I think. Kaia said he told her something about 'looking into' the sheriff."

"Why does any of it matter? Malaki confessed. He said he… killed her."

"That won't fix things forever. I think the funeral…" I exhaled deeply. "Well, look, I know this town, and I can read it. And I've got a theory."

"Go on."

I cleared my throat and finished off my glass of water. "Funeral happens, right, and people are gonna feel all the ways they did before. Angry, confused. They're gonna want someone to blame, yeah? And you know… Malaki's the hometown kid, right? Confession or not, there's no body yet. Plus…" Cliff exhaled deeply. "I heard his dad's getting a lawyer. You know, the Brooksville guy. He's… he's good, they say."

"They're not gonna come after you, Ben." Naomi squeezed my hand. "Nobody is. You're a local, too. Malaki can only plead insanity, if anything."

"Sure. But they… or somebody, might go after the Dawes. No, I know, but it's a possibility. And the fact that we brought in Rhys… I don't know, Naomi. I just think we've been underestimating people. Anger and fear… it can make people do things they normally wouldn't."

The boys walked back toward the porch soon after. Nate peeled off his shirt and stretched his arms.

"What's for dinner?" he called as they approached.

"Just make a sandwich," Naomi said. "It's too late to cook anything."

With disappointment, he shuffled inside. I reached for something to say as they went, but my focus was miles away. A dozen problems on a carousel in my brain. A dozen fears or things that could go wrong.

Naomi stared at me as the screen door slapped behind us.

"Do you think people in town…" Naomi hesitated. "If they're isolating you, are they gonna do that to our kids, too? Do you think Kaia and Nate will be okay?"

"I don't think it'll affect them," I said. "Well, not him, anyway."

"But Kaia?"

I shrugged. "She's in a weird spot because of Allison and…"

"She wants to stay here for another year," Naomi said. "She doesn't wanna go to college yet."

"Because of Allison?"

"She didn't say it, but I think so. Kaia's taking it really hard. Obviously. She won't talk about it, and I get it. It's not easy. I just don't know how to bring it up, honestly. Or if I should."

"Maybe there's nothing we can do," I said. "If she's grieving…"

"But what if she isn't?" Naomi drank the rest of her water and set the glass on the table. She stared into its emptiness. "What if she's still looking?"

<> <> <>

The day after Kaia had escaped from the house on the hill, Jeremy saved some choice words for me. He'd called me the next night at almost eleven, yelling through the phone. His voice had been slurred and there was a lot of fire behind it.

"I knew it," he snapped at me. "Right away. When George — the store caught on fire. I knew this was big, Cliff, and you — "

"It's done, Jeremy."

"It's not!" he hollered. I heard something clatter to the ground on his end. "It's not done. You're gonna see. You're gonna…" He paused, gasping for breath, but revved up again. "I knew this was real bad — you just wanted to sit… get *off* your *ass* and — "

I held the phone away from my ear as his voice blasted obscenities. As he went on, I stepped outside onto the back porch, listening to his rant. Pinching the bridge of my nose, I took a deep breath.

" — always following, but you never *start* things. You wait for someone else to do the hard part. You jump on board at the end. You goddamn coward — "

"Well, if you *knew*," I finally hissed back, right into the mic, "you should've stopped it. Things have only gotten worse since you got involved! How's that work, huh?"

"I'm doing more to protect your kids than you are, dumbass!" His voice was definitely slurred by this point.

"Hah! Yeah, okay. Go to bed, asshole."

"Old Cliff Woods, too scared and dumb to take a shit."

"What are you even saying?"

"Go to hell, Cliff! I'm the only one who took this serious, and now I'm in over my head, busting my — "

"You go to hell!"

I hung up before he could say another word. In the darkness, arms crossed, I'd paced for a few minutes on the back porch.

It'd been nearly three weeks since our shouting match, and Jeremy hadn't spoken to me. I'd seen him in town, made eye contact, but we never spoke. I heard about him from other people. Now, those people were talking to me less and less.

What's going on in this town?

<> <> <>

After our conversation, Naomi and I went to bed. I woke up the next morning before dawn. For a moment, I forgot what I had to do. Everything pressed on us. But it rushed back as soon as I stood.

I still remembered the time in my life when all our friends were getting married. Everyone having babies and some moving away. Eventually, the weddings and the births slowed down. Divorces popped up. And now, it seemed, I was on to the next phase.

Now, I'd be attending everyone's funerals, until I eventually slept through my own.

George's funeral—my first one in years—was only a day away. I stumbled into the bathroom, bleary-eyed and yawning. Stretching my arms, I turned back and saw Naomi curled up, her back to me. She didn't stir as I shut the door.

I splashed cold water on my face and let it drip from my beard. Today, I needed to finish my maintenance on the tractor. Burn through my to-do list, go to sleep early. Tomorrow, I'd wake up the kids and we'd sit in a church pew with the rest of New Haven, mourning a man and his son. Wondering who to blame.

I knew this town better than most. I wanted to say I had the answers, but...

Kaia insisted Malaki couldn't have started the fire. He was getting married that day, after all. She was there with him and Allison. I thought he *could've* done something the day before. A wedding wasn't a stone-cold alibi.

George and his boy were tied up, I reminded myself. *Malaki couldn't have done that.*

Or could he?

Doesn't matter right now. I shook my head and left the bathroom, pulling at my beard, water droplets clinging to my face. *This isn't a weekend to investigate. We're grieving.*

In the dark, I threw on a pair of jeans and a shirt. Naomi slept in the bed, unmoving. Her jewelry box rested on the dresser below the mirror. I caught a glimpse of myself and looked away quickly.

Trudging out of our bedroom and down the hallway, the house was silent. It smelled clean, soft carpet between my toes. I always enjoyed quiet mornings like this. Everybody here, no one rushing out for school. Those days would end soon, and the mornings would be chaotic.

I heard nothing upstairs. It wasn't even seven, so the kids wouldn't be up for a few hours. Probably not until I woke them.

I passed our family pictures hanging on the walls. For a moment, I paused there and looked. The four of us, smiling wide, in different locations. First in our backyard by the huge oak tree. Then by my barn, sitting on a trailer hitched to my tractor. The faces that stared back were less than a year old, taken last fall. Yet they were so different.

In the photographs, Nate looked like a child. His arms weren't as muscular. His jaw had a layer of kid-fat that burnt off during baseball season. Kaia's bright smile was full of hope. She looked free and unburdened.

Naomi and I had a few pictures taken of just us. The first time we'd had professional photos since Nate was born. She looked up at me adoringly. I smiled back. And I seemed more confident in the image. Less afraid of things.

I groaned and moved away. *Need to make some coffee.*

In the kitchen, I was surrounded by digital clocks reading 6:52. I was already counting down the hours, even though the day had just started.

Just over three weeks ago, George and his son had died. It still didn't feel right. Like a thick curtain with a tear down the middle, light streaming through into the darkest corners. Nothing could ever be the same.

While the coffee brewed, I flicked on the television to the weather channel and busied myself in the kitchen. A few dirty dishes waited in the sink. The floor needed swept. And I would water Naomi's plants on the back porch.

I did all of this quickly, deftly. I spent my whole life now doing meaningless chores just so my wife would notice. —For some reason, I thought of Jeremy while I cleaned, and I envied him. I'd never tell him, of course, but maybe he had some things right.

When the coffee was finished, I filled a mug and carried it outside. On the back porch, steaming coffee in hand, I looked around and breathed in the crisp, morning air. It brushed past me, and I savored it. Today would be another miserable one, record heatwaves, but for now it felt great outside. Like a fresh start.

The soybean fields were greener every day. I could see the strawberry patch, full of vibrant red, would probably need picked that afternoon. And after the big storm passed through, the hay fields were waiting.

I took a gulp of coffee. These days, my to-do list threatened to suffocate me. I needed to work in the barn and in the fields and get ready for harvesting. I needed to find answers about Rhys—I still hadn't called anyone, despite what I told my wife—and keep the sheriff from breaking down my door. I needed to mend things with Jeremy and my kids and help Naomi as much as possible.

Taking deep breaths, I said out loud, "There's still this week. Today and tomorrow are about George."

But wasn't everything about George and the Davis shop? Wasn't that how this whole thing started? We still didn't know why it burnt down. The motive or anything.

You never practiced with me, Dad.

I shook my head vigorously and moved on. Time to start.

I left my empty coffee mug on the porch and shuffled away, crunching over the gravel. Birds circled above me in the trees, landing on the house. Tiny but loud, their songs went in one ear and out the other. A warming wind smacked me across the face, dew sparkled on the grass, and I wandered into the barn, the only place I felt completely comfortable.

I knew what needed to be done. In here, I could block out everything else. In here, there was always a second chance to do things right. It usually took a few attempts, because nothing ever worked the first time. I was used to it. The mistakes and the try-agains.

I guess I was worried—with Nate and Kaia and even Naomi—that I wouldn't always get another chance. I felt paralyzed, and this paralysis led me to even more mistakes.

Entering through one of the side doors, I passed by our chickens and through the familiar smell of hay and feed and animal shit. There was a wire fence outside connected to their pen. I stepped through a small gate and opened the door for them so they could roam their fenced-in grassy patch.

I could barely see in the dark barn, but I found my way by instinct to the center, the open area where I kept all my farm equipment. When I pulled the long, hanging string, a light flicked on above me—pale yellow, casting unclear shadows. The whole building was packed with junk. The tractor was closest to the big, double doors, with a combine nearby—my main focus for the day—and my cultivator and planter wedged behind it.

In the small, side bays, I had various tool collections, equipment heads, other attachments I hardly ever touched. The whole floor was spread with dirt and hay. We used to have pigs in one bay. That was a bad idea, but back then I thought of myself as a real, New Haven farmer. The kind my grandpa and dad would be proud of. The kind that wouldn't end up selling the family farm.

I mean, if Jeremy Adams could manage huge plots of land, chickens, pigs, *and* two cows, why couldn't I? My whole family line had done it forever, why couldn't I? Well, I couldn't.

And the family line… I guess Jeremy Adams and I had one thing in common. Neither of us had a son who wanted to take over the farm. We'd both die, and the farms—family farms—would get snatched up by a corporate machine for pennies on the dollar.

As I set to work on the combine—this thing would work a ton in July and then sit untouched for ten months—I had trouble focusing on the task at hand. I'd typically start my preseason inspection with the feeder house, checking the chains for wear and ensuring the slats were parallel. I'd move on from there to the bearings, then the rotor. There was always residue buildup I had to clear out.

I was in the middle of this when I heard someone enter through the side door. The chickens were clucking noisily and flapping their wings. I perked up and listened. There were footsteps, the sound of a cup dipping into chicken feed.

"That you, Nate?" I called out.

There was no answer, but the footsteps drew closer. Kaia emerged, her hair in a bun, wearing a sleeveless shirt and a bandana.

"You know that boy isn't awake yet."

I chuckled and wiped both dirty hands on my jeans. "You're right. I forgot you all were taking turns doing the feeding."

She shrugged and looked around at my mess of farm equipment. I knew to her the machines weren't significant. She probably could've told me what a combine and cultivator did, but that was about it. I didn't mind, though. I dealt with all this—the grimy tools, air choked with dust, toiling away in the dim, yellow light—so they didn't have to. And anyway, she probably knew more than Nate.

"How are you… doing today?" she asked. Her tone wasn't quite normal.

"I'm fine. Did you sleep okay?"

Kaia was standing in the shadows, so I couldn't make out her features. But she said, "Yeah, I'm alright," and it sounded like the truth.

"Is your mom up yet?"

"No." She shook her head and kicked absentmindedly at a clump of dirt. "I think I'm gonna… head into town, actually."

"Oh, alright. George's funeral is tomorrow, you know. Might be busy there. But anyway, if the store's open, could you pick up a blade for the disc-bine? Save me a trip."

"Oh, definitely. I'll definitely get you a blade for your disc-thing." She laughed. "Think I know what those look like?"

"Okay, okay." I moved to my workbench and started shuffling through my toolbox. "I can send you a picture."

"I've gotta run a couple errands first, so you got time," she said. "Oh, right. Um… Can I take Mom's car?"

"I'm sure that's fine. I'll say yes for her since you're getting me the disc-blade."

"Yeah. If you figure out how to send pictures on your phone," she teased.

"Oh, come on. Have a little faith."

She was always running into town these days. Sometimes with Nate, sometimes by herself. I wanted to ask why. What did she do there? Why didn't she tell us? But I didn't want to press too hard. And more importantly —

"Well, I guess I'll see you later," I said. "You wanna help me pick the strawberries maybe?"

Kaia nodded. "Maybe. Probably." She headed out the same way she'd come in and called, "Bye, Dad, love you."

"I love you too, Kaia. Be safe."

CHAPTER 6
KAIA WOODS

Way back in June, at the beginning of the summer, I'd asked Dad about going to college. He'd done it before, and it was weighing on me. All those last-minute college decisions and stress packed into one summer… I was freaking out.

We'd been on the back porch. Just the two of us. Mom had taken Nate into town for his first game of the summer season. Dad and I were about to head that way. But he'd stopped for a minute to carry a few empty buckets to the barn, and I'd helped him because I'm like that.

"It's never easy to leave home," he said as we marched across the gravel driveway. "But it's for the best. And college is… pretty fun once you get adjusted." He turned and grinned at me. "Trust me. In four years, you'll be sad it's over."

"But is Mom gonna be okay when I leave?" I asked. I bumped my knee against the bucket, bouncing it rhythmically. "Who's gonna… chill on the porch with her? And go grocery shopping with her?"

Dad smiled warmly. "Your mom's gonna be okay, Kaia. I promise."

At the side door, he held it open, and the smell of chickens and dirty hay wafted over me. I stepped inside, careful not to whack my head, and turned right to avoid the chicken shit.

"She's just gonna be alone with you… boys," I said, forcing a short laugh.

Dad followed me into the back storage room and set his buckets on the floor. I placed mine there, too.

"She's been through a lot worse than boys. Your mom's incredibly strong. When you do go, it might be harder for me than her."

"Nah, don't think so." I led the way back out of the barn, talking over my shoulder. "I just know it's gonna be hard for me. So, I'm kinda worried for her."

"Well, you could talk to her about it. I'm sure she'd like that."

I nodded. "Yeah. I've still got a few months here, so…"

How things change.

The summer after high school was supposed to be a little weird. To go by fast. The first half was all about fun and moving on and out-of-school fever. Weeks would go by. Graduation parties. Then it was *really* about moving on. Saying goodbye.

It was supposed to be a little weird. It wasn't supposed to be anything like mine.

<> <> <>

Just over a month later, everything had changed.

Mom told me a little about when she went into the house. Not specific details — she'd barely been holding it together for a few days. But when she did talk about the house, she played it off lightly. Called it a bad trip, something unnatural but not real, not physical. She really tried to be as vague as possible and make it sound less dangerous. I knew she wasn't convinced.

One helpful bit: She said it was the same for her. Everything changed afterward. She became a new person.

This new version of me was always scared. Looking out for danger. I felt a weird power after I survived the house, but also like part of me was left up there. Like I was missing something.

Afterward, nighttime scared me. The darkness. In the country, it dropped like a heavy, choking curtain. Hid everything. It wasn't the kind of thing I'd ever admit. High school graduates didn't say they were afraid of the dark. But I couldn't lie to myself anymore.

During the day, I could see so far. Huge trees marked the edge of my world—tiny, distant playthings. They made a wall around us, filled in with tractors, baseball games, and family dinners. I could see danger coming from a mile away. But when night fell, the opposite was true. Everything felt close, suffocating. A foot away, invisible, there could be anything.

I woke up in the middle of the night drenched in sweat, bed sheets sticking to me. I lay there, shivering, and thought about the police lights.

<> <> <>

Running onto the old, rotting porch. The wood is soft and unsteady as I race across. There are police lights all around the house, like a disco sea. Rain falls from the sky in waves. I sprint to the cold, wet grass and fall into Mom's arms. Jeremy and the sheriff are nearby. Everything and everyone is soaked.

All those voices, rumbling. Everyone staring at me. Lightning flashes in the sky.

They shout, and I turn around to see Malaki in the doorway. He drops the knife and strolls across the porch like he owns it. The deputies grab him. He doesn't fight. His eyes find me, and his dead smile burns into my brain. I'll never forget it.

They handcuff him. Five officers clutching his arms and shoulders. They lead him away, but he glances over toward me. I hide my face in Mom's shoulder. I feel her arms around me, tight. She's talking, soft words. She's saying it'll be okay.

I only look back once as they're shoving him into a police car. His grin never fades. As the car turns around in the grass, he's still smiling. I don't look away until he's gone.

The police car fades into the darkness until it's only taillights, trailing away.

Jeremy asks, "Are you okay?" and squats next to me.

"Fine," I insist. "Fine. I'm fine."

Mom asks, "Are you okay?" and squeezes me tighter. Her tone isn't calm anymore. It's shaky and angry, and I hug her so hard it hurts me.

"I'm fine, Mom. I love you. I'm fine, and I'm sorry."

Sheriff Wheeler approaches later. He asks, "Are you okay?" He apologizes for "how things went down." And he promises to leave the Dawes alone.

I feel Mom tense.

"I'm real sorry 'bout Allison, too," he adds. "I know you two were close and all."

"She's not dead!" I scream. "She's in that fucking house!"

"We'll look," he says, nodding. "Swear on my father's grave, we'll look everywhere. But… Kaia, you've got to know it's unlikely."

Jeremy snaps at the sheriff and pulls him away from me. I hear Jeremy yelling as they head toward the house, and he's going on and on. Sheriff Wheeler takes the abuse calmly.

"Your dad's coming," Mom says. "Your brother, too. It's gonna be okay, Kaia."

They show up. The truck arrives, rattling up the hill, breaking the silence. All the cops are inside by now except for two, and I can hear the crickets again until his truck comes rushing up.

Then it all turns blurry. They bring me home. I wobble inside and fall asleep on the couch. I think Mom and Dad stay up all night, by my side, because whenever I wake up from my nightmares they're with me.

When things were too much and too heavy, I usually sat in my room, lit a stick of incense, and tried to focus on the happier memories. I'd been Googling different ways to deal with anxiety and trauma and all that stuff. Some of it worked, some of it didn't, but when I focused on Allison and only thought about the old versions of us, I felt better. For a while. And then even worse. Wasn't that just how shit went?

I was lying in my room on the floor, holding up a Polaroid. The old versions of us. A picture from our graduation party — yeah, we had one together. In the memories worth anything, we were always together.

Before long, it was five a.m. My room smelled like a campfire and a garden mixed together. I held the Polaroid and replayed that day in my mind. Every single detail I could recall. The colors were dimmed, but it didn't matter. I could taste her again. How different things had been. Only a month ago.

Allison had shown up an hour early so we could get ready together. Dress up, makeup, the whole thing.

"Wait 'til you see my dress," she said, hopping out of her car with a smile. "Mom thinks it's too short, but you know." She flattened it against her thighs. "I can do what I want. We're graduates, right?"

"That's right," I said. "The worst part's over."

She laughed and hugged me. Then she pulled away. "Have you heard the new Bruno Mars album?"

"No? Why would I—"

"Come on, girl." Allison clicked her tongue. "Keep up. Let's head to your room. We can listen while we get ready."

"Only if you promise not to sing," I teased. "It's *his* album, let's keep it that way."

"Hey! Don't be cruel."

"You still haven't listened to Beyonce or Alicia Keys, but you're throwing some guy named Bruno on me? I can be cruel if I wanna."

She punched me in the shoulder as we headed for the house. "Oh, *whatever.*"

Out here, at my house. We had tables set up in the backyard. Mom and Dad cooked for everyone who showed up—most of the town. There were lots of gifts, and I'd been coasting on that graduation money ever since. But more importantly, so many people…

Family from out-of-town I rarely saw. School friends. Church people. A few of our teachers showed up. Ms. Houchin brought us handmade potholders. Even Ms. Hargrave turned up for a minute and left a card on the table—a card with crystal on the outside, probably from her shop.

"You two look lovely," Ms. Hargrave said, beaming. "Congratulations and best of luck."

"Thank you!" I said.

Then Malaki's uncle asked about my future plans—"Environmental Biology, Dave. She already told you that."—and Allison's parents were stressing about the presents getting mixed up. Malaki was nowhere to be seen; just his annoying aunt and uncle, and I was thankful.

For three hours, Allison and I couldn't be separated. We moved through the party together, laughing, making the rounds. We were both barefoot, and the grass was warm and soft. Allison wore a cute dress, short and colorful. I tried my best, but she always had a way of outdoing everyone. The makeup, the dress… she couldn't have looked better. So gorgeous I could drop dead.

"Kaia, why do you keep staring at me?" she asked, squeezing my hand. She smiled, showing every pearly tooth.

"I'm not!"

"Do I have something on my face?" She reached up with a hand and anxiously felt around. "Barbeque sauce?"

"No," I laughed. "No, nothing on your face. Just look at yourself. How could I not stare?"

"Whatever." She smiled and rolled her eyes. I could never look away.

The two of us walked around for a couple hours. The feeling of grass under our toes. A warm breeze, perfect weather, cloudless sky. Everybody wanted to talk, of course, and I think we introduced each other about fifty times. In quiet moments, we chatted about her wedding plans and what we'd do next in life.

"It's coming up soon," she said. "It's crazy. This year has just been… crazy."

"Graduating. Getting married. You're just doing it all, girl."

"So are you." Allison stopped walking and turned to face me. "You're gonna go to college. Change the world. You're doing more than I am, *trust me*."

"I mean." I shifted from foot to foot. "It's just college. Doesn't feel like a big deal. I hope it's not a waste of money."

"Speaking of money…" She grinned mischievously. "Let's go check out the gift table again."

"And maybe the food table," I said. "I'm hungry. I needa stuff my face before someone else tries talkin' to us."

The day could not have been more perfect. Malaki couldn't even come. It was *that* perfect. Toward the end, once most of the guests had left and only our two families remained, I remembered the camera.

"Hey, I have this Polaroid camera," I said. "Mom gave it to me. And I... I meant to ask earlier. But... can we take some pictures?"

"Hell yeah! Good idea."

So, we did. We went out to the oak tree and burnt through two rolls of Polaroids. We took some pictures of each other, ridiculous poses and goofy smiles. My mom took a couple, too, of us together.

We were on the ground for the last one, both on our knees. I wrapped my arms around Allison, and she put hers around me. Pressed together, squeezing each other, we faced the camera. I smiled so wide.

Afterward, we split the Polaroids evenly, each taking eight.

At the end of the day, the sun had nearly set, and we were laying in the grass. We stared up at the sky while it changed colors. Everyone else was inside. Nobody else existed. And when I looked over, Allison's face was glowing in the golden lighting.

I had the strangest feeling, but one I'd never forget. I didn't understand it then. I fought against it, but... I wanted to reach out and hold her chin. Pull her closer to me.

"Kaia..." She leaned her head against mine. "What about if... if things don't go like we planned?"

"Like what?" I asked. "What things?"

"Just... you know, in general. Stuff happens. What if our plans don't work out? Will we...?"

I reached over and held her hand. It wasn't the first time that day, but this time it sent waves rushing over me. We were alone on the warm grass. Allison didn't comment, but she didn't pull away, either.

"I don't know about plans," I said, "but you and I aren't gonna 'not work out.' I care about you too much. You're my person."

"Aw, thanks Kaia." Allison sighed. "I'm so glad this is all over. To be honest, I'm tired of talking to people. I just wanna… talk with you." She squeezed my hand.

"I need you." I stopped smiling and concentrated only on her. Everything else fell away. Curtains closed. "In my life. Sometimes, you're like… the only thing keeping me together."

"I love you, Kaia."

"I love you, Ally."

And then I reached out—my hands, my move—and cupped her face.

"Ally?"

She smiled, showing teeth. "Okay… Do it."

I kissed her underneath the oak tree, and then I kissed her again, harder, wrapped in a perfect sunset blanket.

<> <> <>

On the back of the Polaroid, she'd drawn a heart and signed her name to the left. I added my name on the right.

I tried not to think about the next day. When she'd called me, crying.

"I shouldn't have done that," she said, sniffling. "I'm getting married."

"It's not a big deal, Ally. That was just… like a graduation thing."

"Right. Yeah, you're right. But what if—?"

"It's not. I mean… people kiss in Europe all the time, right? Like we're friends. We're fine. Okay? I love you." I took a breath and forced myself to add, "Like a friend."

"Yeah. Okay, Kaia."

And I had asked myself for weeks afterward if we should've. If I regretted it. I'd wanted to… like tease her that it happened. And I wanted it to happen again. But whenever I brought it up, she had tried to pretend it hadn't been real. Eventually, we'd stopped talking about it, and we had covered the potholes without filling them.

But I kept the Polaroid and the memory forever.

When I checked the time, it was half-past six. I knew I couldn't sleep any longer, and if I lay in the dark I'd start to spiral. So, I got dressed quickly and tried to keep my mind blank.

Put on deodorant. Brush teeth. Wash face.

I went through the list over and over to avoid thinking of anything else.

Go downstairs. Make breakfast.

I rubbed my eyes, trying to force some life into them. They stared back, vacant and red.

Without a word, I passed Nate's door, still closed, and headed downstairs. Sunlight was just starting to peek through the windows. The soft carpet under my feet and smell of frying bacon brought me back to life. I tried not to think about George's funeral that afternoon or the entire world pressing against me. Instead, I walked into the kitchen, smiled widely, and thought about bacon.

"Ready for later?" Dad asked from his spot by the stove.

I groaned as I reached around him for a glass. "Let's not talk about the funeral yet. It's so early."

"Alright, alright." He shrugged. "I've been up for an hour."

"Good for you." I threw four ice cubes into my glass and filled it with tap water. "It's only six-thirty, psycho."

"Hey, I'm the one making *you* bacon."

"Good point." I yawned loudly. "And… thank you, Dad."

I asked him about his farming and let him rant for a while as he cooked. He'd talk forever about it, and Mom got annoyed. I didn't mind listening, though, and it usually got me on his good side.

"You'd do a good job," he told me after. "You know… farming. You seem to understand it all."

"Oh, yeah?" I smiled and thought about it. A life of overalls. "I don't know about that."

"Sure you would. You're… you're wicked smart."

"Nobody says 'wicked,' Dad."

"Well, still."

He served me a plate of bacon and eggs.

"Gotta shower," he said. "Orange juice in the fridge if you want it."

"Thanks, Dad."

I ate quietly and stared out the window. From the kitchen table, I had the same view as the back porch. I saw the sky over the distant forest turn from light red to blue. Dad reappeared about twenty minutes later, his hair still dripping wet.

"Is Mom awake yet?" I asked.

"She just got in the shower."

"I'm gonna head into town at nine," I told him. "I need to return a library book, so I'll just meet you at the church. Ten o'clock, right?"

"Yeah. It's… at ten." Dad grabbed a plate and tongs. "You know, I've got some work to do in the barn after I eat if you wanna help."

"Um… not today. Sorry."

As he stacked bacon onto the plate, Dad rolled his eyes. "Kids."

"Don't roll your eyes," I laughed. "You look like a… I don't even know, but it's weird."

He scowled at me and left the kitchen, leaving the plate on the table. I grabbed another piece of bacon.

For almost an hour, I sat in the living room, watching the morning news. In the huge, cushioned armchair, I was a zombie with only four hours of sleep. I drifted off a few times. When Dad woke up the boys, they came thundering downstairs and woke me up, so I yelled a bit. Mom appeared from her bedroom as I grumbled to myself. She said a quick good morning and started making coffee.

"Can I take your car into town before the funeral?" I asked her. "I've gotta run to the library, and I figured you're gonna ride with Dad."

She frowned at me with tired eyes. "Huh?"

"Your car."

"Oh. Uh…" She pressed a button on the coffee machine. "I'm not going. I'm gonna visit Anne Dawes while you all are at the church."

"Oh. Alright."

I needed to know if there was a new letter. It hadn't been two days since I wrote my response, so probably not, but I still needed to know. And this person, this letter-writer… They'd probably attend the funeral, since *everyone* would. So, if I got one in there real quick, I could do two in a single day.

The sooner I got some real answers, the sooner I would do something real.

Eating bacon. Watching baseball games. This was all pretend. Nothing mattered to me except finding Allison.

As Mom waited on her coffee and stared out the window, I felt my heart beating faster. The itch again. I needed to go up there soon.

I need to know what happened.

No matter what it costs.

"I guess you can take my car anyway," Mom said after a couple sips of steaming coffee. "I'll just ride in with Ben."

"Thanks, Mom."

<> <> <>

There was nothing like a first-time rush.

When I got the first letter, I felt something new. Something I'd been chasing since. It grabbed me by the collar and shook. It woke me up.

Before it came, I'd been feeling guilty. All the time, non-stop. I couldn't sleep or eat. For a few days, I was puking and worried. I kept expecting the phone to ring downstairs with horrible news. She's dead. She's gone. There's nothing left.

You should be looking for her.

How can you just lay there?

You should be at the house.

You're giving up. After all your promises.

I was in New Haven at the local grocer on a sleepy day. It was on the near edge of town, a few blocks down from the crystal shop. There was dust blowing around the street that day, and I wanted to be home, in bed. But Mom needed a few things for dinner. She always volunteered *me* for little errands like that.

Allison's missing-person poster was in the grocer, too. On their large corkboard where everybody pinned community fliers or sign-ups. Allison's face was right next to the meal drive sign-up for her grieving family — put on by the local church.

When I came out of the grocer, back into the blazing hot sun, I was carrying one of Mom's oversized, reusable bags, stressed and sweating, and I almost tripped, almost dropped everything.

I would've screamed.

Then, after a few steps, I saw it.

On the windshield of Mom's green Malibu, there was a dirty envelope wedged under the blade. I snatched the paper from the rubber grip and let it slap back against the glass. Checked both sides, but no writing, no address.

Setting the grocery bag on the car hood, I ripped open the letter, standing there on the side of Main Street. Yellowed paper. Promises made. All the envelopes and letters afterward were the same, aging color.

The handwriting was thin and stiff. Ink the color of three a.m.

A tiny, gold key fell into my palm.

Dear Kaia from New Haven,

I hope you are doing well. I'm sorry to introduce myself in such a strange manner, but these are cautious times.

I know about you, Kaia. I know you have been to the house, and you've seen what has slept for a hundred years. As well, I know you seek answers.

Tell me, what do you search for and why? How does the house interest you?

There are things I can tell you.

Simply write back with your answers. If I can trust you, and if I know you seek good and not evil, I will you tell more. I will tell you everything.

Stay safe.

CHAPTER 7
NEW HAVEN (SECOND STREET)

When their dog started barking for the last time, Sheriff Wheeler and his wife Ellie were in the sitting room, staring south. Their three-year-old boy — their only child — played on the shag carpet, rolling a toy truck bumpily and chattering to himself. The adults were in armchairs, his wife drinking wine, while Sheriff Wheeler kept watch on the fire.

Their house was "in town" but on the very edge of it. A two story, light blue abode with clapboard walls, it sat on the end of Second Street. One section stuck out from the rest: a sitting room and a tall chimney. This was the kind of house that showed its chimney with pride and looked better than almost all the rest, because it was.

Only a hundred years old. Practically new by New Haven standards. And until Sheriff Wheeler, it had never left his family. Until him, it never housed a coward.

Most nights, Sheriff Wheeler liked the privacy of his sitting room. It stuck out from the original structure — his great-grandfather had expanded it in the mid-20th century — and faced the endless fields to the south of town.

In wintertime, he'd have the fireplace roaring and smoke

drifting out the tall, brick chimney. He wasn't the kind of man who suffered from seasonal depression. In fact, he didn't believe in it.

Separated from the whole town, with everything to his back, he would pull aside the curtains and stare out the huge, wall-to-wall windows as the fireplace crackled to his side. Out here, there was nothing to see. The hills were far behind him, distant to the north. And he was heading south in his mind.

In the summer, it was often too hot for a fire, but tonight he'd insisted. He'd felt cold for days, and in such a small room, the fireplace worked like a heated blanket.

His wife took a sip from her wine tumbler, holding it with both hands, her feet pulled up on the chair, when the dog started barking in the other room. "Honey, can you please let the dog out?"

Sheriff Wheeler stood up, groaning. "Yeah, I got it."

"Are you almost ready for bed, Gage?"

Their three-year-old glanced up from his truck. He smiled innocently. "No."

"Well, I think it's that time. Come on. I'll get you ready."

While she placed her wine glass on the side table and led the toddler upstairs, Sheriff Wheeler opened the back door.

"Come here, Slider."

The dog sprinted across the house, wagging its tail. Sheriff Wheeler sighed as it ran past and outside, into the dark yard. He shut the door and walked back to his armchair.

"Damn dog must really gotta pee."

He sat there for a moment in the warm room. The curtains were shut again, so he couldn't see outside. He didn't hear Slider barking anymore. They had a fence around the edge of their yard, so he didn't worry. Something to separate his home from the fields.

Sheriff Wheeler always rented out the land around his house to local farmers. It was too vast, and he was too busy. But those farmers, they could use it, and *he* could always use a little extra cash.

It used to earn him some goodwill. He was a stalwart in the community. But things were changing now. Not everybody trusted the sheriff's department. And not everybody wanted to follow orders. Things were certainly shifting. Some days, he felt like one foot was already out the door.

Ellie returned and took up her perch across the room. They made eye contact, and he waited.

"I looked at tickets," she said, "and I don't think we can afford it. Not with Gage."

Sheriff Wheeler frowned. "Why not? We have a whole year to save up."

"Do you realize how long of a drive it is?" Ellie drank her wine and shook her head. "That's at least sixteen hours. Maybe more. And hotel rooms aren't cheap on the way."

"What about flights?"

"We can't fly with Gage!" she said. "He doesn't even like driving to Brooksville. And the tickets, like I said. Disney World is too… it's too damn expensive, honey."

Sheriff Wheeler nodded. He didn't argue the logic or doubt it. Ellie was always better with these things.

"Well…" He gulped. "In a couple years, right?"

"Yeah." She swished her glass and stared into it. "Couple years."

"I just wanted to… do something for him. Something he'll remember."

"We can, honey. We'll have time."

Sheriff Wheeler nodded, but he didn't look at her. The sheriff stared at the closed curtains and thought about Slider. He'd named the dog after the baseball pitch, but the older he got—the dog, not himself—the more his name became associated with terrible farts and accidents at the worst times. And Gage… his own kid saw Slider—the untimely, farting dog—more than he saw his own dad.

Probably would remember him more, too.

If anything ever happened.

"Um… guess I'll get the dog." Sheriff Wheeler shook away those thoughts—the dark ones that crept up when the curtains were closed—and went to the back door.

"You know he loves you, honey. Gage does."

"I love him, too." The sheriff saw himself in the dark panes of glass above the door handle. He wouldn't believe that man, either.

He opened the door. Slider wasn't sitting there.

"Hmm…" He called out, "Slider? Here, boy!"

There was no sound of paws padding closer. He pushed the door open wider, and light spilled out onto the grass. There was something wet and sparkling there. Maybe dewdrops.

"You okay, honey?" Ellie asked from behind him.

"Yeah…" He rummaged in a side table drawer for a moment and found a small flashlight. "Be right back."

When he stepped outside, the temperature didn't drop much from the bright sitting room, but there was a bitter wind rolling out to the fields. Sheriff Wheeler hugged himself and headed for the fence surrounding their yard. Slider would sometimes jump over and sit there, tongue out, until the sheriff came to find him. The dog could always jump out of the yard for some reason but never back into it. Whenever Sheriff Wheeler lifted him up and back inside their property, the dog also had a tendency to fart.

The worst, pent-up ones.

"Slider?" He clicked on his flashlight. There was nothing across the fence.

He followed it out, away from his house and then to the right. Still nothing. It wasn't until he followed the entire fence — right back to the house — that he found it.

Slider was sprawled out in the grass, laying on his back. And besides his back, there wasn't much left.

Something had torn through him. Ripped him apart. Entrails hung from the fence and a long strip of skin. He recognized the dark hair, matted in blood. There was a puddle in the grass and red streaks on the blue clapboard wall.

Sheriff Wheeler screamed.

Ellie rushed to the back door, but he was already stumbling inside.

"What's wrong?" she asked. "Honey, what's wrong?"

Sheriff Wheeler stumbled through the doorway and bumped against her, falling to the carpet and clutching at his chest. There was a terrible, pressing feeling. His breathing was out of control. Chest burning, eyes popping. He heard himself yelling, horrified, but it was a different person.

He fell on the floor after a minute, heart trying to burst through his chest. Sheriff Wheeler pulled at his hair. The ceiling went blurry. He saw Gage, standing across the room, pointing at him.

"What's wrong with Daddy, Mommy?"

Sheriff Wheeler closed his eyes and prayed for it to end. He kept thinking he would pass out, but he never did. Ellie took Gage in the other room. Eventually, the attack ended, and he pressed his face against the carpet.

"Coward," he choked. "You're a coward. And now he knows it, too."

CHAPTER 8
NAOMI WOODS

"This thing's the worst," I mumbled, turning onto First Street. Cliff's rickety blue truck crawled toward the church, his steering wheel, caked with dirt, quivering under my grip. "Hate driving it. Sorry, but I do."

The tall steeple and clock tower stabbed the sky. Our church with the stained-glass windows — old enough for the state to care about it — sat in a crowd of people. Everybody wore dark colors and trudged up the concrete steps. There were a few trees in the church courtyard, a couple flowerbeds, and some people clustered there, hiding from the sun.

"Sure you don't want to come?"

"I'm sorry, but I really gotta see Anne," I said. "Just call me when it's over. I'll swing by."

"Alright, that's fine."

I smiled and nodded, but he was looking at me weird. What did he expect me to say?

"I just didn't know him really. And I've already talked with everyone at the prayer meetings. Not much difference, right?"

The cars in front of us had stopped as people crossed the road. I'd never seen this many people gather by the church. The crowd… had to be half of New Haven.

"I guess they're similar."

"I've just been putting off talking to Anne."

I pulled over beside the church building. Nate and Rhys were sitting in the truck bed, wearing dark pants and button-up shirts. Ben, to my right, wore a full suit. I'd cut his hair the night before and trimmed his beard. He smelled like the forest-green soap I'd bought him for Father's Day.

"No problem. Thanks again for driving." He pushed open the door and climbed out slowly.

In the mirror, I saw the two boys hopping over the side and down to the sidewalk.

"You gonna be okay?" I asked him.

He nodded. "I gotta be."

"I love you," I said.

"Love you, too." He closed the door without expression. "Good luck."

The sound of muttered conversations and birds chirping went silent. I pressed on the gas and drove away from the church, leaving the crowd behind. The truck engine rumbled as I drove down First Street—so much louder than my Malibu. And this seat was twice as high from the ground.

More people were walking toward the church and others jockeyed for side-street parking. I drove past them all. I didn't feel guilty, either. I was doing enough trying to put this town back together since the awful June we'd had. I hadn't known George very well, and it was all such a terrible tragedy, but Anne Dawes needed my attention today.

I hadn't seen her since everything happened with Malaki. On that night, they'd been holding her at the police station. Judy from church had watched her kids as she sat in a windowless room while all the chaos was going on.

I hadn't been there. I had imagined, though, the moment when they released her from the station. Her kids waiting outside to wrap their arms around her, crying and shaking. I was sure nobody else cared, and I was sure it was a beautiful scene.

I'd been holding onto my own daughter when it happened. Up on the hill. Catching her as she ran out from the house.

I shuddered and focused on the road.

As I crossed town—it was so empty on the far side, not a single car out—the church bells rang behind me. I'd been hearing those same, deep vibrations for years. Only this time, it had an extra wave of mourning. The start of George's funeral.

The Dawes house had changed a little. Still homely and isolated, on the very edge of town, it stood next to a cracked sidewalk with weeds growing through. Just past it, Main Street turned into a winding, country road, slicing through corn fields, and the abandoned railroad station waited on the side. The stalks were high enough to stand as a measuring stick to the Dawes' single-story, tiny home.

The roof still looked rough, and the house could use a new paint job, but their yard was cut. Dead grass thrown around like confetti. Their porch, too, was cleaner than I remembered. Only a few pieces of furniture rested on the concrete slab, with no random toys or trash in sight.

When I knocked on the door, I noticed two baseballs, a bat, and a glove were tucked away behind one of the outdoor chairs.

The pale door swung open, and Anne Dawes peered out. Her short hair was pulled back, and she had a broom in hand. She wasn't a very tall woman, but she had some power behind her stare. She could wear a smile while she made you feel uneasy.

"Hi, Anne."

"Come in! Sorry for the mess." Anne ushered me inside and placed the broom against a wall. "Boys! Come get your cars out of the living room."

I saw Smith Dawes scurrying around the stained carpet, pushing two toy cars. His younger brother—I didn't know him at all—picked up his own and walked out of the room.

"Here, have a seat," Anne said, gesturing to the couch. "Smith." She lowered her voice. "Can you go play in the kitchen, please?"

He glanced up at her and then me. "Oh… hi."

"Hello," I said, smiling wide. I tried to sound as cheery as possible. "How are you doing?"

"I'm… good." He avoided my eyes and rolled his car back-and-forth.

"I remember seeing you on Nate's team. Do you still like to play baseball?" I asked him.

He frowned. "I quit the team."

"That's okay. I meant do you like playing with friends?"

He didn't answer. Smith turned to his mom with a confused expression.

Anne sighed. "Go on, sweetie."

He moved out of the room, and Anne Dawes took a seat on the couch, gesturing for me to sit, too. When I did, she pulled her legs onto the cushion and faced me, sitting like a child would.

"New couch," she said. "New to us, anyway. It's amazing how generous people are… after they throw you in jail for a night."

The living room was mostly like I remembered. The fireplace still missed a few bricks, though the cobwebs were gone. Framed pictures hung on the walls, one of each kid. On a small end table by the couch, there was an antique lamp and another photograph. This one showed Anne and the kids, but the right edge was strangely jagged, like something had been cut off.

"Are you doing okay?" I turned to look at her. "Since… everything happened."

"We're doing better," she said. "The kids were very upset at first. Watching me get arrested. Having that strange lady here for a night… You know how kids are."

I nodded.

"Smith wanted to quit the team after. I let him. And people still don't talk to us much. We're alone over here, but I like it. And the church gave us this couch someone had donated, so that's nice."

"It's pretty comfortable." I didn't mention I was the one who set up that donation plus a food drive—although people only made the Dawes meals for about a week. For Allison's family, people had signed up through Halloween.

Anne smiled. "Look, Naomi, I appreciate all you did to help get me out. But why are you actually here? Not to talk about my couch, I know."

"I just wanted to stop by."

"On the day when everyone is at the funeral for that poor man and his son?" She frowned. "I'm not dumb, Naomi."

"No, of course, I know you aren't."

I took a deep breath and tried to collect my thoughts. Anne drummed her fingers on her thighs and stared at me. She had a steely, strong stare.

"I guess I just wanted to check on you. I figured you'd be… scared." I looked at the floor.

"Should I?"

When I glanced up, those eyes were drilling into me again. "I won't lie to you… So, maybe."

"I was scared, Naomi. Very much. And maybe I should be.

That man, Wheeler… He'll try again. He needs someone to blame."

"They did get a confession—"

"Give it time. I know he'll try again. He has good reason to. I didn't start the fire, but neither did the boy they arrested." She leaned closer to me, lowering her voice. "I've talked to someone. I know that boy can't be guilty for it. So that means they'll turn to me, confession or not. If he's lying about the fire… who knows what else he's lying about."

"Maybe he's learned his lesson," I suggested. "He's been under some heat. Since his mistake."

"I don't think men ever learn. Not men like that. Besides, Wheeler has *other* reasons to go after me."

"What? Why?"

She shook her head. "Some things in my past. I moved here to get away. My ex-husband was the worst man alive, so I had to defend myself. And the kids. But it might get dragged up again. Or maybe he already knows."

"Well…" I paused. "Well, you aren't alone. He might come after us, too."

Anne cocked her head.

"My husband and I… we have a kid staying with us right now. He's harmless. But he's not from around here, and if Wheeler needs a scapegoat, he might use us. If things… don't quiet down, he's gonna need somebody to blame. Like you said."

Anne frowned. "Let's hope things quiet down then."

There was silence for a moment. I could see her digesting my words. And I thought about what she'd said, how she *was* running from something. But it didn't matter right now, because for now we still had time.

"Do you think Smith would wanna come over?" I asked. "Like I said, Cliff's nephew is about Smith's age. And I know

Nate and him were on the team together."

Anne's face twisted with shock and happiness. "That's a great idea."

"Maybe day after tomorrow," I said. "Tomorrow's the fourth. So, fireworks in town, cookouts, all that. Are you going?"

Anne frowned. "No… We won't be going to that."

"You think Smith would go with us?"

Anne paused. "I… He…" She cleared her throat and straightened up. "He doesn't do well with big noises like that. He wears his headphones around town, even, because the… the loud cars."

"Well, if he wants to, I'd love to take him." I smiled and tried to sound reassuring. "Might be good, you know, for the boys to meet before he comes over."

Anne nodded and clenched her jaw. She gently scratched her forearm. "You're right. Okay. I'll ask him, but he definitely would wanna go to your house."

"Okay, good. You know boys. They can play baseball for *hours*."

She smiled and reached for my hands. "Naomi, thank you. See, Smith…" Anne lowered her voice to a whisper and looked at the doorway behind me. "He doesn't have many friends. He's on the spectrum, you know. So, it's hard for him, being here. I think it would mean so much."

"I'm sure Nate and Rhys would love to hang out," I said confidently. "And I love Smith. He's the sweetest kid. What's the worst that could happen, you know? They're just kids."

<> <> <>

When I left Anne's house, she waved from the doorway as I climbed into Cliff's truck. She shut the door and I sat there for a moment, the car keys resting on my thigh. I couldn't help but think about the other home visit I'd made. Same side of town, vastly different result.

A few days ago, carrying a casserole, I'd walked up to the front door of Allison's family home. Her parents—Jeff and Laura—had lived there for twenty years. They'd bought this house to put a family in it. They told me so, years ago, with wide smiles.

I still remembered the day they found out Laura was pregnant. They'd been trying for a few years and had started to give up hope. But then they got the news, and they were so excited. We found out the same week, actually. Kaia and Allison. They were inseparable from the start.

When they opened the door, it was the first time I'd seen them in weeks. They'd aged ten years. Jeff was slouched with thinning, wispy hair. Laura—she'd always been the most beautiful girl in town—had bright red cheeks and her dark, wavy locks were tangled in knots.

For some reason, I thought of the *American Gothic* painting. Maybe it was their blank, unsettling expressions, the way they crowded together in the doorway. Or the fact she never spoke.

"Hi, Laura. Jeff." I extended the casserole toward them. "I just thought I'd stop by. Bring you this. You've been getting the other meals, right?"

Jeff nodded. Laura stared at him and avoided my eyes.

"How are you all holding up?" I asked. "Is there anything more I can do for you?"

Jeff shook his head. He lowered his eyes. "No. Nothing."

"I know the meal drive can get… repetitive. Is there anything you all might want? I can suggest—"

"No," he interrupted. "No, thank you."

I nodded. "Alright."

"We don't eat, anyway." His jaw tightened. "Please go, Naomi."

"I'm sorry, Jeff. I was just trying—"

"Please go." He stepped back and lowered his chin. He looked heavier than I remembered. His voice dragged. "Forget us. We have nothing left."

And then he closed the door.

CHAPTER 9
NATE WOODS

After the funeral, I couldn't wait to get outside with Rhys and he felt the same. I could see it on his face while we rode home. The two of us hunched in the back of Dad's truck. Him and Mom were up front, talking about grown-up things. Probably rehashing the funeral. I didn't think there was much to say about it.

"Pretty sad," I said to Rhys. The dusty wind swirled around us as we left Main Street and headed home.

He chewed on his lip. "I didn't know that guy."

"It's still sad though, right?"

He nodded. "Yeah. Just not as much."

"Could've been shorter, that's for sure," I said, laughing. As soon as I said it, I felt something in my stomach clench. "I mean… I was just bored."

Rhys didn't answer. He gave me a strange look, eyebrows raised, while sitting as straight as a board. His expression made me feel guiltier. I hadn't *meant*… I *did* care about Mr. George and his son. It was really sad. But I'd had so many sad and awful things happen since school ended, a funeral didn't really make the list.

"Can we play baseball when we get back?" Rhys asked. "You can just hit if you want. I don't mind throwing to you."

"We'll take turns pitching," I insisted. "It's not fair if only I hit."

"But you're better than me." Rhys leaned back slightly. Then we hit a bump and he straightened up again. He asked innocently, "Why *are* you so good, anyway? Is it 'cause you're darker than me?"

I frowned. "What?"

"Well… like your skin's darker." Rhys rubbed his head. "Sorry, I'm just asking."

"No, you're fine. I've just… Nobody's ever asked me that before." I shrugged off the feeling. "I'm just better 'cause I practice harder. And more. More than anyone here ever has."

"Really?" His eyes got big.

"Definitely. You think there's ever been a big-league player from *New Haven?*" I laughed.

"What's a big-league?"

I shooed away the question. "Just… nobody from here ever does *anything*. That's why I practice so hard. I wanna be the first one. I'm gonna get away from here, and I'm gonna go big."

"Wow. That's so cool."

I smiled at first, but he looked really sad when he said it.

"What's wrong?"

"I just don't think I'll ever be good at stuff. And… I'll never get away from here."

"Well… you're already getting better at baseball." I leaned against the side of the truck bed. "Just in the last few weeks."

"Really?"

"Yeah. Trust me. I'm the best, so I *know* if you're getting better, and you are."

Rhys grinned to himself and stared down at his hands. "Okay. If you say so."

<> <> <>

When we got home, we didn't waste any time.

Kaia pulled into the long driveway right before Dad, and Rhys and I covered our mouths, bumping over the gravel, as Mom's car kicked up clouds. As soon as Dad parked, we jumped out of the truck bed and headed to the porch.

"You boys want something to eat?" Mom asked, climbing out of Dad's truck.

"We're gonna play baseball," I called back to her.

"Alright. I'll make something."

"You wanna play, Dad?" I asked as I grabbed my bat from the porch.

Kaia and Mom both turned to watch him answer. Dad, standing by his truck, waved his hand through the air and smiled at me.

"Sorry, not tonight."

"He will on Wednesday," Mom said loudly, looking at him. "Anne Dawes is gonna let Smith come over, so you all can play two-vs-two or something."

"Oh." I nodded, fidgeting with my bat. There was some weird tension between them. It popped up every few days, and it always bugged me. "Alright, cool."

As we moved away from the porch and over toward the oak tree, Rhys asked, "Who is Smith? You know him?"

"He used to be on my baseball team," I said.

"So, he's… good, then?"

"Nah." I chuckled. "You might be able to beat him. Let's just practice some hitting tonight. You'll see."

We spent the next hour in the backyard. I fetched the tee from the barn, and Rhys started by hitting off it. After I set the ball on the tee and reminded him how to hold the bat—a daily reminder, at least—Rhys started swinging. He sometimes held the bat too far back, right against his shoulder, and he usually swung too high.

It took him five or six times to really hit it. Twice, it dropped dead in front of the tee. Then, with a loud *crack!,* he sent the ball flying to the left. It flew about one second and then rolled on the grass, but it was a hit.

"Nice job," I called, jogging over for the ball. I set it on the tee again. "Try to hit straighter. Just stand a little closer. Yeah, like that."

Rhys hit a few really good ones and smiled each time. I collected the balls (we only had two) and let him keep swinging. I didn't need a turn. This was for him more than for me.

While he was going at it with the bat, I noticed my mom on the back porch. She waved at me, and I waved back, then she disappeared inside. Dad returned from the barn not long after, his head lowered, scratching his chin. He didn't look over.

I let Rhys keep using the tee for another thirty minutes. The longer we stayed out, the less hot it felt. This was the perfect time of day to be outside. The sun dropped lower and lower, finally buried by the trees, and a cool breeze picked up, rustled the oak leaves, then died away. Everything smelled fresh.

Rhys really seemed happy. He was laughing and talking a bunch now, asking me all sorts of questions. "How do I hit it higher?" "How heavy is this bat?" and "Why can't I swing it like this?" He listened to the answers carefully and nodded along.

After he struck three good ones in a row, I asked, "Now pitches?"

"What?"

"Where I throw to you."

"Oh, right."

"I'm gonna try throwing overhand today." I demonstrated. "Like this. Instead of the underhand way I've been pitching to you."

He took a deep breath. "Okay, yeah, I'll try."

"I won't throw them hard."

"But I do like this thing," he said, tapping the tee. It wobbled back and forth, and he chuckled. "I wish they used these in the games."

"Yeah, yeah, sure you do."

We continued to play, or as I called it "practice." Rhys didn't make contact with very many pitches, but it was fine. His form looked better and better. Mom and Dad were sitting on the porch by the time we finished, their lips moving.

"Why are they talking about us?" he asked.

I glanced over and saw he was staring intently at the porch. His eyebrows were furrowed, almost angrily.

"They aren't," I said, knowing it was probably a lie. "They always sit on the deck and talk."

"Oh. Alright."

"Hey, you've never been inside the barn, right? Do you wanna see it?" I pointed in the direction of the big, red structure.

"Sure."

Leaving all the baseball equipment in the yard, I led him over there. Rhys kept glancing over his shoulder at my parents. They weren't watching anymore, thankfully. Even though they *did* always sit there and chat, I knew they'd been talking about Rhys. But he didn't need to worry about them. They would do whatever was best, and once they wanted to ask questions, they'd do it to his face, not go behind his back.

"So, these are the chickens," I said, leading him up to the wire fence. "I've gotta feed and water them every other day. When Kaia doesn't."

Rhys nodded, watching them strut around, clucking loudly. His eyes were glazed over, wearing a vacant expression.

"Let's go inside," I suggested. "I know you've seen these dumb things before, but Dad also has tractors and stuff in there."

Rhys didn't respond.

I let my eyes drift away from the chickens, followed the wind, carrying to the end of our driveway and across the road. The field over there, which no farmer owned or used, was growing taller every day. I hated going through it. Once the grass got knee-high, it left me itching and cut up.

We hadn't gone there in a while, mostly biking to the hills now. We hadn't been in a few days, so we should go again soon. Just as I was about to tell Rhys, I noticed something.

There was a figure standing in the tree line. A dark shape. It shocked me to see a person out there in *our* space. And that person seemed to be staring at us.

Maybe it's Kaia?

No, Kaia had gone inside with Mom. I would've seen her come back out.

Whoever that was, it couldn't be my sister.

"Hey, Rhys." I nudged him with an elbow and pointed. "Do you see that?"

Rhys glanced up and peered in the same direction as me. The figure didn't move.

"Yeah. Who is it?"

"I don't know." I shook my head. "I never see anyone out there. Only me and Kaia use that part of the woods."

I watched the dark figure step backward into the trees and vanish from sight. Chills crawled up my arms, and I forced myself to turn away. It was probably a hunter. Or someone from town. Other people *were* allowed to use the forest, even if I'd never seen them do it.

"Pretty weird," I said.

Rhys shrugged. "There's some weird people out there. Gotta be careful these days."

"Yeah… I guess you're right."

Mom called, "Boys! Dinner's ready!" from the back porch. Rhys and I trudged in her direction. I glanced back one time at those trees across the field, and nothing unusual showed itself.

"Do you think I'll get along with the new kid?" Rhys asked.

"Sure you will. He's pretty nice."

"But I don't get along with lots of people," he mumbled.

"Don't worry about it. We'll just play some baseball, it'll be fun, and you'll have a good time."

"Well, I hope so." He opened his mouth to say something else but closed it. "Yeah. We'll see."

CHAPTER 10
BENJAMIN "CLIFF" WOODS

On the back porch, in the dying light, our whole family was clustered around the table. Everyone had a plate boasting a BLT sandwich, a huge bowl of salad in the middle of us. Everything we ate — besides the bread and bacon — was fresh from the garden.

I took a bite of my sandwich and groaned.

"Oh, God. Amazing."

Everyone looked at me, and Naomi laughed.

"Yes, hun. It's good."

"But like… the tomatoes are incredible. And the lettuce is so… crisp."

"Have you ever thought about being a food critic?" Kaia joked. "I feel like you rate every meal we have."

"Well, I give this five stars."

Nate frowned. "Five? That's not good."

"I mean five out of five."

"But you grew most of it," he said.

"Well, then *ten* stars out of five." I took another bite of my sandwich and savored it. "Mmm. Crops."

Kaia stifled a laugh and squeezed her eyes shut. Naomi patted my knee underneath the table.

"Can you pass the salad bowl, Kaia? Thanks." While Naomi grabbed bits of salad with the tongs, she asked, "Nate, do you have any extra backpacks?"

"Backpacks?"

"Like… the ones you use for baseball stuff. You have old ones, right?"

He nodded with a mouthful of food.

"Could Smith maybe have one?" Naomi asked. "He has baseball stuff but nowhere to keep it."

"Oh. Yeah. That's fine." Nate glanced over at Rhys.

I asked, "Rhys, would you ever want to play on the team? Baseball team."

He looked up, holding a fork in one hand, poking at his salad. "I… can't."

"I think you could," I said. "Only if you want to, I mean."

He wrinkled his nose and picked up a piece of lettuce. "Maybe."

"Do you want any ranch for your salad?" Naomi asked him. She held out the ranch bottle. "Or we have other dressings inside."

Rhys shook his head quietly. "No, thank you."

"I'd take some Italian dressing," I said.

She chuckled. "Then you can go get it."

"Eh. I'll just take ranch. Any dressing works when the crops are this good."

"*Stop,*" Naomi groaned.

Rhys didn't talk much during dinnertime. He was a pretty quiet kid overall but especially when the whole family got together. I didn't blame him. It must've been weird—moving in with a random family. I knew it was awkward for me, so I could only imagine how he felt.

I didn't know how to talk to the kid. He shared some interests with Nate. They were always chatting, but whenever I came around, Rhys backed into a shell. He wasn't mean or anything, just quiet. I wasn't sure we'd ever had a long conversation. Not since the first night.

"Do you have a family?" I'd asked him. "Where are you from? Where are your parents at?"

I never got a straight answer to any of the questions. He said, "I just need to stay here for a while. Just a few weeks." When I had pressed harder, he'd added, "I'm not waiting for them. They're waiting for me. My parents are fine with it. I promise, sir, they already know. And thank you."

And that was all.

Call CPS. I need to call CPS.

What if I didn't? What would happen? Was that illegal?
Probably.

But sometimes, way out here, it felt like the laws didn't exist. Still, my window was closing. I needed to get everything sorted out.

At dinner, Naomi asked the kids how the funeral had been. I'd already told her my point of view — lots of old people crying. A terribly depressing event. Everyone seemed to look around at others. Everyone was suspicious of someone — but the kids were more straightforward. Nate told her about some of the people who'd spoken. Like George's wife. She had a rough time talking between sobs, and I felt embarrassment for her.

Her husband just died. Wouldn't you be the same way?

When I went forward with the whole "I'm so sorry for your loss. You have my condolences," George's wife had given me a tight hug and cried on my shirt. Then she'd pulled away abruptly. Stared into my eyes, frowning.

"What is it?" I'd asked.

"Go, Cliff. Just go."

She shook her head and pushed me away. I didn't know why.

Jeremy did come up to me, though. We shook hands and talked. It wasn't like old times, but it was something. He apologized, and I promised to take things seriously from now on.

"I want to help any way I can. Whatever you're thinking. Just keep me in the loop."

He smiled when I said it — a strange smile for a funeral — and then we parted ways.

Kaia mentioned some of the other people who'd attended. "The Turners. Cassy. And —"

"And," Nate interrupted her, "you were crying a bunch!"

Kaia glared at him and took a sip from her water glass. She stopped talking and clenched her jaw.

Naomi said, "Lots of people cry at funerals, Nate. It's a sad time."

"Yeah, but Kaia was full-on —"

"That's enough," Naomi snapped. She looked at him with more confusion than anger. "Don't... Let's not talk about it right now."

Kaia grumbled something under her breath and ate her sandwich in silence.

For a few minutes, nobody talked. The atmosphere had totally shifted after what Nate said. The tone of his voice. It had been... cruel, really, and it confused me. He'd never been mean-spirited, especially toward his sister.

"Hey, Mom and Dad," Nate asked in his normal, innocent tone. It broke my train of thought. "What kind of music do you two listen to?"

"Oh." I fumbled. "Um..."

"My friends were just talking at practice. I was thinking about what you'd answer."

"I like Tom Petty," I said. "And... um, Bruce Spring — well,

I don't listen to music very much."

"Of course you'd say Tom Petty," Naomi teased.

"Hey. I didn't hear you answer."

"ABBA," she started, "and Grateful Dead."

Kaia snorted. "So cliché, Mom."

"Well… what about Johnny Delaware?"

"Oh, right. The guy that literally ten people know."

Naomi held up her hands in defense. "Yeah, so, it's not cliche."

A fly buzzed around my ear and I swatted like crazy until it flew away. Kaia and Naomi smirked as I battled the insect.

"We really should get a bug net," I said.

Naomi snapped, "For the hundredth time, I don't want one."

"It's so easy!" I protested. "Just have to staple the screen to the edges of the porch. I could do it in… an hour or less, I think. So easy."

"I *know* it's easy," she said. "I just don't want one."

"But these flies—"

"I like the open air."

I frowned. "It'd still be open air."

"Can we not argue about bug nets right now?" Kaia cut in. "You two can do that on your own time."

"Fine." I hummed a little tune and brushed my fingers against the table edge. "Then why don't we talk about… how amazing these tomatoes are?"

"You're ridiculous, Dad." Kaia smiled, the way she used to, wide and bright. "You and your tomatoes."

"I might be, but my tomatoes *are* seriously the best."

"They're half mine," Naomi interrupted.

"Oh! Now that they're good you want—"

"I'm done." Nate stood up from the table, holding his plate.

"You don't wanna sit and talk?" I asked. Naomi and Kaia

were staring at him, too.

"No, I wanna shower," he said. "Come on, Rhys. You can go after me."

The two of them went inside the house. Nate muttered, "PlayStation while these old —" and the screen door slapped shut. Through the window, I saw Nate rinsing off the plates, and then they took off toward the stairs. Probably to play video games for two hours straight until I hollered for them to go to bed.

I looked at Naomi and Kaia once they had gone. We were all finished eating, but nobody stood up to leave. I sat facing the house, eyeing the deck, tracing the grooves in the wood. Naomi and Kaia stared past me, out to the world.

I started to think about my to-do list for tomorrow. I needed this next storm to come through so I could finally cut and bundle the hay. Every day, it threatened to rain, but it never did. Just kept building and building. So, I churned through little to-dos.

"Do you think Nate seems different lately?" Kaia asked. She glanced at me and then Naomi.

"What do you mean?"

It was Naomi's turn to look over at me. "You haven't noticed?"

"Haven't noticed what?"

The two of them shook their heads at me.

"He just seems… meaner," Kaia explained. "Ever since Rhys got here. Nate's been acting older, I guess. I don't know. He's just rude sometimes. He keeps talking about how some of his teammates are 'fat' and… stuff like that."

"He's just maturing," I said. "Right, Naomi? It's a phase."

Her jaw moved as she ground her teeth. I always hated that sound. "Maybe. But I'm not sure."

"Come on. He's gonna be an eighth grader. Everyone gets a little… a little mean in eighth grade."

"I didn't think *he* would," Naomi said quietly.

I opened my mouth, but there was nothing else to say. I didn't need to defend Nate. He wasn't in trouble or anything. And... I knew they were right about him.

He's just a kid. Kids are like that sometimes.

"Don't you think you've changed this summer, too?" I asked Kaia. "It makes sense... for him to change also."

She lowered her eyes to the empty plate in front of her and squared her shoulders. "Yeah, guess so."

Naomi shot me a look. "Kaia, we're really glad you'll be around for a while."

"And you can help me with the harvesting later this month," I added. "Unless you're looking for a job in town. *Are* you trying for a job?"

Kaia shrugged.

"I just think if you'll be here for so many—"

"*Cliff.*" Naomi placed her hand firmly on my knee. She mouthed, "Not now."

When I turned to Kaia again, she was watching us. Her eyes were red, and she had both arms wrapped tightly around herself. Her expression reminded me of a wounded deer on the side of the road.

"I know what you want," she said in a dead tone. "I know you both want me to talk about it. And I just can't. Okay? Not like that. You don't... understand... how hard things are right now."

Naomi interrupted, "Kaia, honey, it's okay. You can—"

"Everything reminds me of her," Kaia went on. "Every road sign. Every store."

The floodgates had opened it seemed, and everything poured out.

"Even the songs… I hear Frank Ocean, and I think about us… us driving down the highway, listening to him, talking about life… life after graduation. She's everywhere in this town. Everywhere."

Kaia's voice started to crack. Still hugging herself, she grabbed her own shoulders like a life raft. "I can't take it anymore. Being here, being around her. But I also can't leave. I don't know where she is, and I don't know if she's still alive. I know you say she isn't — everyone says so — but I won't believe that. I just can't."

Before Naomi could speak, I jumped in. "Kaia, I'm really sorry. I didn't mean —"

"No. No." Kaia pushed back her chair and stood up. She steadied herself on the table. Tears marked her cheeks. "It's not… your fault. I just… I can't. I'm sorry that I'm…" She backed away, toward the door.

Naomi offered, "Kaia, honey…"

"I wanted to be better," she said, full-on sobbing. "But I love her too much. I'm so sorry."

Then she vanished inside, and the screen door slapped against the house once more.

We were left in silence, Naomi and I, side-by-side. The wind whispered through the fields, and a bird sang in the oak tree. I put both elbows on the table and buried my head.

"Damn it, Naomi. Why do I do this? Every time…"

Naomi stood up, too. She placed a hand on my back. I didn't look up.

"You're not the victim here, Ben." She leaned down and kissed my cheek. "I'm gonna go talk to her, okay?" Again, she patted my shoulder. "Take it easy on her. We can talk about… jobs and stuff later. Just give her time."

I heard her footsteps on the porch and then the screen door

opening and closing. Straightening up, for a couple minutes I didn't move, sitting alone, twisting my wedding ring. I thought about my grandparents and parents. They'd all lived in this house for decades. They'd all divorced before they could leave or die, but at least they never had to sell the farm. Kept it in our broken family.

What could I have done better? What could I do now?

More and more, it seemed we were out of options. Nothing else had happened since Kaia went inside that house, and yet every day it got worse and worse. We were drowning, and we were isolated. I had nobody to hold on to, and I couldn't save anyone else.

I stood up, finally, and began collecting the dishes, stacking the plates, carrying it all inside. The sky was nearly dark by the time I loaded the dishwasher. I made one final trip to the barn, crunching over the gravel, hands in pockets. Right before I went in, I noticed.

In the distance, beyond all the fields and trees, the house in the hills. Maybe it was a reflection from the setting sun. Maybe I saw what I wanted to. But behind one of those distant windows… I saw a flickering light.

I watched it for a moment. A faint glow, like a candle, hidden behind a curtain. It could've been nothing.

And I realized, for the first time, I *wanted* the house to be alive. Our whole family was stuck. We were waiting for something to happen. I wanted us to be safe, but even more… I wanted to prove myself. To fix things.

I wanted something in there to live. So I could kill it.

CHAPTER 11
NEW HAVEN (FIRST STREET CHURCH)

"Good afternoon, everyone. Thank you for being here." Susan gripped the podium in front of her. Her voice wobbled at first, but she steadied herself. "Let's begin with a word of welcome."

Standing at the front of the room, she faced the gathered church members. Three-dozen people sitting in the stacked rows of folding chairs. It was a smaller crowd than usual — to be expected on Fourth of July. But like always, they looked around at each other and whispered breathlessly.

"Take a few moments and greet those around you in the name of the Lord."

The crowd collapsed on itself and shook hands. Most people said a few hellos and then sat with no expression, straight as logs.

One woman in particular — sitting alone toward the back — didn't move at all. She had a wide frame, hunched shoulders, and kept her eyes glued to the gray carpet.

Another woman walked up to her and stuck out a hand. "Hey there, Beth."

Beth reached up and shook it, but she didn't smile. She had circular glasses resting on her long nose, and stringy, graying hair dropped to her shoulders.

"How are you doing?" the other woman asked.

Beth shrugged. "I'm okay. I apologize, but… it's been a rough day."

The other woman frowned. "Oh. Sorry to hear that." She returned to her seat.

Can't admit you need prayer at a prayer meeting or you freak people out, Beth thought to herself. *Imagine that.*

These meetings had started as six round tables on an old, gray carpet. Twelve women and three men, creating a list, praying their way through it. Beth had been coming her whole life, but the meetings had died off for a while until Naomi and Susan revived them.

Nowadays, everyone could use it. Everybody left feeling a little better. They'd done their part—they'd closed their hands and opened the heavens. But for some reason, the list kept growing.

As it grew, so did the crowd. By mid-June, after the Davis family's tragic fire—George and his son—there were twenty people who gathered on a regular basis. They dragged out folding chairs and scattered them around the tables. When Allison went missing, the crowd grew again, and Beth helped them store away the tables. They meticulously laid out six rows of fifteen chairs.

By the time Malaki was finally arrested, the prayer meetings consisted of almost fifty people every Tuesday.

Nobody felt much better after he got arrested. In fact, things were turning worse. The Davis shop was a glaring scar on Main Street. Jeff and Laura hadn't been to church since their daughter went missing. Malaki's family didn't come either, and nobody knew what to think of that.

None of it worried Beth as much as the Clarks. That was a *sure* sign. Things were getting much worse very quickly. Even if nobody else wanted to take her seriously, she wasn't gonna let them forget. She wouldn't give up on her sister.

"Before we dive into our prayer list," Susan began again as everyone in the room focused on her, "let's give thanks and share in our gratitude. Does anyone have any thanksgivings to start with today?"

Beth folded her arms and listened as a handful of people stood up to share. Every meeting, there was at least one man who stood up and thanked God for something about his fields. Good harvest, good weather, whatever. A mother stood up and praised the Lord for her children. Others mentioned their prayers previously answered — a successful surgery for one. For another, strength and peace through tough times. Many people mentioned the wonderful funeral for the Davis family.

And then the tone shifted.

"Let's move to our prayer requests," Susan said, looking down at the podium, where she must have held the master list of prayers. "From last week, we have some standing requests. Of course, we will pray for the Davis family in these dark times, and we will pray for Jeff and Laura as they confront these challenges. As well, Sarah's cousin, who is battling a serious illness in Brooksville, and prayers for our community in general."

"Don't forget to sign up for the meal drive!" someone from the crowd said. "Jeff and Laura have sign-ups available in October."

A woman stood up down the row from Beth. "Have we thought about a meal drive for the family of Malaki Banks?"

Nobody spoke. Everyone peered around, craning their necks to see who asked. Beth recognized the woman standing — dark hair, sharp features, and small glasses under her thin eyebrows. It was Malaki's aunt, but Beth didn't know her name.

Murmurings came from the crowd.

"Um..." Susan tapped on the podium as the awkward silence

stretched on. "If… Well… We normally discuss the meal drives in the board meetings on Monday mornings. If you… would like to come next week, we can consider that."

Malaki's aunt took a seat, huffing.

"So, moving forward…" Susan took a deep breath. "What, um… Are there any other prayer requests to add to the list?"

Beth stood up right away, but a man near the front was quicker. He was wearing overalls and a straw hat. She didn't have to guess his occupation or his prayer request.

"Yes, sir," Susan called on him.

While Beth leaned on the seat in front of her, the man rambled for five minutes about his crops and the lack of rain recently. Just as she expected. Everybody listened attentively, and when he sat down, there were some affirmations.

"Thank you, sir." Susan clicked her pen and wrote on the paper. "Anyone else? Yes?"

Beth took a deep breath. She waited a second longer, as some people turned around to face her.

"The Clarks are still missing," she said. "I said it last week, too. So, it's on your list. But they still are."

There were murmurs again. Some people shot her nasty looks but most were puzzled.

"Ah, yes. I see it here." Susan tapped her pen. "Um… Alright, we will pray for Roland and Mallory and their continued safety."

"It's been over a week," Beth went on.

"They're just outta town." The farmer from earlier turned around and shook his head at her. "Come on, now. Those two are always going away.

"My sister wouldn't just—!"

Someone interrupted her, "They spent half of December in Florida. Remember that?"

"She would've told me!" Beth protested. "My sister… She always—"

"I'll add them to the list," Susan said loudly. "Roland and Mallory Clark. Their safety and their quick return home. Alright, who else?"

And that was all. Beth sat down, grumbling. There was some minor commotion as the double doors opened behind her and Naomi Woods hurried in. A few people said hello, but most avoided her eyes. Naomi took a seat near the front, as Susan went on taking prayer requests.

She would've told me, Beth thought. *Mallory tells me when she does that kind of stuff.*

Beth's husband was great friends with Roland, too. He always gave the Clarks discounts whenever they stopped by his pizza restaurant on Main Street. They had missing posters all over town for that girl Allison, and they'd run her story on the news for a while, but when somebody as old as the Clarks went missing, nobody cared. Not even enough to pray.

As old as the Clarks. As old as me.

Beth continued to grumble as the prayer meeting went on. She noticed the crowd around her shooting dirty looks at Naomi, even though she was nothing but pleasant. She usually led these meetings—as well as organizing the meal drives and the church's outreach program. But some of the churchgoers didn't appreciate it. Especially the men.

"Shouldn't have a woman doing that much, if you ask me," Beth had heard them say on their way out of the prayer meetings. "She's got a lotta power, huh? Almost like she's making up for something, huh? Something she's done?"

But maybe… Beth had an idea. *Maybe she'll take me seriously.*

Because what Beth *hadn't* mentioned was what worried her

most. The Clarks were certainly not at home. Roland's truck was gone. Her sister wouldn't go on a trip without giving Beth at least *some* notice, even last-minute. And now Beth had a gut feeling she couldn't shake.

Her sister and Roland lived outside of New Haven. Right by those hills. Closer than anyone to that house. Her husband wouldn't even consider it, but Beth wondered…

Maybe Naomi would believe her.

Susan started to wrap up the meeting. The prayer list was longer today, and it would take them fifteen minutes to pray through. Right before she started, the dark-haired, sharp-nosed lady to Beth's right stood up again.

"Yes?" Susan asked.

"One more item." Malaki's aunt cleared her throat and curled her fingers together. "Pray that… the new lawyer in Brooksville can help my nephew. Pray the truth will win, like God says, and the new lawyer who my brother's hiring can save—"

"You better pray Allison turns up!" Naomi snapped, leaping to her feet. "*Alive.*"

People gasped. Some of them glared. But nobody dared say anything out loud.

Even Malaki's aunt simply waited and curled her upper lip.

"Pray on that," Naomi said. "That's the only thing gonna save his ass. 'Scuse my language. Sorry, everyone."

And without waiting for the meeting to end, she stormed out, just as quickly as she'd entered.

Susan barely kept things together after that. People were so eager to gossip, they could hardly wait to pray. But while they ran through the list, Beth couldn't help but feel disappointed.

Missed my chance. Dang it. She didn't want to wait until next week. She needed somebody to listen, somebody who had *been* up there and might know.

And suddenly, it clicked in her mind. A conversation she'd overheard at the library. A familiar face who kept showing up there.

Beth had an idea.

After the meeting, she headed straight for Second Street.

CHAPTER 12
KAIA WOODS

On the day of George's funeral, I got more emotional than I'd expected. So much so, I was wiping away tears, sitting in those too-familiar pews. I'd attended church—that exact church—ever since I could remember. In the last few years, we hadn't gone much, but every couple months, I'd go with Mom. Now I was sobbing for a man whose last name I hadn't even known.

I pictured the tall steeple without even trying. The courtyard outside with a beautiful view of the stained-glass window and a few skinny trees. Birds were always chirping in the branches after church. On hot July afternoons, I'd stand under them, greedy for shade, and the birds would sing to me. Just me.

Sitting in the pews, hearing about George Davis and his son, I couldn't *not* cry. It was more emotion than I'd ever felt in a church before. A sadness with sharp claws and long fingers. Wrap one hand around your throat and squeeze your heart with the other. For the entire hour, every choir song, every low, tearful mourner, it wouldn't let go.

The day before, I'd found my dad in the barn. It had been early morning, and I was feeding the chickens. When I said goodbye to him—"Bye, Dad, love you," and "I love you, too Kaia.

Be Safe." — I had to hurry outside. A heavy weight pressed on my chest without warning, and I felt myself choking.

Ever since I'd drowned under sirens and lights, I'd been crying more and more often. I didn't want to be ashamed of it, either, because I had every right to cry. But I still hid it.

When I took Mom's car into town, right before the funeral, the post office had been empty and so was the PO box. I'd stuffed the little key into my pocket angrily and went to the crystal shop to waste some time. All around me, little reminders. The clear quartz crystals like the necklace I made for Allison. Ms. Hargrave's ancient, wavering voice. It hurt too much. I left the store in a hurry and saw the church on the next street over.

They were preparing for the funeral. Only a month ago, I'd played bridesmaid in a wedding there. A beautiful wedding. Those memories, those pictures, everybody in their dresses and suits — everything torn to pieces and seared in fire.

I hid it until the funeral. At some point, during one of the songs, I stopped wiping the tears away. Those old-ass, wood pews had hurt my butt, and I couldn't bear the weight of everybody's grief. I stared ahead, unmoving, and let myself cry.

Go ahead and watch me. I don't give a fuck.

<> <> <>

On the day after the funeral, the day after I broke down in front of my parents, I hid in my room until it was time for Nate's practice. Mom talked to me the night before, and I told her… I told her everything. About my feelings for Allison. About our kiss. I told her every damn thing, and she cried a little, holding my hands.

"It's okay, Kaia," she said. "You don't need to… feel bad about it. That's beautiful. You're both beautiful. I'm just… I'm so sorry for how things… for what happened."

You mean that I never admitted it until she was gone?

I nodded. "Me too."

The next morning, I dashed downstairs, said quick goodbyes, and hurried Nate outside to Mom's car.

"Don't forget about the fireworks tonight!" Mom said as I was rushing onto the porch. "I need you back so I can go pick up Smith Dawes."

"Right, right. I won't be long."

Fourth of July. I'd forgotten about it. Every year, the town put on a fireworks show, and with each year it got more underwhelming. There was only so many times I could watch a bunch of explosions above some guy's farm before I lost interest.

"Are you excited for the fireworks?" I asked Nate, opening the driver's door.

He stood on the opposite side, looking at me over the car. He was getting so tall.

"I guess so." He opened his door and squirmed into the passenger's seat. The ceiling in Mom's old Chevy Malibu was low, and every week Nate seemed closer to brushing his head on it. "I just don't wanna go to practice today."

"Why not?" I asked him, starting down the driveway.

"We're doing defense, mostly. And I always get put with the fat kid."

I cleared my throat. I didn't wanna talk about it right now, so I ignored it. "I mean, defense is important."

"I know, I know." He grunted. "But I just wanna focus on offense. Our team needs it, too. Those guys *suck* at hitting, but they're okay at fielding. For middle schoolers, you know."

It was usually easy to talk to Nate — besides his random, mean comments. He kept the conversation focused on himself and his baseball team. I didn't blame him. He was pretty good, and for an eighth grader, sports were number one on the list.

The conversation lagged as we moved through the country roads and into town. I tried to pay attention to him—always talking about the other boys on his team, how skilled or unskilled they were, how he felt about them—but my thoughts were racing ahead to the post office and if there was another letter waiting.

"Are you excited Smith's coming over tomorrow?" I asked him as we reached Main Street. The town was a lot emptier than yesterday. All the mourners had closed themselves away. "And it sounds like he's coming to the fireworks, too."

"Yeah. I am. But Rhys seems nervous."

"Nervous? Why?"

"He doesn't think they'll get along." Nate shrugged. "I dunno. They're both kind of weird, so I figured they'll be fine."

I frowned. "Don't call your friends weird."

"Sorry. I just meant… I know they're gonna get along."

"Does Rhys think Smith will be mean to him?"

"I don't know? Chill." He rolled his eyes. "He's just nervous. That's all I know."

I let Nate out at the baseball field, and he jogged away, catching up with two of his teammates. They started laughing right away, all three of them hollering. I backed out slowly, watching my mirror for any idiot drivers.

Without hesitation, I headed for the post office, trying not to think about Nate, his friends, and how boys changed when they got closer to high school. In my experience, they got worse, like something dark clung to their shoulders.

I just hoped Nate wouldn't get *too* mean while he was trying to fit in. Sometimes, once it happened, it never stopped.

<> <> <>

When I had the envelope in hand, I walked straight from the post office to the library. Didn't bother jumping in the car. Finding a parking spot in New Haven could be hell. I moved so fast my heels were pounding the sidewalk. Only five minutes between me and the library.

Fingers squeezed together, I looked around at Main Street. All the vacant shops and empty display cases. I'd gotten really familiar with it over the last three weeks. Spending more time here than ever. Shaving off the hours.

With each letter, I felt a little closer to her. To the end.

Being stuck in a place like this, I couldn't help imagining New Haven in the 60s. Maybe those stores were alive and these streets were filled. Maybe they played live music in the bars. All the music was gone, now. Most of the stores, too.

If I come back in twenty years… will this place just be gone? Nothing left?

A house in a field. Abandoned in a sea of corn stalks. A setting sun. A sleepy death.

I shook away those images and walked faster. I had about an hour until Nate's practice ended, and I'd need every minute. I had to really think about my answers now. Every time I wrote another letter, I chose my words carefully. I needed this stranger to keep trusting me. I couldn't push too hard.

But time was running out, and I'd never forgive myself if…

"There's a stupid motorcycle," I said out loud, as it roared up Main Street. "There's the church and the big tree. It's always right here, huh? When I start to freak out?"

Someone passed on the other side of the road and gave me a look.

"What?" I called over. "You people be talking to yourself more than me!"

They lowered their head and shuffled along.

I didn't care what these people thought of me anymore. I was gonna get away, soon. Drive out that interstate exit and never come back. I just needed Allison to go with me. We were gonna leave for good.

The thought of her kept me going.

I hurried to the library, putting everything else behind me. I found an open table. There were ten of them, all small, each with a computer. Old people always clustered here, moving slow, dragging their cursors like snails.

Ripping open the envelope, I wiped a hand across my forehead and devoured the new letter.

They're starting to get suspicious.
I'm running out of time.
Just wait.

I placed the paper flat on the table and reached inside the envelope. As always, there was a second one tucked inside.

What the hell am I supposed to write back?

There was a pen on each library desk. Deep blue with "New Haven Public Library" on the side. I reached for it and started tapping on the desk.

What a waste of my time? Is this a prank or something?

I felt a hand on my shoulder.

"What the—?" I jerked around.

But it wasn't Jeremy or anyone I recognized.

An older lady stood there, shifting on her feet. She had hunched shoulders, a wide frame, circle glasses perched on her nose, and stringy, graying hair dropped to her shoulders.

"I'm sorry, I..." She paused. Her voice was like sandpaper.

Did she see the letter? I wondered. I kept eye contact and tried to look upset.

"Look, sorry, but I'm busy."

"Oh, I apologize." She wobbled a bit. "My name is Beth. Beth Turner. I was hoping you'd... I just wanted to ask you some questions... about..."

The older lady looked both ways in the library and took a seat in the empty desk beside mine. I pulled the letter and envelope closer to me, scowling at her.

"Okay, what?"

She gulped. Her two hands gripped the desk's edge. They were shaking wildly.

"What's it like up there?" she whispered, lowering her chin. She stared at me with crazy eyes, dark bags underneath. "Why do people go up there?"

"Up... where?"

"The house on the hill."

"Oh." I tried to force a smile, but she watched me in dead concentration. "What... why do you care?"

"I've seen you here before," she said, growing more intense. "I know you're the girl who went up there. Asking around town. My husband owns the pizza place, and he's seen you, too. And I... my sister... The Clarks are gone, and I think they've been taken."

"Listen, I'm just—"

"Taken up *there*. You understand? It's happening again!" She shook her head and gripped her knees with both hands. "I don't trust the police. Nobody's taking it seriously. And I just know... They're—"

"Wait," I stopped her. "What do you mean? 'Happening again.' What is?"

She leaned closer. "I remember it. Just barely. When I was little... People go missing here. It used to happen more, and now..."

"Do you know who does it?" I asked breathlessly. "Or why? Do you know—?"

"I don't know anything!" Beth lowered her head, shoulders shaking. "I just know my sister's gone and her husband and now nobody thinks it matters, and I'm so... I'm so..."

"I don't think I can help you," I said. I reached over and patted her forearm. "I'm really sorry. I wish I could. Maybe... if you find out more, you can tell me, right? But—"

"Please!" She leaned forward and reached for me. "Please, Kaia, I need your help—"

I pushed back my chair and stood up. "Get off me, okay?"

The lady stared at me, sniffling, and a new expression settled on her face.

"You have to help." She frowned, holding back tears. "You have to stop it. Before more people are gone."

"What do you think I am?" I asked. "Go talk to the cops. I don't know? I'm not here to save anyone except—"

"I can't," she said. "And if you're not gonna help, I'll try myself. But you've gotta do something. You remember that. You're the only one who can now."

Then she stood up and walked away. Not even looking at me.

I felt bad for a while, but people were bound to start acting like that. Everybody was going a little crazy around New Haven. Though, maybe she was right. Maybe this kind of thing had happened before. I just needed to find Allison and get out.

I planned my response to the letter—saying I was gonna be

pissed if this was all some prank and they'd regret it—as she walked out the door. I flipped the page over to the blank side. Then I'd mail it. Head home. I looked up at the clock and cussed loudly.

Beth Turner left the library. I never saw her again.

CHAPTER 13
NATE WOODS

Mom picked me up from baseball practice in Dad's truck. She was grumbling about "Your sister promised, and now… and your dad's too busy too…" and took us home. I didn't really listen to her complaints, because I was starving, and I just wanted to rant about my practice.

When we got home, I ate three chicken sandwiches, because I was *literally* starving, and then took a quick shower. With a fresh shampoo and a full belly, I hurried down the stairs.

Mom was in the kitchen, sweeping. I jumped from the third step and landed with a boom on the carpet floor, making our family pictures rattle.

She looked up and snapped at me, "Will you quit doing that?"

The broom kept swishing across the hardwood floor while she frowned.

"Sorry, forgot. I was just gonna ask if we can bike to Mr. Turner's house."

"Mr. Turner's? Why?"

"The other day, he asked if I could feed his animals while he's in town. He's extra busy today. Getting ready for the fireworks tonight."

Mom stopped sweeping and rubbed a fist against her forehead. "Yeah, that's fine, I guess. We're leaving in a few hours, but don't bike too fast. You just ate all that food."

"I'll be okay," I smiled. "And then I'll have some money to buy cotton candy with."

She chuckled and focused on the hardwood floors again. "Alright then, honey. Go on."

<> <> <>

Biking was like everything else. It was so hard to get started, but eventually you did. And then there was a rhythm to it—legs pumping up and down, flying through the countryside—and then it was like nothing ever happened.

Half an hour later, Rhys and I were pedaling down the road and caught sight of Mr. Turner's house. It was almost as far as Jeremy's but not quite. When the country road started to curve, just before you came around the bend of trees and saw New Haven, there was Mr. Turner's house.

A small, tan house. The most boring I'd ever seen. His roof had shingles like ours—I always remembered that word after Dad complained about having shingles but "not the kind on our roof"—but it was sort of orange-brown color. There was a tall maple tree in the front yard, an American flag on the right wall, and a white screen door on the left.

Behind the house, there was a small barn. Smaller than Dad's, anyway. Those bikes we rode came out of it, and I knew from feeding his animals before there was a door on the left side. All I had to do—and I'd done it three times before—was go through the door, throw some food into two buckets on the inside of the pen, and leave. Feed for the cows, hay for the goats. Mr. Turner had three cows and four goats, but no other animals and no crops.

We rode up to the left side of his house and set our bikes against the brick. On the sides, Mr. Turner's house was half-brick on the bottom and some material like plastic boards on the top. From the left side, I saw a stretch of curving, country fields all the way down to Jeremy's house.

"I wonder if Jeremy owns all that," I said to Rhys. "All that land." Rhys didn't answer. "You remember who Jeremy is?"

"Not really."

"Oh. Sorry. He's um… Dad's friend. Has a beard. Usually smells like beer."

"Oh, right." Rhys chuckled. "I call him 'Hairy.' That sorta rhymes with Jeremy."

"Right, yeah." I laughed as we walked across the yard toward Mr. Turner's barn. "I guess it kinda does."

"Why doesn't your dad have more animals?" Rhys asked. "Seems easier than all those fields and tractors. Couldn't he see your mom more? If he had animals instead?"

"Um… Yeah. Maybe so. I… don't know why. They see each other, still."

"Yeah, but they don't seem very happy," he pointed out.

I didn't answer this time. He was absolutely right, but I didn't wanna admit it to myself.

The barn was only as tall as Mr. Turner's house. It wasn't very wide, but it stretched back far. Fences lined the back, a chunk of green grass on a slight hill. Beyond the fields, I could see all the way to our biking hills. It was all so green and bright and perfect.

"I think Dad tried to have some animals. But they kept dying or something."

Rhys clicked his tongue. "Yeah. Animals. They do that, huh?"

We approached the left side of the barn. I stared out to the field, but there were no animals in sight. None of the cows or goats.

"Maybe they're inside," I said. "Oh, God." I pinched my nose and turned back. "Did you fart, Rhys?"

"No?"

"Do you smell that?" I frowned. "It's like… bad milk or something?"

"Cow poop?"

"No, worse. I mean. It is pretty hot today. Does cow poop smell worse when it's hot?"

Rhys laughed. "How am I supposed to know that? You're the farmer kid."

I walked up to the side door and unlatched it, trying to ignore the smell. "I'm not a farmer kid."

"You're getting paid to feed this guy's cows."

"Yeah… but… that doesn't make me a farmer. I'll never be a farmer."

I pushed the door open and took a step inside. Right away—the second I looked—I felt my stomach go sick.

Three huge piles of chunky red meat and brown strips. All near the edge of the pen, almost in the grass. A hundred sheets of flesh were around the pile, hanging from the walls and drooping over the gates. Dark red dripped down the walls and pooled on the ground. A million flies buzzing around like the angriest lawn mower. And the smell… worse than ever. Worse than anything.

Then I saw it. Propped against the wall—smashed against it, actually—was half of a goat head.

I stumbled back, tripped over Rhys. Landing on the grass, I vomited onto a patch of dandelions.

"You okay?" Rhys asked.

I pointed at the open door, shaking my head. I gagged again

and threw up more.

"Oh. Right." Rhys looked back through the doorway and clicked his tongue. "They do that, huh?"

CHAPTER 14
KAIA WOODS

I'll admit, I thought, after everything I went through—I'd like to order a couple traumas, one house, and an attempted-murder, please—my parents *might* take it easy on me. Just maybe.

I was proven wrong again and again. Basically every day.

No, I didn't pick Nate up from practice. I had to text Mom because I knew I wouldn't make it. After sending the letter off, I stuck around town and tried to find that Beth lady. I checked everywhere—all the shops, the bars, and even the church because people went there during the day if they were really upset—but no luck.

So, I got home at almost four o'clock. *Way* later than I'd said at first. Nate was in the living room, looking green. And Mom was standing in the kitchen, holding the house phone to her ear.

"Yes. Yes, I understand," she spoke into it. Her voice was serious. "Okay. Alright, thank you, Sheriff."

She hung up the phone.

I raised my eyebrows. "Sheriff?"

"Don't even start with me." Crossing her arms, she glared. "What happened to 'I'll be in town, I'll get him,' huh?"

"I…" I gulped. I'd been trying to think of a good lie since the moment I texted her. "Ms. Hargrave at the... the crystal store needed my help."

"Well, *I* needed your help. Now I'm running late to get Smith, and Nate's as green as mushed—"

"Don't talk about mush," he whimpered from the other room.

"What happened?" I asked. "I don't... Sorry, but I was—"

"I don't have time," Mom snapped. She marched over and grabbed the keys from me. "Just try to make sure your brother doesn't puke anymore, will you?"

Then she headed outside.

I moved into the other room and found Nate the color of old peas.

"What's up with you?"

He shook his head, cheeks bulging. "I can't talk about it."

"Mr. Turner's animals," Rhys said.

I turned around. He was leaning against the stair railing and shrugged. All the lights were turned off, and his face was hard to read.

"What about them?"

"All torn up. Dead." Rhys sighed. "Such a mess."

"*What?* And you two saw it?"

Rhys nodded. "We were gonna feed them. We didn't... obviously."

I turned back to Nate. His eyes were bulging, and he reached for the orange bucket on the floor. Something nasty swished around inside as he lifted it.

I moved toward the steps, but before I went up, I asked, "Rhys... Do you ever... send letters to people?"

Rhys narrowed his eyes. "Letters? No. I don't write letters." He studied me closely. "What about you?"

"I was just wondering."

I brushed past him and headed to my room.

When Mom got home later, she chewed me out for ten minutes. First, she said, "I talked to Ms. Hargrave, and she hasn't seen you all day." Then, before I could protest, she added, "I don't know why you're keeping secrets. Or what you're doing. But I'm over it. *So* over it."

"It's not what you think! I'm not keeping secrets. I'm just—"

"Don't let it happen again," Mom snapped. "Just go get ready. I'm gonna drag your father out of the barn, 'cause we're supposed to leave in twenty minutes."

She wasn't wrong, of course. But the fact she'd *checked up* on me was infuriating. I wasn't looking forward to the fireworks at all. I'd rather stay home and sob into my pillow.

In the end, it was a good thing I went. Because damn… someone really did set off the fireworks that night, and not the kind I expected.

<> <> <>

So, three hours later, we were in town, *waiting* forever, and I was still in a pissy mood. We were there for *hours* before any shit happened, roasting in the sun.

The sky got darker. Like somebody slowly turning off the lights one by one. We had good spots by the road, but then everybody started filling in behind us. The six of us wedged together. We were at the front. The crowd stretched out along the lane, with cars parked behind us in the fields. It got more and more dense. Rednecks in lawn chairs. Church women carrying coolers. Packed in tight all the way.

Imagine being at the biggest music festival but it's everyone from your town—especially the weird people—and they all smell bad and there's no festival. Just some dumb, ten-minute fireworks.

I'd seen the show *every year* and I was over it. All of this.

We stared at the fields. Endless. Like our wait. But we sat there, anticipating an explosion in the sky. The same fields I'd been looking at my whole life. Just a bunch of zombies. All staring up.

The sky was turning a pale yellow color in the distance. Smith Dawes was beside me on the grass. He wore these big, green headphones and looked around at everyone.

"I've never seen fireworks," he said to me. Only me.

I forced myself to smile. "I've seen too many. But you'll like 'em."

"I hope they aren't too loud," he murmured. "I… it scares me."

"Well…" I hesitated. "Then I think you're very brave."

He turned to look at me. Wide eyed, his lips curved with hope. "Really? You do?"

"Definitely."

Mom, Dad, the boys, Smith, and I were clustered up front and to the right. Nobody talked about what happened earlier. Mom said, "I called the Sheriff. He'll deal with it. *Thanks* for being such a help," to Dad. He scowled. That was all. Nothing else.

We were close to the police station. On a normal day, there was a large parking lot in front and a brick concourse with some benches and mulched plant beds. On the Fourth of July, all the cars were parked in the grass — more arriving every minute. The parking lot and concourse were now a hub of energy, choked with food carts, booths, and people. I recognized Cassy from the pizza-place walking around with a boy. The blonde, skinny waitress waved at me, and it was awkward, but I waved back.

Then it got even wilder over there. A band started playing on the steps of the police station. I watched her move over, holding hands with her boyfriend. Them and the high schoolers started to "dance." (Not a single person over there could, but they kept on trying).

Smith watched them, too. When the band first played, he'd pressed both hands against his headphones. But then he let go and watched as the crowd swirled.

"Wow…" He reached over and tapped my shoulder. "Wow, do you see all those people dancing?"

"Do you like it?" I asked.

"I like the music." He nodded and then he started to drum his hand against the grass in rhythm. "I've always really liked music."

"Do you wanna get closer?"

He shook his head quickly. "No, but I still like it."

A swarm of pimpled high schoolers had taken over the concourse. As they danced, I saw Cassy moving with her man. He had a tight haircut and looked like a farmer's kid but the kind that wasn't too ugly. It was nice, I guess. Them dancing. They were smiling and didn't look as awkward as everybody else.

I'm not one of those girls who gets weirdly turned on by the blues. But it was cute.

"What a nice evening," Mom said from her lawn chair. "I like that music over there."

Dad smiled. "You're right. This is nice. It adds to it."

Nate and Rhys were sitting on the ground beside them. Picking at grass blades or talking quietly. They hadn't talked to Smith much, and I felt annoyed. At all of them, really.

"I wish there was baseball or something," Nate grumbled. "We could play over there. Behind all the cars."

He pointed to the back of the crowd. There was a stretch of grass behind all the cars, though it was filling quick.

"Yeah, true." Dad scratched at his beard. "You could."

Mom and Dad talked about people in the crowd. Of course,

they recognized everybody. And she'd tell a story, and he'd say "Great guy," and she'd agree. Everybody fucking agreed. But none of those "great guys" came up and talked to them, did they.

I just watched the crowd over on the concourse. At least they were interesting.

Those high schoolers danced for an hour. There was some smoke gathering from all the grills and food carts. I smelled it, and I wanted it.

Beside the legit food carts, there were random dads grilling, charging five bucks for a hamburger. I couldn't blame them. Everybody came to the fireworks show. Everybody got there early. Everybody wanted a hamburger, including myself.

Over in the parking lot, across all the cooking, laughter, and music, the cops were letting kids sit inside a patrol car. They had a firetruck, too, and little kids gathered around it, waiting to sit up front. Firemen and cops, giving the kids balloons and shit. Some church people—I recognized Mom's friend Susan—handed out free water bottles from a cheap, plastic table.

"You wanna go see that fire truck?" I asked Smith.

He shook his head. He'd switched between watching the live music and staring at the crowd of people around us.

"No, too many kids. I'm not… I'm more okay over here."

"Alright. Just let me know if you do wanna." I lowered my voice. "I'm getting tired of sitting here, you know?"

Smith laughed. "Yeah. Lots of sitting."

I knew most of the people on the concourse. I was trying to avoid eye contact. When I turned around to look at the fireworks crowd, it had doubled. People were stretched out, following the slight bend in the road. A thick line of people with a thick row of cars behind them.

Can I get away to check the post office? I wondered. *No, I shouldn't.*

I don't wanna leave Smith here.

After a while, our family fell into silence. Very few people came over to chat with my parents. I saw a few stop by to ask about Rhys, introduce themselves. Those people tried to act polite, but it was obvious they were snooping.

"My nephew from out-of-town," Dad lied every time, wearing a fake smile. He'd gotten good at it.

"Oh, alright. Well, nice to meet you! See you around, Cliff."

None of them ever mentioned or looked at Smith. I almost spoke up, face turning red, but he stopped me.

"Please don't," he said quietly before I could even speak.

I frowned at him. "They just ignore you, though."

He shrugged. "I'm not like them. Anyone here. But I'll find people that understand me, one day, and I'll say, 'Hi. I'm Smith.' And they'll want to say hi back."

"You know, I think you're amazing, Smith. You really are. You're just… you're the best."

He beamed at me. "My mom says it's my superpower."

"Your mom is totally right."

Whenever people stopped by for a second, Dad tried to keep the conversation going. "How is your tractor doing?" or "How are the kids?" but they always hurried away. Nobody stayed to talk. Nobody really bothered us. In fact, I'd say they avoided us.

Usually, *everyone* wanted to talk to Dad at these things. And lots of women would come talk to Mom. Church people. Wives of Dad's friends. They'd all chat with Mom. But now, nobody did. She seemed unbothered. Sitting there and glowing like always. But he looked around, sad, like a lost puppy with no owner.

I was still in a bad mood obviously, but the sun was nearly gone, everything wearing odd shadows. Still, people danced around as the band played on. They were moving slower now, and someone shouted, "Grill's shutting off in twenty minutes! Last call!" and the band stopped entirely.

The church bell rang out. I could barely hear it over all those voices.

"I'm starving," I said.

Smith looked over. Nobody else acknowledged me.

After sitting on the grass for an hour, listening to Rhys and Nate have immature conversations, I'd had enough. I was getting hangry anyway, so I stood up, brushing off my shorts. Mom looked over from her lawn chair.

"Getting some food," I said. "Anyone else?"

Nobody answered. Smith shook his head.

"No? 'Kay." *Good.* I leaned down to Smith. "Will you be okay here for a few minutes?"

"Yeah, of course."

"Okay, be right back."

I walked over and eventually found the back of the line. There were people clustered everywhere in little groups, talking about nothing. The line snaked around clusters and toward the food carts. The longer I waited, the stronger those delicious smells became. It was basically dark now, but the fireworks hadn't started yet.

If I can get a big ass hamburger right now, best fireworks show in years.

Waiting in line, this whole event started to get on my nerves. People were *so loud.* Shouting over each other. The food stand workers were yelling to take orders, and the deputies stood in a solemn line on the far side of the courtyard. They all crossed their beefy arms and watched the crowd with little smirks. Before long, I had a splitting headache.

The streetlamps were the main source of light. Everything and everybody had a strange, yellowish glow. The police station had some exterior lights, so people in line for the food were bathed in a harsh, white glow.

After minutes of not moving, there was some commotion near the front of the lines. I stood on tiptoes and tried to see.

"No more!" someone shouted from the front of the line. "No more, we're closed!"

It was a nerdy guy wearing a dark polo shirt. He faced the crowd and waved his arms in the air.

"Go back to your spots. The fireworks are starting soon!"

People murmured and didn't move. I was still trying to wrap my brain around what he meant.

"No more food!" he called out. "We're closed. The line is shut down."

"What the hell!" I yelled. "What you mean 'shut down?' Hey, boy!"

Everybody else started clamoring too. I was shouting some awful things, but so were they.

The workers behind him were loading the equipment, and the smell of grills started to die away. I stood with my arms in the air, burning with rage. And all these annoying ass people crowding me were doing the same thing. *Jesus,* people smelled bad after four hours in the sun. Wear some deodorant.

Out of nowhere, I got elbowed in the back. So hard it shoved me forward. I bumped into the middle-aged guy I'd been next to for twenty minutes.

"Sorry," I groaned. I whipped around as somebody shoved me again. "Hey, *what*? Watch it!"

People were all over the place, shoving against each other. Someone yelled angrily, but I couldn't make out the words. Everybody was hollering now. The whole crowd rushed forward. I saw somebody throw a punch, and then all hell broke loose.

"Back up! Watch it, fucker!"

"Hey, get your ugly—"

Someone knocked me over, lunging forward. I fell to the ground, almost hit my head, and a heavy boot came down inches from my ankle. I scrambled backward as the crowd pushed again. Climbing to my feet, I saw the nerdy guy in the dark polo up ahead.

A few men grabbed him, threw him down. Before I could even process this, they were kicking and stomping, beating the shit out of him.

"Hey, back up! Get back!"

The line of cops sprang into action. They rushed forward, pulling out tasers and heavy batons. A whole group of men actually rushed *toward* them and leapt forward.

"What the hell?" I backed away from the mob quickly, stumbling again.

Dozens of bodies smashing against each other. Some people took off running, trying to get away, but there were at least twenty men locked in hand-to-hand combat now. Throwing punches, lowering elbows. A couple food carts collapsed as somebody toppled onto them, and there was a loud crash each time. I couldn't get back to the fireworks crowd, so I waited for the mayhem to end, wondering, *What the hell is wrong with us?*

Then the old man came into view. He was pushing through the edge of the crowd, holding up a flip phone with a tiny screen. He waved it over his head, yelling, "Have you seen her? Help me, please! Has anyone seen her?"

Nobody answered, of course, or paid any attention. The fights were ongoing. The cops were all busy. Before I could move or speak, he came running up to me.

The closer he got, the more I recognized him. He had wrinkles all over his face and thin patches of dark hair. He was breathing heavy, overweight. Without warning, he stuck his flip phone in my face.

"Please! Please, Kaia, have you seen her?"

I stared at the square image. It was grainy and hard to tell, but I thought…

"Oh my god." I grabbed the phone from him and stared at the face on the screen.

"You've seen her?" he asked, breathless.

"Mr. Turner… I saw her today. At the library."

"She's my wife!" he wailed. "Beth! She's not home. She's gone!"

"Wait here." I jumped up and down, waving toward the cops, who were still caught up in the chaos. "Hey, cops! Need help over here. Please, quick, I need help!"

I kept shouting until one of them came over. He was sweating profusely. He looked young and buff, but more than anything he was overwhelmed. I could see it in his eyes and his trembling jaw. This dude was in over his head.

"Thank you, thank you." I gently pushed Mr. Turner toward him. "Can you listen to this—?"

"What?" The officer frowned. "No, I need to get—"

"You guys got that under control," I said, although it wasn't totally true. "Look, it's all fine. This is important."

Mr. Turner stuck out his flip phone and latched onto him. He was still yelling and not fully coherent, but I saw the officer lean down and start a serious conversation. I thanked him.

Another officer shouted something about "postpone the show!" and someone else responded, "It's too late!" I took this as a warning. The fireworks would launch any second now.

So I backed away toward the road, across the parking lot—there were a handful of fights going on and a few arrests being made — and I saw everyone lined up. Blank faces watching a dark sky above a vacant field.

So now Beth Turner's gone missing? I shook my head and reached back to massage my neck. I had such a bad headache from all that noise and no food. *What happened to her?*

The Clarks. She mentioned the Clarks. Who are they?

I started moving through the slush of people again, toward my family, but someone reached out and grabbed my arm.

"Kaia!"

I glanced over and found Cassy. She was crying and holding onto her wrist.

"Kaia, please help! I… I got knocked down. My wrist… I think it's broken, and I can't find Matt, and I don't—"

"Okay, okay. Calm down." I looked around, groaning. "Who's Matt?"

"My boyfriend! He got caught between these two guys going at it—"

"He's probably fine," I assured her. "See that table over there? With the women around it? They're from the church, and I think Susan's a nurse or something. They can help you, okay?"

Cassy nodded tearfully. "Okay… but is Matt okay?"

"I'm sure he is. They'll help you find him, okay? I can't. I don't know—"

The exterior lights on the police station shut off. Everybody gasped "Ooh" and held their breath as we waited for the sky to explode.

"Thank you, Kaia." Cassy took off into the dark.

I bent down, hands on my knees, overwhelmed and stressed the fuck out. After a minute, I straightened up and started walking toward the crowd, trying to find my family before the show started. The more I pushed, the thicker the crowd became. Everybody pressed together, nobody moving.

"Move, people! I'm trying to—"

The fireworks went off, and my voice was lost in the excitement and explosions.

I watched for a moment as the sky turned into an ever-shifting rainbow. Then a voice—cold as ice, firm, and right behind me—said, "Kaia."

I froze in place. Lost my breath. Their hand reached to my shoulder and hot breath pushed into my ear. Shivering, goosebumps—my heartbeat thundered.

"Take this," the voice behind me whispered.

I felt a hand reach down and grab my own. It pressed a balled-up paper into my palm and closed my fingers around it.

"Stay safe."

Then the hand slipped away.

I whipped around, but nobody was standing there. On both sides, dark figures were everywhere. All moving together. A group of men passed, giving me odd looks, and then a couple with a stroller.

I didn't move for a few minutes. Gripping the ball of paper, I watched the fireworks, more numb than ever before. There were so many thoughts in my brain. I unfolded the paper and tried to read it, but there wasn't enough light. I almost lost my cool for a minute. Standing there with something, some answer, and unable to read it. I never felt so frustrated.

I need to know what this says. And I need to know about the Clarks.

I'd seen the show my whole life. The same damn show every year. They would paint the sky in brilliant colors. It rattled teeth and shook the ground. But I hadn't been impressed for years. Especially not now.

Before I knew it, the show was over, and I wished I'd paid attention more.

What if this is the last time I ever see fireworks?

What if this is it?

Without meaning to, I stumbled into my family, and it was like they'd never noticed I had left. I didn't pay them much attention, either. I couldn't stop thinking about the paper, now slipped into my pocket.

"Wow, that was awesome!" Rhys yelled when they ended.

My parents and Nate laughed. They talked non-stop. Smith moved with them, fully engaged now, waving his arms around. The whole crowd started to leave, pushing toward the field of parked cars. My own family and Smith packed up our lawn chairs and got caught in the current. Three hundred sweaty people pressed together and struggling to escape.

I slumped along while they whooped and cheered. Nate and Rhys were having the time of their lives. Smith hung on, talking fast and excited. Mom and Dad were holding hands again. But I couldn't stop thinking of the Clarks and Beth Turner, who nobody knew about.

What if I go missing and nobody cares about me?

What if nobody cares about Allison?

The voice continued in my head. Gravely and slow, like a longtime smoker.

Take this.

As soon as we got home, I ran up to my bedroom. Everything was a blur until I closed the door behind me and worked gently to unfold the wad of paper.

She's still alive.

Things are going to change. It's happening again, but we have time.

What you saw inside the house is real. The woman. The lights. It's all real. It's the aftermath. The house has starved for years. Now it wants more.

Things are in motion. You will see where everybody falls.

I cannot answer for three days. I apologize.

Stay safe.

It has starved for years. Now it wants more.

<> <> <>

I had to tell someone about everything. And I wasn't gonna talk to Dad.

The next morning, I was out in the barn helping him. I didn't know anything about the part he was replacing—nothing had more stupidly specific parts than a tractor—so he'd ask me to hand him a tool or a different-sized wrench. In that barn, it could get so hot and stuffy. Even after I got used to the smells, I never adapted to the heat.

"Thanks for helping me, Kaia," he said at one point, taking a break. Dad wiped both hands on his jeans. They were so dirty I wouldn't call them "blue jeans" anymore. He scratched at his beard and smiled.

"No problem." I shrugged. "Got nothing else to do. Think maybe… is there anything I can help with and you'd pay me?"

He raised his eyebrows.

"I'm looking for a job, but until then, you know." With pursed lips, I added, "I've been making up for Nate slacking, anyway."

"You're right." Dad sighed. "Yeah, lemme think later. I can find some jobs worth paying for. They might be pretty bad, though?"

"Hah. Yeah, okay. I've been helping you with the worst jobs for years."

He laughed and got back to work. Underneath the tractor, he had a white-knuckle grip on his tools and kept clanging away at the underside. While he was busy, I crept over to the workbench where he kept all the nuts, bolts, and wrenches. It was the least disgusting workbench of his three, so he kept his phone there.

I opened up his contact list—probably faster than he could've—and found Jeremy's number. Without a sound, I added it to my phone and then put his away again.

"I've got something you could help with after dinner," he called out from under the tractor. "It's on the hay baler. Not a hard job. Just annoying and hurts my back."

"What doesn't?" I acted like I was thinking about it. "Yeah, okay, I'll help after dinner."

"Sounds good. Thanks again."

"No, thank you."

What was I gonna tell Jeremy? "Hey, this woman at the library, Mrs. Turner, said the Clarks went missing and something about the house. And now she's missing I think, or Mr. Turner's crazy. And I don't know any of these people. Great, thanks."

I don't know. Something like that, yeah. But I had a feeling he could help. And this way, Dad wouldn't even have to know.

Maybe I would even tell Jeremy about the letters. Part of me wanted to and another part refused. But I would certainly tell him about these missing people, and maybe later on… if I trusted him enough… I'd tell him everything.

PART 2
THE KEYS

CHAPTER 1
KAIA WOODS

When Nate, Rhys, and Smith were together the next day, I didn't worry as much. Nate's recent mean streak faded from my mind. Right away, when Anne dropped off Smith, Nate was introducing him to Rhys, trying to be the middleman. Even though they'd met the night before, they hadn't talked much at the fireworks. Now, he showed Smith his room upstairs, then the barn, and of course within a half-hour they were playing baseball outside.

"I think they're gonna have fun," Nate said to me on the way outside.

"Good, honey."

"And Dad's gonna play baseball with us!" He smiled so wide with his announcement. It sent a warm feeling through my chest and belly.

"Have fun. I'll come out and watch in just a minute."

"Okay, Mom."

Then he dashed outside. Smith and Rhys were standing awkwardly in the gravel waiting for him. They both chuckled at something Nate said, and the three of them were off toward the oak tree.

Ben walked into the kitchen just then. He pulled one arm across his chest and stretched it, then the other one.

"You're unretired, huh?"

Ben grinned sheepishly. "I figured it was time I do something right."

I moved closer to him and kissed his lips. "Even if that means getting all sweaty and losing to your son?"

"Oh, yeah. I'm definitely losing."

I grabbed his hands and pressed myself against him. "Well, sounds like you'll need another shower later. Maybe I'll join you."

"Oh, yeah?" He laughed quietly. "I won't argue with that."

I was in the kitchen opening canned vegetables and preparing a big pot of vegetable soup. While I worked, I'd glance outside and see the baseball game. Before long, it was in full swing. Nate and Smith were on one team, facing off with Ben and Rhys.

At one point, I looked over to find Smith and Rhys both standing at second base. Rhys gave him a nasty look, and Smith reached out with one hand, pushing the other boy's shoulder. He backed away, and Rhys said something else. I couldn't hear any of it, just see their actions.

A minute later, I saw Cliff standing, facing second, talking right at Rhys and Smith, very animated. They both nodded their heads, and then the game resumed. Rhys and Smith stayed away from each other after that.

When I went outside ten minutes later, the game wasn't as heated. Ben threw a slow pitch to Smith, who hit it short but still managed to get to first base. (With only two people on each team, I didn't think there were very many outs.) Then Nate hit one really good, up and over, way out to the vegetable patch.

"And that's a homerun," Ben called, sounding like a PA announcer. "That's the run limit, and the first inning is over. Score 5-5."

"I'll get the ball," Nate said. "You're a terrible announcer, Dad."

"And Nate's team is trying to get *kicked* out of the game," Ben went on, still in a deep, faux-announcer voice. "They'd better watch out, or the referee-pitcher-Dad won't take it so easy next time."

"Don't step on my cucumbers!" I called to Nate as he jogged off.

He gave me a thumbs-up on his way to the garden.

"Do you all want some lemonade or water?" I asked the boys. "There's some on the porch. The clear pitcher is water. The other one is lemonade."

"Thank you," Rhys said, walking toward the porch.

Smith nodded at me with a toothy smile. "Thanks, ma'am."

As they passed, I turned to Ben.

"Having fun?"

"Yeah. It's fun." He rubbed the back of his neck. "I said they should let me hit from the tee, but Nate wasn't having it."

"Yeah, 'cause you're too old to use a tee!" Nate said, returning with the baseball. Specks of dirt clung to the ball and his hand. "Why'd they go to the porch?"

"Drink break," I said. "Go get something, and then you all can keep playing."

He moved along and I turned to Ben once more. "Have you seen Kaia today? She didn't go into town, did she?"

"Not since this morning. Your car's still here. And she was helping me in the barn earlier." He used the bottom of his shirt to wipe sweat from his forehead. "I guess she's inside."

"I hope she's okay. She didn't wanna talk much last night after…" I didn't explain the short conversation we'd had. It hadn't been long, but it'd been a lot.

"She wasn't super talkative this morning. But we were working."

Neither of us spoke for a minute. I pressed my bare toes into the grass and wiggled them. Ben stared past me, at the porch, where the boys were probably talking about the game.

"Smith's a pretty quiet kid." Ben scratched at his chin while he spoke. "Even more than Rhys."

"Well, Rhys is more comfortable here. Now, anyway."

"I've only heard Smith talk three or four times. He just sort of… nods, usually." Ben frowned. "He said something to Rhys, though. Earlier. I dunno what, but Rhys was on second base, and Smith was standing out there, you know. Then they just started shoving each other."

"Oh, yeah, I saw part of that, I think."

"I went out and told 'em to quit or we could stop playing, so they stopped."

"Were they shoving… hard?"

Ben shrugged. "Not super hard. But not like friends, either. They were fine after, though."

The boys returned and we didn't have a chance to talk about it anymore. I watched another inning, sitting in the grass underneath the tree. While they were playing their mini game of baseball, I didn't notice any anger from Smith or Rhys. I hoped they were getting used to each other and it'd been a one-time thing.

They kept going, sun beaming down. I was more than happy with my shaded spot, but my thoughts kept drifting to Kaia. I worried about her. It was definitely the right choice—and *her* choice—to stick around for another year. But I wanted her to have space to heal, and I wasn't sure we could offer that. I couldn't imagine how she felt right now.

And the whole job thing. She couldn't get a job right now. Not until she healed, not until the whole town wasn't covered in missing posters. Cliff should've kept his mouth shut on that idea.

For Kaia, I knew it must be hard going into town. There was too much Allison there.

Maybe that's why she keeps going, I thought. *The memories are bittersweet. They hurt, but it's all she has left.*

Either way, she didn't need a job until she dealt with that trauma. Maybe in a few months. School would start, things would settle into a routine, and I'd find her a therapist. Not in New Haven but in the city, Brooksville, and I wouldn't mind driving her forty minutes there and back. We'd try it, see if it helped her.

Yes. That's a good idea. Definitely try that.

With a month left before Nate started school, I knew things would calm down. As soon as we made a decision on Rhys—I was getting impatient with Cliff. He still hadn't found any answers, despite all these phone calls he said he'd made, and I started to wonder if he wasn't trying very hard.

Gonna have to do it myself, I guess.

Maybe I should've. But I had so much going on with the church and organizing meal drives and trying to help out wherever I could. I wanted Cliff to do something for once. Something to help the whole family.

Either way, things would go back to normal. In a way. A new normal, maybe, but better than our last couple weeks.

Will they have a funeral for Allison like they did for George?

I pushed the image away.

The screen door opened. I glanced over and saw Kaia standing there, wearing jeans and a colorful top. With a headband on her forehead and hair in a messy bun, I felt like she was me twenty years ago.

I waved. She lowered her head and started toward me, crunching over the gravel.

I looked back at the two-on-two baseball game. Behind it, I

couldn't help but notice the twisted house. It was the backdrop to everything we did. It didn't scare me as much, now. Not like before. Kaia going in there had been my worst fear, but she'd survived it. She was so strong. We were dealing with the aftermath, sure, but the worst had passed.

Whenever I saw the house, I still got a feeling in my stomach. Like a dead weight. It wasn't as bad as before, but it was there.

Sitting in our yard, on a perfect evening, the dead weight feeling returned as Kaia walked closer. Her face was emotionless. A shiver rolled through me.

"Hi, baby. If you're hungry, there are some leftovers in the —"

"Mom." She squatted down. No expression. No fear in her voice. "Jeremy called."

"What? He called you?"

She hesitated. "No, he called the landline, but you all weren't in there. I answered, 'cause I didn't know who it was, and…"

I stood up, and she did, too. "What'd he say, Kaia?"

"He said… Um, it's about Malaki."

The weight in my stomach turned into a boulder. "What about him?"

"He told the cops he'll talk. But he'll only talk to Dad… and me."

"Oh, God."

Kaia took a deep breath, then reached out and held me by the shoulders. It was strange and straightforward. My daughter, trying to steady me.

"Jeremy's coming right now. He's gonna pick us up. We're going today."

"But…" I fumbled over what to say. After our conversation the night before, this felt surreal. So much worse. "What do you think he wants?"

Kaia shook her head. "I have no idea, Mom. But he… I mean, Malaki knows stuff. He could tell us a lot."

"Well, you…" I ran a hand over my face. I felt like my head might explode. "You can't go, though. I mean… right? You're only…"

"I'm going, Mom."

She didn't say it angrily. Her voice was firm. She wrapped her arms around me and pulled me into a hug. I felt like I was a puppet, like I had no control anymore.

After everything I've done? Everything, and I can't stop this?

The oak tree whispered above us, leaves trembling. No birds sang anymore, and I couldn't find strength from the grass under my bare feet.

She squeezed me tightly and went on. "I need to do this. Please don't be mad, Mom. You have to understand. I love her. I love her more than I've ever loved anything. And I didn't want to admit it to myself… but I know it now."

I opened my mouth, but she kept going.

"And it's safe. It's at the police station. All the… all the cops will be there. The sheriff. Everyone's watching. Jeremy can keep me safe. Just let me do this, please, because I have to. And I really don't wanna fight with you, Mom."

It took everything in my power to nod. To let go. It went against every instinct in my body. And yet I knew she was right. Kaia needed this chance more than anything. If I said no, she'd go anyway, resent me forever, and I would never forgive myself.

It's safe. It's at the police station.

But if something happened… If this wasn't all…

"Okay. Okay." I breathed out, counting to ten. "But I need you to be *extremely* careful. More careful than you've ever been. Do you understand me?"

Kaia nodded frantically. "Yes. Yes, I will."

"This isn't the same Malaki you remember from school, okay? This is…"

This is the man who tried to kill you.

"I know. I know, Mom. I'm going to be so careful."

I stared into her eyes for another moment. I had the feeling of two heavy magnets being pulled away.

"I love you, Kaia. And Allison would be so proud of you."

She choked up. "I love you, Mom." Then she ran back and vanished into the house.

Without any idea what would come next, I turned to the baseball game. All those happy, smiling faces. Any minute, Jeremy's truck would roar down the driveway, throwing up dust clouds, and everything would change.

"Ben!" I yelled, heading over. "Ben, come here, quick!"

CHAPTER 2
NATE WOODS

"Through here." I led them both into the forest, dodging under some low-hanging branches and stepping around a thornbush.

Rhys and Smith followed slowly. They weren't sold on this idea, wandering out into the woods. They'd liked baseball more, I think. But after Dad left in a hurry—didn't tell me why and probably never would—the game died off. I didn't wanna play anymore. After you get a real game going, like we did with two-on-two, it's not as fun to play with less people.

"Is it safe out here?" Smith asked as he moved around the thorns.

Rhys snorted. "What, you've never been in the forest before?"

"It's safe," I assured Smith.

Leaving the field behind and our last view of my house, I led them deeper in. Even with the trees overhead, it was easy to see. Middle of the afternoon, with enough sunlight, I almost didn't notice a difference.

"We just go on this path here," I explained. "You'll see."

I felt like the leader of a safari. There were thick trees on every side of our little group and huge bushes that reached above my head. It was like walking through a hallway, but the walls were natural and green. Everything smelled like a garden.

It was never quiet in the woods—constant chirping and rustling, and sometimes animals would shake the bushes so loud, like a jump-scare.

"I think I like the hills better," Rhys said as we moved farther in.

"I know, but Smith has never been out here." I glanced over my shoulder.

Smith stared around, wide-eyed. He took each step slowly and kept both arms tight to his body, as if the trees might reach out and grab him. But he didn't look unhappy. I think I caught him smiling a little.

"*Have* you ever been in the woods?" I asked him.

"Yeah, I…" Smith paused. "Um, kinda."

"Kinda?" Rhys rolled his eyes at me, but Smith couldn't see. I asked, "What do you mean, Smith?"

I was trying to be kinder than Rhys. He seemed to have something against Smith. All day, he'd been making little, snide comments, and they'd started shoving once during our game.

"I've been in a little woods," he said. "Before we moved here. But not big like this."

"Where'd you used to live?" Rhys asked him, sneering.

"Where'd *you* used to live?" Smith countered. "I've known Nate since school ended, and you weren't around then."

Rhys scowled at him and shut up.

Thankfully, we reached the log bridge soon. We came to the creek and found it moving quickly but not deep. It bubbled across the rock bed, but the rocks were still very visible.

"So, we have two choices," I explained, putting on my safari guide voice. "We can either cross the creek and our shoes get wet, or we can try the log bridge."

"I think I'll get hurt if I fall," Smith pointed out, his voice shaking a bit.

Rhys chuckled. "Come on. Don't be a pussy."

Smith stared at him, confused. I shot Rhys a look and shook my head.

"What?" He laughed. "Come on. Go. Let's go across."

Rhys led the way over the log bridge. I went second, and Smith followed behind me. Once we were on top, I took my time. The fall *did* look dangerous. There were tons of rocks — some big ones, too. I didn't feel like breaking an ankle and missing out on months of baseball.

"See, not bad," Rhys called back once he'd reached the end.

Smith and I finished crossing a moment later. We hopped down, landing in soft soil, and breathed easy.

"Let's keep going a bit," I said. "There's something up here I wanna show you. Rhys, you've already seen it."

"Oh, right." He nodded. His expression changed, and he rubbed his neck. "Smith… sorry about what I said. It's… I'm just not used to being around kids this age."

Before I could speak, Smith answered, "It's alright. You didn't hurt my feelings."

"Okay, good." Rhys blew a raspberry. "Honestly? I was worried about meeting you."

Smith wrinkled his nose. "Me? Why?"

"I just thought you two were good friends already, and I didn't think I'd fit in." Rhys lowered his eyes to the trail.

"Well, I think you're cool," Smith said. "Maybe even cooler than Nate."

"Hey! Why am I catching strays here?"

We moved along with less tension after that. They took turns commenting on weird features we saw. A tree with a gnarled trunk or a thick bush in the shape of a dick. Smith asked about my dad and the farm, which I tried my best to explain, but I honestly didn't know much. The three of us were finally getting along. Dunno *why* Rhys apologized like he did, but I was glad. I'd been hoping for this kinda day.

The path got more rugged and narrow the longer we went. It had been weeks since Kaia and I had used it. Thorn bushes stretched out over the path. Tiny stems grew from the dirt wherever we stepped. At least we didn't see any snakes.

"So many rotten leaves," I said once the silence became awkward.

"They're decomposing," Smith said. "Not rotting."

"Oh." I cleared my throat as we approached the end. "Well, anyway. Here's this."

We emerged from the thin path to find a cleared area. It was mostly grass here, not dirt. A little creek bubbled to the right, and on the left stood the hut.

"Woah…" Smith headed for it right away. "Did you build this?"

"Kaia did." Then, "But I helped," which wasn't true.

The structure had a domed roof with shingles on top. The hut was circular, built around a large tree trunk helping support it. There were two big wood planks holding up the front, dug into the ground, and the far side had an actual wall of wood. Lots of beams lay across, with a little shelf. Some large stones propped up the back, extra support. Lawn chairs sat inside, under the roof, with a clear view of the creek and our patch of grass.

Smith turned back and asked, "Can I… go in?"

"Definitely. Sit down." I beamed with pride as he entered. His eyes were so wide.

Rhys stood in front of it, staring at the shingled roof. He scratched his chin and didn't smile.

"What's it called?" Smith asked.

"Um…" I hesitated. It was the Wolf Cave… "It doesn't have a name."

Rhys laughed, and not in a happy way. "How? You two built this, and it doesn't have a name?"

"Well…"

"Let's name it!" Smith yelled from inside. He was sitting in a lawn chair. "Got any ideas, Nate? Since it's yours."

"No, not really."

To my surprise, Rhys spoke up. "How about…"

All eyes turned to him. He walked to one side, checking out the back of the structure, and then to the front again.

"How about the Silent Hut?"

"Huh?"

"Well, you know." Rhys waved his hand in the air, turning to face the creek. "The whole forest around here is connected to the Silent Forest."

"The Silent Forest?" Smith asked. "What's that?"

"I'll show you guys sometime," Rhys said. "It's up by the hills. That's what everyone used to call it."

— A memory jumped out at me. Sitting in the dark, next to the house on the hill. Police lights all around. I glanced over to the right, to the trees. Next to the house, the dark forest went on forever and ever. There were depths to the night, there. Endless depths among the trees.

"I'm getting hungry," Rhys said, and my memory burnt down. "Think your mom made anything?"

"Probably, yeah. Wanna head back and see?"

Smith stood up from the lawn chair and walked toward me. "Yeah, I'm hungry, too."

"Alright. Let's go back."

Rhys and Smith led the way. I followed them onto the narrow trail. They were talking about food or something, but I didn't pay attention. Rhy's voice stuck in my mind, and I couldn't shake it.

"...connected to the Silent Forest. ...what everyone used to call it."

I turned back to look at the Wolf Cave one more time. It seemed lonely now. Bathing in sunbeams, sitting beside the creek, but more and more we forgot it. And if Kaia went to college, maybe I *wouldn't* ever come back.

Something caught my eye.

"Wait. Rhys, stop."

I grabbed his arm. He stopped beside me, staring back toward the hut.

"What?" he asked loudly.

"Shh. Look, there." I pointed a shaking finger.

Behind the Wolf Cave, there was something in the trees.

"What the hell?" He stepped in front of me, squinting.

"You see it?"

"Yeah. But... what is it?"

I turned to look at him, and I had this choked feeling in my throat. Heart pounding, legs shaky, but like I could run for miles.

"Is that a... person?" Rhys whispered.

"Remember that guy we saw over in the field yesterday?" I said, keeping my voice low.

"Oh, shoot." I heard Rhys breathing, sharp and unsteady. "Let's... let's get home. Quick."

I nodded. "Okay. Let's go. But... all at the same time."

We turned around. Smith was staring at us.

"Wait, what?" he asked.

"Go on three," I said. "There's someone behind us."

"What—"

"One, two—"

At that moment, I heard something crashing. At first—a terrifying image—I thought the Wolf Cave had fallen over. But then I realized it was the sound of someone trampling bushes and breaking sticks.

I glanced back. A dark figure, tall and lean, was sprinting through the forest. Closing in quick.

"Shit, run!" I yelled.

The three of us took off. Rhys passed Smith, and I was right behind them. Thank God Smith wasn't one of those slow kids. The path was too small. We were stuck in a single-file line. I couldn't hear anything behind us. Just our footsteps, our gasps. Everybody sucking wind, and I panted, "Go! Go faster!"

We plunged through the trail. Nothing could stop us. I was an athlete, but I'd never felt my heart scream like that. I felt it vibrating in my throat. I almost threw up.

"Can you see them?" Rhys called back.

I slowed down enough to turn and look. I didn't see anything for sure. Maybe in the distance, there, on the trail, or possibly—

Choking on my words, I sputtered, "No. But it… just go… the bridge."

By the time we reached the fallen log, I was doubled over and heaving.

"Go across. You two." I waved my hand at them, clutching my stomach. "I'll watch back."

Smith went first and then Rhys. They were moving fast over the log bridge. None of us even thought about the rocks. We were focused on running away. Getting home safe.

"Maybe it was nobody," I said loud enough for them to hear. "I don't see anything now. We're probably—"

"Ahhhh!"

A terrible, spine-tingling scream cut through my words.

I'd never heard a kid scream like that before. Like the end of the world. Like they were going to die.

I whipped around to face the log bridge. The screaming continued, mixed with sobs.

Rhys stood on the bridge, hands against his chest.

Smith was in the creek bed, cradling his elbow. When I looked closer, I gagged and felt queasy.

His forearm was split where it shouldn't be. Like a second elbow.

"Oh, shit…"

CHAPTER 3
KAIA WOODS

I'd never been in a police station before.

From our house, driving into New Haven, the police station was on the close side of town. Right at the edge. When Jeremy pulled into the lot, my breathing picked up. I felt lightheaded. Later on, Jeremy explained the men inside were actually deputies, not "cops." Only real towns had cops. We had deputies, and they were all selected by the sheriff. But to me, it didn't make a difference.

"Remember what I said." Jeremy paused with his hand on the door handle. He turned back to face me. "Don't let him get to you. Don't answer any questions he asks. And if you need a break, you can take one. *You're* in control here, not Malaki. You're not the one going to prison."

I nodded without meeting his eyes. "Okay."

"Same goes for you," he said, turning away from me.

Dad stared back at him, jaw clenched.

There'd been this tension between them ever since Jeremy picked us up.

"Guess you really are serious, huh, Cliff?" Jeremy had asked. There was a strange smile behind his bushy beard. "About what you said at the funeral?"

Dad had nodded. "I wasn't lying."

"Well, let's see if you'll be useful *and* serious."

Dad hadn't talked the rest of the way. But I didn't think on it too long, 'cause I was freaking out about what I'd agreed to do.

Jeremy opened his door and hopped out. Dad followed his lead. I opened my own—Jeremy had one of those nice, spacious trucks with backrow seating—and dropped to the hot pavement.

Deep breaths. Stay grounded, I reminded myself as we approached the police station. *You've been waiting for this. Just chill out.*

A terrible sun beat down on us. I followed Dad and Jeremy, happy to third wheel. I didn't need to ask questions. I didn't know what I'd even say. The whole ride over, I'd tried to imagine seeing Malaki again, face-to-face. I knew it would upset me, and I'd probably start to freak out, but I just needed to survive, get through it, and it would be worth it for some answers.

The cops will get answers. You'll get nothing.

First, we went through double glass doors. Jeremy held one side open. Dad passed through, murmuring thanks. I reached for the handle and motioned for Jeremy to go on.

"I want to be last," I said quietly.

He offered a kind smile and let me follow. The door swung shut behind us.

It was one of those in-between spaces—a single bench and a pamphlet display. A corkboard on the wall with fliers, posters, and Allison's missing poster—I didn't look.

There was another set of doors just ahead. This time, a cop waited. He held one side open for us. As we passed through without a word, his eyes fixed on me. I looked down at the floor.

In the air-conditioning, I realized I'd been sweating. I adjusted my headband and clasped both hands in front of me. Dad looked back.

"I'm okay," I mouthed.

He nodded, but his face said he didn't believe me. I wasn't sure I did either.

I'd never been in a police station, but I imagined they were nicer in other cities. The floors were all pale tiles, and the walls were white, decorated with cheap office decor. To our left, there was a huge front desk with mug shots behind it (I didn't look closely, but Malaki's probably hung there). No officer at the front desk, nothing but cluttered papers, with a few empty waiting chairs, it made a small lobby.

"Do we… sit?" I asked Jeremy.

He shook his head. "Sherrif knows we're here."

A few cops drifted around, watching us curiously. Some had manilla folders, some had coffee mugs. I heard phones ringing toward the back of the station and rehearsed voices answering. I wondered if they were calls about Allison or if they'd buried her under all the other manilla folders.

Sheriff Wheeler came around a corner, chewing on a toothpick. He wore his star-emblazoned hat and a frown. His eyes drifted over Dad and me, staying on me. His features were lined with age, shadows under his eyes. Even though they were roughly the same age, Dad seemed about ten years younger.

"Good. So, everyone's here." Sheriff Wheeler crossed his arms and rotated his intense stare between the three of us. "Here's the deal. Cliff… you and your daughter are going with me. Malaki's agreed to talk but only to you two. I'll be in there, of course. We'll keep it short and sweet. This is just a start, 'cause the hope is we can get him talkin' more in a day or two. Maybe this'll start something."

I gulped. The sheriff focused on me.

"You gonna be okay in that room?"

I nodded. I had both hands locked together and squeezed. "I'm fine."

"If you ain't, you can step out," he said. "Nothing wrong with that. Don't hurt yourself or nothing."

He cleared his throat and went on for another minute, explaining how everything would be recorded and captured on video. Malaki would be seated across from us, chained to the floor and wearing handcuffs. There would only be a table between us.

"I thought…" I hesitated. "I thought there'd be… like… a telephone or whatever. Like the…" I stopped myself before I said *movies*.

Sheriff Wheeler frowned. "Not here, no. This isn't a prison."

"Are you gonna have any trouble holding him?" Jeremy asked.

Sheriff Wheeler shook his head. "We've got a confession to arson. Confession to attempted murder. Not to mention, we think it could be… uh, racially motivated." His eyes flicked toward me for just a second. "But besides that, he hasn't been any help. Hoping to change that now, 'cause we don't have many holding cells. Soon, he'll be sent to Brooksville."

"Has he said anything?" I asked. "Anything about… Allison?"

The sheriff shook his head. "I'm sorry, Kaia," he said, and in a way like he meant it. "I've been trying. Trust me."

From the corner of my eye, I saw Dad glance over at me. I didn't acknowledge it.

The sheriff glanced at his watch. "Alright. Let's head in. You two, follow me."

He led us through the middle of the police station. A dozen men watched from their desks. Some of them were curious and leaning forward, others scowled, and a couple laughed quietly. I tried to ignore them all, reaching up and feeling the quartz stone hanging around my neck. I had it tucked under my shirt, pressed against my collarbone. For a moment, I gripped it tight between two fingers and thought about her.

This is all for Ally.

Sheriff Wheeler led us down a wide staircase with a rail in the middle. Blank, brick walls lined both sides. He mentioned something about, "…historic section, built by my great-great-grandpa, with the add-on near the front," but I didn't care to listen more. The farther we went, with each step down, the lights seemed to dim.

We met a hallway running left and right. The air was cold here. More isolated. I imagined how a scream might echo around this space. How chains might clang against these hard floors.

The sheriff led us to the left toward a door at the end. The thickest door I'd ever seen, made of iron, like the entrance to a bank vault. To the side, there was a normal-sized wooden one.

"Go through there, Jeremy," the sheriff said, pointing to the right door. "A couple officers are waiting. You know 'em."

"Yes, sir. Good luck." Jeremy gave me a solemn nod. "Kaia, if you need to step out, I'll meet you out here. Okay?"

I couldn't find the words to answer or even nod. He opened the door and vanished into the dark room behind it.

"Here goes nothing," the sheriff said.

He knocked on the thicker door and after a moment—I imagined the sound of locks turning—it swung open. A female deputy beckoned us through with a hand resting near her holster.

I followed Dad and the sheriff in. It was all gray and concrete. Streaks of yellow marked the walls, possibly old paint. Nothing in the room except for a table in the center. The whole place smelled like bleach and sweat.

When I stepped inside, I saw a mirror wall on the right, just like in TV shows. I could imagine Jeremy behind it, watching intently. The thought made me smile a little.

Malaki was on the other side of the table. His hands were in his lap. He sat rigid, impossibly still, and wore the same, thin, unbreakable smile from that night.

On the near side of the table, there were three chairs a few feet back.

"Have a seat." Sheriff Wheeler motioned at them.

Dad took the center one, and I settled into the rightmost.

I crossed my arms and felt the cold metal against my elbows. When I looked up, Malaki was staring right at me. Those emotionless eyes never wavered. Again, I reached for the crystal hanging around my neck.

For Ally.

"Malaki Banks," Sherrif Wheeler started, using a more formal tone than I'd ever heard from him, "we got a few things to ask you about. This won't be a long interview, understand, so if you've got details to share, don't wait."

He paused for a moment. Malaki glanced at him, then focused back on me.

"Keep in mind any information you share could result in a more lenient sentence," the sheriff went on, sounding rehearsed.

Malaki snorted. He still didn't speak.

"We're joined by two members of the Woods family."

Malaki rolled his eyes at me, smiling, as if we shared some inside joke. I tried my best to show disgust and not shake.

"I'm certain you remember Kaia Woods?"

Malaki looked over at the sheriff, cocking his head. "Come on, Sherrif. Skip this boring shit."

His voice didn't sound the same anymore. Familiar but different. Like it had been frozen. It lacked any emotion, except for sarcasm. "Course I remember Kaia." He turned to me again and licked his lips. "Who could ever forget a hot black chick like that?"

I didn't answer. I glared back, not breaking eye contact, not wavering.

"Well, last time, you sure were happy to see me," Malaki went on. "You said, 'What the hell are you doing here? Did you check down there?' Oh, you were so close, Kaia. So close."

"As you seem to already know, Mr. Banks," the Sheriff continued, raising his voice. "We've had a string of missing persons reports lately. First, George and Mallory Clark. Next, Beth Turner. Do you have any idea who might be responsible for either of these?"

Malaki adopted a fake British accent. "Well, it's the same person, innit?"

"Do you know who that person might be?"

"Nah."

"Do you know what might be the reason for these—?"

Malaki rolled his eyes and returned to his normal voice. "Looking for motive on a century-old kidnapping? Idiots."

"Mr. Banks, these happened last week."

"But it's been happening, right? Always been happening."

"So, you do have information?" Sheriff Wheeler, stone-faced, didn't take his eyes off Malaki for a second. "Information you'd be willing to share?"

"Nothing you don't already know." Malaki faked a yawn. "Everybody knows it, right? They know they're in danger. Getting worried, too, and especially good folks like the Woods here. Must be *real* worried."

"That's enough," Sheriff cut in. "If you don't have anything to share, we'll move on."

Malaki leaned his head back and waved a hand in the air. "Proceed, your highness, but I can't promise shit."

"Mr. Banks, you *told us* you had important details to share. That is why the Woods are here. Do you still hold to what you promised?"

"Come on, Sheriff. Can't a guy have a little fun?" Malaki cackled. He looked past me at the mirror wall. "See, he knows what I'm talking about."

The sheriff furrowed his eyebrows. He glanced over at the female officer guarding the door, exchanged a look, then returned his focus to Malaki.

"Next, I would like to ask simply about the night of your arrest. It's been over two weeks—"

"You know what Allison did, baby?" Malaki started again. He watched me closely now and leaned forward a few inches. Both hands were still in his lap. "The first time we *fucked?*"

He was laser-focused on me. I squirmed in my seat, but I couldn't turn away. And I wouldn't run out, either.

You don't… you have no power over me.

"She moaned 'Kaia. Oh, Kaia.' Can you believe that?" Malaki smacked the table and leaned back, laughing. He motioned for the others—like frozen sculptures—to chime in.

"You're lying," I hissed under my breath. I felt uncomfortably aware of Dad right beside me.

"Oh, okay, play it like that." He showed those ugly, yellow teeth as he went on. "On my *wedding night,* Kaia. And she told me, you know that? She told me about the graduation party. Crying and begging… 'Forgive me, Malaki.' Begging, baby!"

"That's enough!" Sheriff Wheeler tried to cut in, "Malaki, you listen—"

"No!" Malaki screamed. He thrashed for a minute, hair flying.

The chains on his legs and arms rattled and shook. The chair didn't move an inch as he moved wildly. Then he settled again and was impossibly calm.

The sheriff began. "Malaki—"

"No, Sheriff." Malaki smiled. "You listen to me. Boy, have I got a *story* for you." In a sing-song voice, he went on. "Oh, such a *story*, Mr. Sheriff. A very *sexy* story." Malaki cleared his throat. He glanced at each of us. "Oh, yeah." He nodded at Dad. "You'll like it, Papa Bear."

My dad growled, and Malaki shivered.

"Mm, stop, I like that. Anyway. There was a mommy and a daddy in the woods. They were hiking, you know. People do weird things in these weird times. Everybody can feel it... The wind turning. Everybody gets anxious, worked up. There was a big fight, right? That's what I'm talking about. Worked up bastards."

He sighed. "Anyway. Sorry. So, there's a mommy and a daddy and their little girl Luna. Well, only Luna came back." Malaki's cheeks twitched. "Mommy and Daddy were swallowed up whole. Swallowed up, up, up. They came down, down, down. Everything goes down, you know. In those hills... Everything goes down."

"We want actual information," Dad said out of nowhere. "Not little fantasies from your drugged-out brain."

Malaki's eyebrow twitched. Then he smiled and his voice grew deeper. "Oh, you couldn't handle my fantasies. Especially Papa Bear."

Sheriff Wheeler cut in, raising his voice so it echoed around the room. "Malaki Banks. If you don't have more *important* details to give, then—"

"*Please* don't take them away yet," Malaki whined. He started cackling.

I could tell from the sheriff's face he was almost done with this shitshow. He was turning bright red and a vein throbbed in his neck.

"Malaki," I said, leaning forward. "Malaki, hey! Shut the fuck up!"

He blinked once and narrowed his eyes.

"Allison loved you," I said. "She *trusted* you. And you…" I stretched my neck out and said in a deeper voice, "You made a *vow*, Malaki. I was there. She really did love you, and you know it, too. But you don't wanna admit it, because… because of what you did."

His eyes got really wide, then. He jerked his head to the left and right, settling on me.

"Oh, no… Oh, Kaia…" He gaped at me. "They still haven't found Ally…"

I nearly choked. Everything seemed to pause. For an instant, I thought I saw something genuine in his face. Something like regret.

"Do you know where she is?" I asked, breathlessly.

Everyone turned to look at me. Malaki's face twitched again, and he closed his eyes.

"Oh, no…"

"Malaki. Where is she?"

"I know… I know about the silence under… Ohhhh, no," he wailed, like he was in pain. Malaki shuddered in the chair again, rattling the bolts which held it to the ground. "All their darkest… All the things our fingers touched… Oh, no, Kaia." He opened his eyes, and they were bloodshot. "They're never going to find her down there."

"Down where?" I was about to explode.

"You can rot in hell, Malaki." Dad stood up from his chair,

clenching his fists. "You piece of shit. I don't care anymore. I don't care. You deserve whatever you had and whatever you've got coming. I hope your aunt and uncle spend their whole lives, all their money, lawyer after lawyer… and…" He heaved, out of breath. "I hope they end up homeless, broke… in a gutter somewhere. For raising something like you."

"I'm… I…" he stammered.

I was sure this time. Malaki had torn off whatever mask he wore, and he was on the verge of tears. Something had broken through. Some actual, real person. With his lips quivering, he turned to me. "Kaia… I didn't mean it…"

"Where is she, Malaki?" I leaned forward even more, catching the scent of his foul clothes. "Tell me where she is. You can still help us. We can still save her."

He shook his head, and he started to cry. The tears were streaming out, dripping onto the concrete floor and the chains around his ankles.

"I can't save her, Kaia," he blubbered. "Nothing down there ever comes back."

"Down in the hills, right?" I asked frantically. I was closing in. "Is she there? Malaki, she's in the hills somewhere? Isn't she?"

"Down… down, down, down…" His chin dropped to his chest as he sobbed. "The streams. The streams come down in the hills. You'll find them there."

"Them?" Sheriff Wheeler snapped. "Who is them?"

Malaki turned his face upward again. He stared at the ceiling. "Please take me back to my cell. I can't have nothing else."

"Malaki, answer me."

"Please take me back. I can't have nothing else."

I tried again, undercutting the sheriff. "Malaki. It's me. It's Kaia. Is Allison in the hills? Is she?"

He cocked his head, cheeks wet, and stared at me. He opened his mouth, hesitated. "Please take me back. I can't have nothing else."

CHAPTER 4
BENJAMIN "CLIFF" WOODS

On the ride home, nobody said anything for a while.

Jeremy navigated back toward our house, deftly passing through the wide-open fields. He didn't talk much after leaving the station. I guess we still weren't on the best of terms. Just working toward the same goal.

I looked out the passenger's window, watching the countryside rush by. Our stretch of land became familiar after fifty years and there was never any surprises. Clean-cut fields and soybeans pushing out against tree lines. The short, leafy plants were like a dirty green ocean. Such a sharp contrast between everything. Clear and simple.

Kaia was in the back seat. I looked back once. She was lost out the window, same as me. To my surprise, she looked okay.

"How are you doing, Kaia?" Jeremy asked before I did.

"I'm… okay." She kept staring out the window. "I feel weird. Part of me's like… happy that's over with. But I wish he would've told us more."

"He still might," Jeremy said. "They're taking him to Brooksville this week, but the sheriff wants to bring him back soon. Ask him some more questions."

Kaia nodded.

"You did amazing," Jeremy assured her. "You got him to talk more than anybody else has." He glanced over at me. "And you held it together better than your dad, here."

I felt my cheeks grow hot. "He didn't get to me too bad."

"Oh, yeah?" Jeremy smiled behind his thick beard. "Not too bad, huh?"

I didn't answer. I knew I'd sort of lost my cool, but the way Malaki kept poking at my daughter... and the way his eyes lingered... "At least I didn't punch the son of a bitch."

Kaia snorted from the back seat.

"I mean it!" I said. "Could've been a lot worse."

"True." Jeremy chuckled. "Especially with his uncle and that new lawyer, huh?"

"Do you..." Kaia's voice trailed off. We were passing by Jeremy's house now, less than minutes from our own. "Do you think he's actually... sorry?"

"Sorry?" I laughed darkly. "No way in hell. He seemed to enjoy talking about everything he's done."

"But... you don't think maybe it was real? At the end?"

I opened my mouth to repeat what I'd said, but Jeremy cut in first.

"No way to know," he said. "But we can hope. I've never hated Malaki. And I really hope he comes around to... to being sorry, like you said."

"No chance," I grunted. "He did what he did."

"You're right." Jeremy clenched his jaw. "But he... kids... he didn't know what he was getting into."

A couple minutes from home, we saw another vehicle heading toward us. I realized I knew the blue minivan right as it sped by, going toward New Haven. It roared past, dust everywhere. I watched in the rearview mirror as it continued racing toward Main Street.

"That's the Dawes, right?" Jeremy asked.

I nodded. "Smith was at our house."

"Guess he went home."

"Yeah... guess so."

<> <> <>

Jeremy dropped us off. I thanked him for the ride as I climbed out. He didn't answer me but told Kaia again how well she'd done. She smiled politely and turned cold as soon as he left.

Naomi met us before we'd even reached the porch. I looked behind her. Nate and Rhys were sitting in silence around the outdoor table. The air seemed tense, and I didn't know why. Kaia and I both stopped in the grass as she approached.

"Smith just left," she said.

"We saw them driving, yeah."

Naomi crossed her arms. "The boys were out in the woods, right. And... Smith fell in the creek. Anne's taking him to the hospital."

"Hospital?" I gaped.

"His arm's broke. Badly. It was... it wasn't pretty." Naomi groaned and pressed both hands to her forehead. "I've been talking with the boys. But I figure you should, too."

I nodded and scratched at my chin. This wasn't exactly the welcome home I'd expected.

Naomi looked at Kaia. "How did it go? Are you okay?"

She nodded. "I'm gonna go shower. I feel gross."

"Okay, honey." Naomi stepped forward and hugged her out of nowhere. It was quick. She didn't hang on for long, but she said, "Let me know if you need anything," and then backed away.

"Thanks, Mom." Kaia rushed across the porch, not stopping to talk to the boys, and headed inside.

Slowly, I made my way toward the outdoor table. Nate and Rhys were both watching me with something like fear. Or maybe guilt. I frowned at them and folded my arms. They were seated, but I remained standing.

"So…" I cleared my throat. "What happened out there?"

The two of them exchanged a look. It was hard to read their expressions because they weren't at all the same. Nate looked nervous and jumpy. Rhys stuck out his bottom lip, but his eyes were focused on me and never wavered.

"We were crossing the creek," Nate said at last, looking across the table at Rhys, "and we were hurrying because… because… we were hungry. Wanted to get back here."

Rhys looked toward him and nodded. Then those unnerving eyes refocused on me, and a shiver ran down my back.

Nate turned his face up. "Smith fell off. That log out there. And…" His voice wavered. "I just heard him screaming."

Naomi jumped in to explain, "It was his forearm. Pretty bad. They'll get an x-ray, but it looked so… It was definitely broken bad."

The idea made my blood curdle. I liked Smith. He was a sweet kid, and it was just terrible luck, sounded like. I looked around thoughtfully and took a deep breath.

"That's awful. You guys… you can't rush across the log like that. Don't get hurt doing dumb—

"It was me," Rhys blurted out. He had both hands covering his face. His voice was shaky, and he went on, "I bumped into him. I was falling, so I just… reached out. Instinct. And he fell because me."

Naomi raised her eyebrows at me and rushed to him. She

leaned over and put her arm around Rhys. "It's okay. You didn't mean to."

Without speaking, Nate watched the scene unfold. He frowned and looked up at me for a second.

"I'm so sorry," Rhys went on, "I didn't mean—"

"Of course not. Accidents happen. It's okay."

She stayed there for a minute until Rhys had wiped his face. Still rubbing his back, she said to Nate, "Why don't you and Rhys go get changed? I'll fix you something to eat in a few minutes."

"Alright."

Nate stood from his chair, and Rhys slowly did the same. They were silent as they moved inside and the door closed behind them. I watched through the window as they trudged toward the stairs, and then they were gone.

Naomi took a seat at the table and propped her elbows on it. I settled across from her.

"Lots happening today, huh?"

She groaned. "It was awful. Anne was freaking out. Which, I get it. But when I saw the boys comin' up the driveway, stumbling, you know..." She shook her head. "Nate and Rhys didn't even help the poor kid. They were just walking up, like nothing happened, 'til I saw his arm hanging halfway off."

"I mean, what could they do? They're just kids," I pointed out.

Naomi scowled at me and changed the topic. "How'd it go at the station?"

"Oh, um..." I turned to the right and stared at my barn for a minute, avoiding her eyes. "He gave us some confusing clues. Something about the streams that runoff from the hills."

Her eyes widened. "What kind of clues?"

"Something about... about finding answers out there. Or

bodies. It was confusing, like I said. And Kaia said a few things, and he started crying at the end. It was real weird."

"What'd she say?" Naomi pressed, leaning forward.

"Just asking about Allison, you know."

"You think she'll be okay?"

"I mean, yeah. She said she was."

"But was she okay afterward?"

"Geez, just ask her, Naomi. Not me." I exhaled.

"Ben, look at me."

Naomi stared at me, palms flat on the table, forward in her seat. Behind her, the window reflected our whole, darkening property.

"Did she seem okay? Not what she said, how she acted."

"I guess so. Malaki tried to get under her skin, of course."

"And did he?"

"No. I mean." I shrugged. "You know how he is."

"Don't shrug your shoulders at me," Naomi snapped. "This is your daughter, Ben. I know you wanna run off and play hero with your best bud Jeremy again, but Kaia is more important than any of that."

"I'm not trying to 'play hero.' Come on." I scoffed.

"You think you're invincible with Jeremy." She pointed a finger at me and then folded her arms. "It's not a good thing."

"I know she's important. I'm trying to protect her." I paused for a moment, trying to choose my words. I didn't want this to explode in a full-fledged fight.

"And have you even called CPS like you said?" she asked coldly.

"I... yeah, I did. They're looking into some things," I lied. "I can call again if you want, but I don't think it'll help. Everyone's trying their best, you know? But this whole thing... it's a shit situation. Like what am I—What are we supposed to do?"

She grabbed her head and groaned. "I know, I know. There's just too much right now, Ben. And I'm worried about Kaia. Worried as hell."

"I know. Me too. But she shook it off. She's tough, you know." I added, "She's like that. Like you."

"Or she *acted* like she did, Ben." She pinched the bridge of her nose. "I think you're so caught up in 'protecting' our kids that you aren't taking care of them. 'Cause protecting them, that's what heroes do, but taking care of them? That's what dads do."

"Hey."

"Just keep that in mind when you're playing through your hero fantasies."

I threw my arms up. "Don't get all angry with me, okay?"

"I'm not angry—"

"Oh, right, just disappointed. That's how it goes, yeah?"

"Real mature, Ben."

"Whatever." I stood from the table. "I've gotta finish something in the barn. I'll be inside in a bit."

"Alright." She didn't move from her spot.

I started to storm off but something held me and I turned back to her. "I'm sorry. It's just been a long day."

She nodded, not looking at me. "I know. I'm sorry too. Go on. Don't let me keep you."

<> <> <>

I was in the barn when I got the phone call.

Sweating profusely, I stepped away from the hay rake. I had the lights on, so I could work another thirty minutes. Still in the process of checking the rake teeth, I wasn't happy to hear the phone ring. I grabbed it, saw the caller ID said "Jeremy," and trudged outside.

There was a cool breeze, and the sun had vanished beyond the trees. It had just become fully dark. If I didn't finish in the next thirty minutes, I'd have to do it tomorrow. I was already running behind with these checks, and things just kept piling on.

"Yeah, it's Cliff," I answered, leaning against the side of my barn.

"It's Jeremy. I've got news."

The fields never looked as peaceful as they did right before things changed. This whole town had a certain beauty as bad storms approached. I'd seen it the day of George's shop fire. And the day Allison and Malaki went missing. A sort of glow coming from the earth. I saw it again when Jeremy spoke.

"What is it?"

He paused. There was static. "Police have confirmed two people missing for almost a week now. Clark couple they mentioned at the station. Lived just outside New Haven, other side of the hills basically."

"Oh, no."

"I don't know what Malaki knew or how. But he wasn't lying to us."

I frowned. "What do you mean?"

"They went missing over by the hills. Where all the rainwater runs down and pools at the bottom. Not on our side, on the train station side. Just like he said."

"Shit. So…" I felt my shoulders sagging. "What do you wanna do?"

"The sheriff's leading a search the area, of course," Jeremy said. "But they've got a lot of ground to cover."

When he didn't go on, I asked, "What are you saying?"

"Look, Cliff… We've had our differences. But I can trust you.

We know this has to do with the house. I say we start down at those ponds and follow the water up toward it."

"Okay. But when?" I ran a hand over my forehead. "I got so much to do with the farm. And Nate's game this weekend—"

"Tomorrow," he cut in.

"Tomorrow?" I thought about Naomi and what she'd said. She definitely wouldn't like this. But the sooner we searched, the sooner I could do what she wanted. Focus on the kids. Actually call CPS. Worry about our little family instead of the entire town. "Okay, yeah. Let's do it tomorrow."

"I'll let you know when I'm coming," he said. "It'll be early."

"Fine with me."

Then he hung up.

CHAPTER 5
NATE WOODS

Later that night, we were upstairs in my room. I sat on the floor holding a controller and watching the small TV screen like it was life or death. Rhys was on the bed holding the other controller. We were playing MLB The Show, of course. I chose one of the worst teams so the game was more fair. I also made a few throwing errors on purpose because I wanted Rhys to have a chance.

Back when he first moved in, I had to take it *really* easy, and he still never beat me. Now, as long as I made a few mistakes, the games were competitive. But I still won most of them.

We were both being really quiet, not talking at all. Dad had called up the stairs for us to go to bed about thirty minutes ago. I'd said we were going to finish the one game, and he'd said okay. But now we were starting another.

The game announcers and crowd cheers were whispers. Rhys groaned as he hit a pop-up, and I made the easy out.

We hadn't really talked about what happened out in the woods. It was an accident, and sometimes it was easier to ignore accidents. I felt terrible for Smith — the whole way back, through the field, he was crying and wincing and holding his arm — and for Rhys because he'd sounded so hurt when he explained everything to my parents. But the worst part was Smith might never come back. I mean, I wouldn't blame him. That was one hell of a broken arm, and he probably blamed us. He probably hated us.

Blame…

No, the worst part wasn't any of that stuff.

Honestly, Rhys didn't seem too broken up about it *besides* when he explained to my parents. When I saw him standing on that log, holding both hands against his chest, I'd wondered, *Did he push Smith?*

And on the way back to the house, he never said sorry. He never said a single word. It was the most awkward walk home I'd ever had. Even more awkward than the time Sherrif Wheeler came looking for Kaia and she got the phone call while out at the Wolf Cave.

Why didn't you say sorry? I wanted to ask him. *Did you push him? Was it on purpose?*

But we ignored it. I ignored it. After talking with Mom and Dad, we'd both eaten a quick snack, showered, and came up here to play video games.

"Are you gonna throw it or what?" Rhys asked, his voice even quieter than the television.

"Oh. Sorry." I realized it was still my turn to pitch. "There you go. Slider, outside. Gotcha."

Rhys groaned. When the inning ended and the game cut to his pitcher, showing stats, Rhys took this small break to reach under my bed. I watched him curiously, until he pulled out a box of Pop-Tarts.

"Where'd you get those?" I hissed.

"Downstairs." Rhys opened the box and threw me one package. "Your parents won't notice. They'll just buy more."

I smiled and felt my heart jump a little. "Right, yeah. Good point."

We munched on our stolen — not stolen, just taken without telling — Pop-Tarts and played through another couple innings. After a while, I yawned and paused the game.

"I'm gonna get some water," I said, crumpling up the Pop-Tart wrapper. Those things always made me thirsty. "Don't start 'til I get back."

"I won't. Can you get me some water too?"

"Ugh. Yeah."

I went downstairs, using all my stealth to avoid making noise. I *could* say I'd just woken up thirsty, but I didn't want to risk it. Especially with Dad. He didn't trust me. He was the type to come upstairs just to check I was telling the truth, and if he found us on the PlayStation a full hour after he'd told us to sleep… Yikes.

I managed to fill two glasses with water no problem and make it back up the stairs. Feeling pretty cocky, I swaggered into my bedroom.

"Here, Rhys."

I stopped in the doorway. Rhys was by the window, peering outside.

"Rhys? What's up?"

He turned around, shaking his head. "Nothing. I was just checking."

"Checking?"

He took a seat on the floor again. "The guy. I was checking if he was out there."

"Oh. Okay."

I handed him a glass of water and sat on my bed a little too hard. The springs creaked. I became a statue, listening carefully for any sounds downstairs. Counted to ten… nothing.

"Why do you think it's a guy?" I asked him, drinking half my water and then placing it on the bedside table.

Rhys held his glass with both hands, staring through it. He didn't look over at me when he answered, "I've seen him before."

"Right, we saw him together."

Rhys shook his head. "No. Before that. I've met him."

"What?" I leaned closer, struggling to keep my voice down. "What do you mean '*met*' him?"

"That night when I was in the rain. And you saved me." Rhys rocked back and forth. The floorboards groaned. "I met him. He was right behind me in the trees. I've seen him watching us since then."

"I… But…" I studied him. Was this a joke? A prank? "Who is he?"

"I'm not sure." Rhys turned to me, frowning. "But he lives in the Silent Forest."

Then I heard from downstairs, "Boys! I better not hear *any* more talking. Go to bed, *right* now!" Dad sounded angry.

"Oh, shit." I switched off the television and collapsed under the covers.

Rhys followed my lead, curling up in his sleeping bag on the floor.

The room was pitch dark now. I listened for footsteps on the stairs but none came. I wasn't sure how long, but I lay there in the dark for at least thirty minutes. Thinking about what Rhys said. Imagining the figure, somewhere outside, lurking under my windowsill.

"Rhys?" I asked much later. "Rhys, are you awake?"

He didn't answer.

CHAPTER 6
KAIA WOODS

I couldn't sleep that night. No surprise, really. After everything he'd said…

You know what Allison did, baby?

I tried to scrub his voice from my memory—it stuck like a leech—and I didn't trust what he'd said. Allison never mentioned telling him about our kiss. Although, we never really talked about it afterward. She felt guilty, I guess, and it was hard for me to handle.

I'd told Mom about it the night after George's funeral, after I started crying at the dinner table. She came upstairs—a soft knock at the door—and sat on my bed. I told her I'd kissed Allison. Months ago. Way before she went missing. And I didn't know until it was too late… I didn't know how I really felt.

"You don't need to feel bad," she'd said. "I think you two always had something special. And now you know for sure."

It helped in a way, but it also hurt worse.

What if I never get her back? And what if there's nobody else like her, ever, in the whole world?

And I missed my chance?

And it's all because of Malaki.

I stood up from bed and marched toward the second-floor bathroom. I was going to scrub my eyes until I couldn't picture him anymore. Take another steaming hot shower, burn my skin, and probably drink some of the whiskey I'd stolen from Dad's liquor cabinet. —My second bottle now. *Really, Dad?*

Anything. Anything to bury his voice and her smile.

When I got closer to the bathroom, I saw the door was almost shut, open just a crack. And there was a low voice coming from inside.

I stopped in the hallway, feeling soft carpet under my bare toes. I didn't call out right away or knock. I wasn't sure why, but after a moment, I was glad I hadn't.

"It doesn't matter," the voice said. "No, it doesn't matter now. He won't come back."

I thought it was Nate for a moment. I opened my mouth to say something, but—

"*No, no,* we aren't sure."

Rhys. It was Rhys speaking. In the dark bathroom, middle of the night… I leaned closer and peered through the crack by the door frame.

"But he was hateful, wasn't he? He would've done anything for it… And he was a smart one, too."

Rhys was staring into the mirror, his knuckles resting on the countertop. I couldn't see his expression, but his voice felt like ice cubes on my skin and spider legs crawling up my shirt.

"He didn't know better. *We* didn't do anything."

"They think we did! They're going to tell the others!"

My breaths were shallow and I didn't dare move.

What if he hears me?

But it's just Rhys.

"But we can't go back now," Rhys continued. "They won't

let us back. They told us last time. They said, 'Never again.' And now, never again!"

What is he talking about?

"But we have to. We might have to."

"We can't! Never again! They said, and they meant it, and they…" He paused. I heard the sound of his tongue clicking.

"Well…"

I held my breath.

"I think…"

And then his voice got deeper.

"Someone at the door?"

My heart skipped. I backed away, almost falling, and hurried to my room.

Someone at the door? Someone at the door?

I couldn't hear a sound except for my hard breathing, my beating heart. I crawled into bed as quietly as possible and closed my eyes.

There was nothing for a moment. My heart was a racehorse, those four words storming through my head.

Someone at the door?

Down the hall, the bathroom door creaked open and then clicked shut. There was no sound for a moment except the hum of the air conditioner.

Then a single footstep toward my room.

Oh, God.

He called out softly, "Goodnight."

And then Rhys walked to Nate's room and closed the door behind him.

CHAPTER 7
NAOMI WOODS

"You don't need to go with them."

Standing by the kitchen counter, I pressed two fingers against the center of my forehead. Kaia was by the table. She *had* been sitting, but we were in a heated discussion now—I've never liked calling it an argument with my kids.

"I do!" she protested. "I'll notice things they won't. I've *been* there before."

"They're only going around the property. It's not even a big deal." I groaned and squeezed my eyes shut. I'd been fighting an excruciating migraine all day, ever since I woke up. It felt like someone had taken a fork and driven it through the back of my neck vertically. Every time I moved or spoke or thought, I felt it twist deeper into my head.

"I still wanna go."

"It's dangerous!" I exclaimed. "Kaia, you're not going."

"If it's not a big deal, how is it dangerous?"

"I'm your mother." I put both hands flat on the table and stared at her. "You are not going. There's... We don't even know if this is connected. It's police business. It's not worth—"

"Yeah, 'not connected.' Okay." Kaia put down her finger

quotes and crossed her arms. "I bet Dad would let me go."

"We already talked. He agrees with me."

"Probably because you told him to."

I would've gaped if I wasn't in pain. I clenched my jaw and tried not to yell at her. "What's wrong with you today?"

She shook her head. "I need to go. I need to know what Malaki was talking about."

"Your father will—"

I stopped when there was a knock at the door. I looked over and saw Jeremy, his bearded face pressed to the glass. He smiled awkwardly and waved.

"Hold on," I muttered. I walked over and opened the door. "Hi, Jeremy. Cliff will be out in a few minutes."

"Can I talk to Kaia?" he asked, adding, "Real quick?"

I glanced over. Kaia's face looked as confused as I felt.

"Yeah. Okay."

I stepped away from the door and Kaia went outside. Because I didn't feel like eavesdropping—or arguing more—I went into our bedroom. Cliff was sitting on the bed, putting on his socks. I marched past him, into our bathroom, and took some Tylenol and Ibuprofen.

"I can't do it, Ben." I leaned my head against the white-trim doorway. "I don't know how I can keep her safe. Without her hating me."

"Don't worry about it right now," he said. Cliff stood from the bed, wearing dirt-stained jeans, a dark shirt, and now both socks. "You're totally right. This isn't the time for her to… to get involved yet."

"But when that time comes? How am I supposed to let her…?"

"We'll figure it out together."

I waved a hand at him. Nothing he said could assure me right now. "Jeremy's outside waiting. Go on."

"Alright. I'll be back before dinner." He walked halfway down the hall, then paused. "I love you."

"Yep. Love you, too."

We exchanged a look, and then he went. I heard the door open and shut, some muffled voices, and then nothing.

I sat on the bed and rubbed my neck for a minute, digging every finger into the tight muscles. It was only a little relief. I got up and went into the kitchen. Jeremy and Ben were outside. I only saw their backs as they left the porch, stepping down together, almost in sync. I watched them go, not sure about this plan.

The night before, he'd explained what Jeremy had said on the phone, and I'd begged him, "Leave it to the sheriff."

"I can't. I don't trust the sheriff. And I don't want Jeremy to go alone."

It hadn't really been a question, but I gave in. Each day, I gave in. More and more, Ben was off playing the "hero," and he left me here to take care of our kids. Our home. Our family. And yes, the two were connected. Kaia was forever connected to that house. But we didn't have to give her to it.

She came back inside right after they left.

"Sorry, Mom," she mumbled. Unlike earlier, there was no anger on her face. She rushed past me and went upstairs before I could get a word in.

I went outside then. I wanted some fresh air. The intense heat—it was in the high nineties—also worked to ease my headache. Or maybe it was the medicine I'd taken. But either way, I leaned back in my chair on the porch and watched the world turning slowly.

As I let out a breath overflowing with tension, a memory wrapped around me. Ben and I, standing out here in the darkness.

I remembered the oak tree rustling and the chilly wind against our faces. That night, I'd convinced him things were serious with the house. The kids were in danger. And now, we'd almost moved on, ignoring it. Nothing had changed. They were still in danger. Maybe *more* danger. But we'd moved on to other things.

There were no easy answers. We couldn't tell Kaia to forget Allison. We couldn't tell Rhys to leave with nowhere to go. And even if those things happened, our family would never be the same. Kaia had seen things, experienced things, which could never be forgotten.

The house on the hill peered at me from the distance. My heartbeat quickened.

I still had never told the kids exactly what happened to me up there. What I saw in those dark hallways. And in the empty room… Maybe it was nearly time. A part of me wanted to explain it away. A bad trip… The wrong mindset, imaginary things… But I knew better.

The door opened to my right and broke my concentration. When I turned, I found Nate coming outside, eating a cold sandwich. He had a glass of water in his other hand and took a seat at the table.

"Hey, Mom."

I smiled. "Hi, honey. Where's Rhys?"

"Upstairs." He grinned. "He's practicing on the PlayStation so he can try to beat me."

"Oh, gotcha. Well, how are you?"

"I'm good." He gulped hard and took another bite. "Do you ever get scared still?"

"Of course, honey. I get scared. Everyone does."

"Even brave people?"

"It's not about being brave." I shook my head. "Just about

getting through it. You've got through all sorts of stuff, right?"

"Yeah… I have."

"And you're growing up, and that comes with new jump scares. If I'm being honest. The older you get, the more there are. But you get better at… getting through it. And you're getting better every day."

"I do feel old sometimes." Nate frowned. "Remember when… I was little and I'd ask you to tell me a story?"

"I do, honey." *Just two months ago. And he says he was little.*

"I kinda wanted to…" He paused and looked around, as if anyone would be out here listening to us. He asked, with red cheeks, "Could you tell me a story?"

"Oh?" My chest turned warm. "What about? Not being scared, I hope."

"No, no way. Just… like… your life." Nate's embarrassed grin turned to a frown. "I forget sometimes that I won't always be able to ask you. And I wanna hear all your stories before… before I can't anymore. I don't wanna forget to ask."

"Well, alright." I took a deep breath and studied our backyard. "I'm sure I can think of something."

The oak tree and the swaying field beyond it. A sharp line of distant trees. A group of birds flying overhead. Nate set his glass on the table, and the sound reverberated for a moment.

"What kind of story, honey?"

"Maybe, like… when you were with those hippies in the vans."

"That was a long time ago, honey. But…" I closed my eyes and tried to recapture the image.

"So, I remember it like this. I was in a hammock, just sunbathing and forest bathing." At his confused expression, I explained, "That's just sitting somewhere with lots of trees and nature. Taking it in."

"Oh, gotcha." He didn't look convinced. "Seems kinda boring."

"Well, we were more boring than normal hippies, but we had it better, too. You'll get it, one day." I went on. "So I was in a hammock, watching the trees swaying, rocking back and forth, and the sky that day was incredibly blue. Not a single cloud, not even the thought of a cloud.

"There were some other people, too. We were all by this huge tree in the middle of the woods. Some of us had hammocks. Others were just sitting on the ground. We'd just been hiking—"

"Hiking?" he interrupted. "Like on a trail?"

"Um, kind of. We were… looking for mushrooms. Uh, but anyway, about eight of us sitting there. And I hear this couple behind me. They're having a quiet conversation, but it sounds really happy. They're in love and so peaceful. Somebody in front of me, a little far off, they're playing a ukelele in a hammock. Everything is perfectly balanced. Not too loud. Not too hot.

"So, the man playing the ukelele, he's singing in this quiet, imperfect voice. It was nice to listen to, really. He plays uncertainly. And then, in the middle of this little song, he sneezes. Real loud. Stops playing, of course, when he sneezes. But a second later, he picks up the song without missing a beat. Right back to it." I smiled to myself. "Like nothing ever happened."

"Hmm…" Nate studied me. "Um… that's nice. I mean, it sounds cool. Did… or do you have any stories that are more… I don't know, exciting?"

I laughed and threw my head back. "Maybe so. I'll have to think for a minute. Why don't you make me a sandwich like you had, and by the time you're done I'll have a really good one?"

He grinned wide and got up from his seat. "Okay." As he went toward the door, he paused. "Mom, why do you remember that story, anyway?"

"Well… it's weird, Nate. When you get older, you don't choose what sticks around in your head. Some memories just hold on. Weird ones, too, and happy moments and terribly sad ones. But to me, the best moments are the ones you never expected to stay so long but mean so much."

As Nate walked into the kitchen, Rhys came out. The door shut, and he leaned against the exterior for a moment, watching me.

"Hey, Rhys. Are you hungry?"

He narrowed his eyes. The little boy looked back inside at Nate.

"What would you do, Miss Naomi?"

"What, honey?"

His cold eyes turned to me. "What would you do if someone you loved was in danger?"

"Oh…" I felt a chill run over my spine. My stomach turned to slime. "Well, I'd try to stop them from —"

"No. If they were in danger already, and you couldn't stop them, and you weren't there, what would you do?"

"I'd find them," I said honestly. "I'd give everything to find them. And then, I'd do anything to keep them safe."

Rhys nodded. "That's a good answer. And you're a good mom."

"Thank you, Rhys. But —"

He reached for the door. "Would you save me? If I was in danger?"

"Of course, honey."

"And you'd give anything to keep me safe?"

"I would."

Rhys sighed. He smiled a little. "Then I think this is gonna work out, don't you?"

The door opened, and Nate came out carrying a sandwich

on a plate. Behind him, Rhys stared me down and raised his eyebrows. Then he stepped inside.

"Goodbye, Miss Naomi."

CHAPTER 8
KAIA WOODS

We are in the forest. The Wolf Cave. In the tiny hut with a shingle roof, Allison and I are sitting in lawn chairs. We watch the creek bubbling past and hear the birds above it, singing to each other.

Straight ahead, we can see through the trees. The sky is a gray blue color, hazy all over, with no clouds. I feel safe with her in the forest. Trees branching over us and forming a roof. Our home and garden. Soft rustling in the underbrush as a squirrel darts through and climbs a tree.

"Nothing bad about this place," I say. "I love it."

She watches me, and she looks at peace. "I know you do."

"It just gives me this feeling… like I've got a place and nobody can touch it. No matter what happens in… in this country or this world. No matter how hot it gets. I got a place they can't catch on fire."

Allison smiled. "That's how you make me feel, Kaia."

I blush and look away. "Do you remember last time we came here?" I put my hands behind my head and breathe deeply.

She turns to look at me. "No? What happened?"

"We were doing homework, I think. And I asked for help."

Allison grins. "When was this? I don't — "

"Senior year. Just last year." I frown. "And then… don't you remember? You moved your chair over here to help me. Like really close.

And we finished it. I think it was math. And you kissed me on the cheek."

"I..." Allison hesitates. "That was in the car, wasn't it? After we got caught in the rain? You were drenched," she laughs, "and I kissed your cheek because you were so cute."

"No way. It was here."

Allison leans over with her wide smile. It's so disarming. "You're my favorite, Kaia."

I blush and turn away. "Thank you, Ally."

There's no response.

"Ally?" I look over and she's no longer smiling.

Her lips are sewn together. Little droplets of blood have collected on them. Her eyes are wide and her mouth is closed forever. She's trying to scream, and more blood leaks out from her lips.

"Ally! What's going — "

With a thunderous crash, the Wolf Cave collapses. The heavy roof falls. We're crushed. The ground shocks me, and I'm pinned. When I look over, Allison's head is gone.

I startled awake, gasping for air. A few streaks of sunlight touched my face. I reached up with both hands and felt my cheeks, neck, and then collarbone.

"Goddamn it." I rubbed my eyes and rolled over, trying to sleep again. It was no use, and I already knew it. Every time that dream replayed, I woke up sweaty, unnerved, and exhausted.

After ten minutes of failed sleep and the image twisting its way into my mind — *Allison's body, trapped under wood beams, blood soaking the ground where her head should be* — I stood up.

It was impossible to think of anything else. Right after the interview with Malaki, I felt some relief but also more tired than ever. By the next day, it'd actually made things worse. I couldn't focus. I couldn't bear *not* being up at the house. I'd give anything

I owned to go with Dad and Jeremy.

But since I couldn't, I took a nap and ended up watching my dead friend.

Dead in the dream. Not dead in real life. She's somewhere. Still alive.

After the argument with Mom, Jeremy had actually taken my parents' side. On the back porch, just us, he explained something to me.

"You'll have a chance soon," he said. "I promise. You're in this, Kaia, whether you like it or not. But for now, just stay here. I promise you'll get your chance. I've never lied to you."

Everyone always told me to stay. Nobody offered help for everything I went through. Nobody considered I might be in more danger, stuck here with my own thoughts, than out there *doing* something.

Allison wore a floral dress and sneakers, showing her smooth legs. She had a messy bun, strands of hair flying out. I couldn't remember the background or the setting, but I remembered her.

"Hey, girl." I grinned. "Who are you trying to look so hot for?"

Allison blushed, and I wanted to feel her. She looked older now. Like she wasn't a kid anymore. Neither of us.

"Just myself, I guess. This is new." She lifted the fabric of her dress, showing her thighs. "You really think I look hot?"

"Um… yes? Are you kidding me?"

I was on the ground, looking at the Polaroid of us on our knees. Right next to that oak tree in the backyard. And I thought about lying under it with her, warm and safe.

There was a knock on my bedroom door. I groaned and stayed on the floor.

"Come in," I called, throwing as much attitude into the phrase as I could manage. I really didn't want to talk with Mom right now. *Just leave me alone.*

Instead, when it opened slowly, Rhys was standing in the doorway.

"Oh." I stared up at him and struggled into a sitting position. "Hey, Rhys."

"Hi." He held both arms at his side and waited, stiff as a board.

"What's up?" I didn't want him to mention last night. I wanted to pretend it was a bad dream… or maybe he was sleepwalking. I didn't need any more questions.

He shifted on his feet. "Is… is everything okay?" he asked. "I heard the… the arguing downstairs. Am I in trouble?"

I shook my head. "No, Rhys. You're fine."

"Oh. Okay." He nodded and looked around my room for a minute. Then he blushed and stared at the ground. "Well, are… are you okay?"

I sighed. "Yeah, I'm okay."

"But it must… be hard."

"Yeah, it is. I was… really good friends with Allison. She isn't the kind of person you can replace."

He gestured at the Polaroid in my hand. "Is that you two?"

I smiled and handed the picture to him. "Yeah. At our graduation party."

When he gripped the picture gently and focused on it, his features changed. His eyebrows stuck up and his lips pressed together.

"I got a text from her," I explained, "a few weeks ago, and so I went to the house. But it wasn't her. It was Malaki. He attacked me, but now… I don't know where she is or if…"

"Wow." Rhys handed the picture back to me. "It's… I can't believe you know the girl who went missing."

"We're best friends. More than best friends."

"Did you love her?"

I nodded. "I still do."

"I…" Rhys rubbed the back of his neck and avoided my gaze. "I knew a girl like her."

"What, Rhys?"

"Sorry, um…" He shook his head frantically and stepped back. "Do you think… If you were like her and you went missing… Do you think your mom would save you?"

I didn't answer at first. "Why would you ask that?"

"Miss Naomi said she would. Said she'd do anything. But… does she mean it?"

"I think she does, yeah."

"Okay. Okay, that's good. Sorry. I just needed to make sure." He closed the door.

"What the hell?" I muttered.

<> <> <>

Later that evening, I wrote out another letter to the mystery person I'd been in contact with.

You said Allison is alive. But Malaki keeps saying she's dead. Are you sure you're right? How can I trust you?

Either way, we need to do something soon. I can't wait any longer. I'm ready to act.

Tell me when and where. What do I need to bring? I'm tired of waiting, so tell me what to do, and let's do it.

I need to do something.

CHAPTER 9
BENJAMIN "CLIFF" WOODS

Jeremy pulled over to the side of the road and parked in the grass. We were truly in the middle of nowhere now, over by the west hills, away from New Haven. All the roads here were empty, but the hills had tall, thick trees blocking out the sun and any view of the house.

"Kinda weird how the hills look so different by us," I pointed out.

Jeremy climbed out of the truck without saying a word. Things still weren't exactly normal between us.

Standing off the road, he tucked a handgun into his waistband and pointed ahead of us. "If you follow this road, around the hills, then the hiking trails start two miles from here. The cops are up there, starting their search."

"So, what are we doing? And why do you need a gun?"

He gestured to the right, where the hills climbed upward. There was no path here, just tall trees with thick underbrush below and a heavy darkness clinging to the branches. Jeremy stared into it.

"We'll cut through here 'til we find the hiking trails. Then follow them up toward the house."

"I thought Malaki said the body was down here."

"Down somewhere. Maybe it's here. Maybe it's halfway up. Or maybe there's something under the house."

"And the gun?"

"It's just a 9 millimeter. I'm leaving my shotgun in the truck." He led the way off the road, and we plunged into the thick shadows of the forest. Vegetation crunched underneath our heavy boots. "I'm not expecting to find anything anyway. But just in case…"

"You sound real hopeful."

We marched through the underbrush in silence for a few minutes. I had on jeans, so the bushes and thorns didn't bother me. Every green surface, both low to the ground and hanging above us, shimmered with raindrops from the brief showers last night.

With no trail, we had to zigzag our way, ducking under branches. Neither of us talked for a few minutes. I heard birds chirping overhead and something rustling in the bushes. A squirrel chattered as it climbed a tree. For a moment, I forgot how morbid our mission was and enjoyed our walk.

"There's no trees by us," I pointed out. "The east hills are just grass and wildflowers."

Jeremy didn't answer. He didn't even mumble. Just moving on wordlessly, stomping his way through a patch of thorns.

It didn't used to be like this. Before George's shop burnt down, Jeremy had been an easy-going, fun person. Always laughing. Always joking. But like everything in New Haven, Jeremy had changed over the past few weeks. He only talked about the case with me now. About the missing people and the house.

I supposed we were all obsessed. But Jeremy more than most.

After plunging through the trees and heading uphill, we

found a thin path winding through the woods. Vines stuck out and mushrooms crept toward the center of the trail.

"Let's head straight," Jeremy said. "There's a spot up here I wanna check out."

"Jeremy, what are you hoping for here?" I asked. "This is… this forest is so dense, I really don't think we can—"

"They confirmed the Clarks went missing from their house, but they don't know where." Jeremy glanced around in every direction. "They're searching everywhere, but with Malaki's clue… Maybe we'll find signs of them. Or even the bodies. I don't know. But there are answers here, somewhere. Malaki said so."

"And we trust him now?"

"Not sure we have a choice. He seems to… know."

I chewed on this idea for a moment. "Jeremy, how do you even find out about this stuff?"

He shrugged. "I have friends. Connections. They aren't afraid to help me out."

"Friends?"

No answer.

Across the path and into the trees again. They were packed so closely here, like they were choking each other for space. But to my surprise, the ground sloped downward, so we were moving along quicker.

"It's been so long since I came this way," I told him. "Not since… I was a kid, actually."

He acknowledged me with a grunt.

"Ever since I moved back, I've been… trying to stay out of these hills."

"Everyone has. Except for me."

We crossed over a little stream, rushing down the hillside. Water trickled over the stone bed and carried on. There was bright yellow-green moss growing around the sides, like two white lines directing traffic on the highway. We stepped over easily and moved past. Jeremy turned to the left slightly, so we were almost following the stream downhill.

"So, what's this spot you wanna look at?" I asked him.

"You'll see."

I didn't know why Jeremy was being so closed-off, and I tried not to worry about it. We both had the same goal. Maybe he was just dead focused on it. Or he was still holding a loose grudge against me.

The deeper we went, the more unsure I became of what I heard. The rustling bushes and squirrels had faded. I couldn't hear any birdsong above us, only a faint wind blowing through the canopy. Twigs cracked all around, like there were dozens of people sneaking up and circling, but nobody ever appeared.

And something else was weird. Mixed in with the fresh smells of dirt and plants from every side, there was another scent. The wind carried it, made the smell more extreme. Undeniable.

I wrinkled my nose and asked, "Do you smell that? Like… something rotting?"

Jeremy faced the wind for a moment and sniffed. He said, "We'll head that way next," and then nothing.

After a minute, still not following any trail but rather Jeremy's judgement, we found a small wooden footbridge. It ran across a creek slightly larger than the first one. Jeremy crossed quickly and without looking back.

When I moved over the footbridge, I noticed how the carved wood was still pale, like someone built it recently. I stood there and looked downstream. Trees reached over the glistening stones, forming an archway. I stared that way and noticed something in the distance. A shape, not even a figure, in the middle of the creek.

I thought it was a tree shadow until it moved to the left and vanished.

"Hello?" I called out.

Something answered. It was a sound, like a deep, ragged breath. And something stepped out from behind the tree.

"Hello?" I leaned forward, over the railing. "Who's there?"

It moved away again, and I was left with a peaceful view.

"Well, shit." I rushed off the bridge and headed the way Jeremy had gone. I kept glancing over my shoulder, listening for anything suspicious, but there was nothing after that. Until the pond.

Following Jeremy, I lunged through the trees and found myself in a strange clearing. Jeremy was ahead, standing at the edge of a small pond. On the far side, I could see a few streams feeding into it. With his back to me, he stared into the water.

"I saw something," I said, rushing up to him. "I thought it was a… person, maybe, but it didn't…" I stopped beside him. "Are you okay, Jeremy?"

His face was blank and colorless. He stared into the murky water. Weeds grew along the edge of the pond, climbing up his shins. The clearing was surrounded by tall trees. I saw the sky above reflected on the pond.

"Do you see them?" he whispered.

"See what?" I followed his eyes and gasped.

Floating under the murky surface, there were two ghostly white faces. Their features were cracked and falling apart. I watched as one rolled over and showed a head full of white hair. They both started floating away from us, toward the center.

"I'll call it in," Jeremy said, but his expression never changed, and he kept staring straight at the water. His voice, too, was flat and emotionless. "Tell the police. Ask someone to come… dredge the pond."

"It must be the Clarks," I told him. "You found them."

Jeremy stepped away from the lake and pulled out his phone. He held it to his ear and started in the same, deadpan voice, "Sheriff Wheeler. It's Jeremy. I'm at the runoff pond…"

I stopped listening and stared at the water. It had ripples when just a moment ago it had been utterly calm.

I looked to the other side where the streams were feeding in… And I saw it again.

Behind a tree, peeking out, there was a dark shadow. I strained my eyes to make out the edges, but I couldn't see clearly. There was something. Something watching me. The same thing as earlier. And that's all I knew for sure.

I pulled out my phone, thinking I might take a picture, but whatever had been standing there vanished like before.

When Jeremy came back over, I shook my head. "This place creeps me out."

"We're not done yet." Jeremy folded his arms and frowned. "Let's get back to that bridge and go up toward the house."

"Which way is that?" I asked. I hadn't been able to see the house since we arrived in Jeremy's truck. This forest was dense, and the steep hills kept it hidden.

He pointed to the right. "That way. We can follow the stream the bridge crosses. It feeds into another pond, lower down, not this one."

"There are more?"

He nodded and started moving away from me.

Once we got to the bridge and followed the creek, I realized the horrid smell had come from this direction. I didn't smell it anymore, just like I didn't see that figure, but I was starting to doubt my senses. And with each silent minute that passed, I was beginning to question Jeremy.

<> <> <>

It took us a while. My legs were aching by the time we reached the top of the hill. The higher we climbed, the farther I could see through the forest. All around us, the trees were less packed. Three times, I thought I saw a building in the distance, and I thought it might be *the house,* but it always swam out of view.

"Are there other buildings in here?" I asked Jeremy.

"You don't have to whisper. And yes." He looked over to the left, where a small, blockish place squatted behind the trees. Then he focused straight ahead.

I kept my eyes peeled, waiting for the house to appear. I'd expected the forest up here to be darker and more ominous than ever, but it worked out the opposite. Leaving the valley and scaling the hill, the air turned warmer. Sunlight poked through the treetops and painted warmth on the forest floor. I smelled an earthy scent mixed with wildflowers and felt okay about things.

"It's kind of nice up here," I remarked.

I thought I heard him chuckle, but there was no answer.

Closer to the house, we ran into a shed with sheet metal walls. There was an awful smell coming from it. I walked toward it. All those warm feelings were gone.

Jeremy hesitated. "We don't need to check there."

"What? Why not?" I reached for the door, plugging my nose. "Could be important."

"I'm not—"

I opened the door—a big piece of sheet metal—and peered inside.

"Oh my god…"

First, I noticed the raw meat. There were chunks of it, some on the ground, others hanging from the roof in strips. A wave of heat rushed over me, a stench worse than anything.

Second, the ropes and chains. There were dozens of chains connecting to the walls and a pile of rope in the center.

While I stood there gaping, I felt a hand on my shoulder.

"Come on, Cliff." Jeremy pulled gently. "We don't need to worry about this."

"What? This is obviously —!"

"Probably locals," he said. "You know how it is."

"The hell do you mean? *Locals?*"

"Come on. I'll call it in. But we don't want to stay here too long."

"Okay, okay."

"Gotta keep moving, Cliff."

So we did.

Before long, I saw the house. We were reaching the edge of the trees. Just beyond them, I recognized the hulking, Gothic structure standing at the hill's crest. The steep, high roof rose in a way I didn't recognize. A whole side of the house I'd never seen. I stood in awe of its size.

There was a garden closer to the front, to our right, the whole plot strangled by weeds. Vines crawled up the back of the house and the near side. But most importantly, on the back, there was a section of stone jutting out from the rest. From the outside, it couldn't have been much larger than a closet sticking out.

"Are we going inside?" I asked Jeremy, trying to hide the quiver in my voice.

"No, we'll just look around. Out here." Jeremy pointed to the left of us, where the woods continued at the back of the house.

"This is weird," I admitted. "I didn't realize they went on so far behind… it."

"This forest can hide a lot."

"I've never been in these woods before. Not this part."

Jeremy looked over his shoulder. I saw a smirk behind his beard. "Most people haven't if they're still alive."

I followed him silently. I didn't like his tone of voice, and everything about him was throwing me off. But I wasn't eager to step foot inside that house, and I didn't want to walk alone, so I wouldn't argue with his plan.

"Malaki said something about below here," Jeremy muttered. "I think we've got... got to get underground somehow."

"Alright..."

He moved around at a furious pace, walking quickly to the left and right. I followed dumbly, looking around. I didn't know what he was searching for or how I could help. As he zig-zagged his way through this section of trees, I glanced to the right and saw another structure. This time, we were close enough. I knew exactly what it was.

"Jeremy! Hey, look at that!"

He stopped and turned to where I pointed.

"That's gotta be it." He laughed loudly and started jogging toward it.

Without question, I went too.

Behind the house, deep in these old woods, I'd found a tiny church building. Intensely rugged and forgotten, hidden away. I'd lived in New Haven my whole life and never knew it existed.

I did get the feeling this was it. Something important. Malaki had basically led us here with his cryptic mumbling. I didn't know if it was good or bad, but it was something. A step.

Among these pine trees, the tiny church building was covered in moss. From the crest of the triangle roof, there was a small cross sticking out with vines crawling up. This dark, compact building had no windows. It was plain and ancient. It could have been four hundred years old or five decades.

As we moved around one side, we found a single doorway at the end. There was no longer a door but instead an empty, gaping hole. Jeremy stepped close to it and pulled out his phone. Lighting the way, he stepped through without a word.

I heard rustling inside like birds. Or bats. Through the doorway, I saw rows of pews, some tipped over. Everything was covered in cobwebs. The floor looked like stone, and at the far end of the church there was a raised, wooden platform with a pulpit.

"This is terrifying, Jeremy."

He was moving farther in, his phone light casting his face in strange shadows. I couldn't tell if he was scared or amazed.

"Jeremy… We probably shouldn't—"

"There's a way down. Somewhere. There's a way down."

He pointed his light to the end and cried out.

"Yes!"

I poked my head inside to look. There was a door in the far right corner. A plain, wooden door.

"Cliff, this has to be—"

And then we heard it. The rumbling. It came from the door, and even it was shaking. Jeremy turned to look at me, and his features had gone pale.

"Let's go!" I hollered. "We've gotta go."

He nodded and started walking, but he kept looking over his shoulder at the door.

"Jeremy, come on!"

I started moving away from the church, motioning desperately. He finally emerged from the dark and sprinted. Just as we were running away, the door inside crashed open.

Gasping for air, we sped away, dodging trees and running for the clearing. I looked over my shoulder twice and saw nothing behind us. Only the church surrounded by woods. But I kept glancing back as we emerged into the clearing.

"Let's get outta here." I bent over, heaving. "Let's… follow that road." I pointed ahead of us.

"My car is way back in—"

"I'll call Naomi." I looked back once more. Nothing was chasing after us. I shook my head and said, "We can come back later. With the cops."

Jeremy frowned at me, but he didn't argue. We made our way along the road, following the hills. They were covered in wildflowers here, and we had left the house behind. But after calling Naomi, I kept looking back. Just in case.

CHAPTER 10
KAIA WOODS

When Mom left in a rush to go get Dad and Jeremy, I thought, *Yes. This is it. Something's happening.*

I made a trip into town. But after I placed my letter in the cold PO box, I expected things to start heating up quickly. I was ready as hell.

She came back two hours later with only Dad, and neither of them spoke to me. I waited in the kitchen, raised my eyebrows when they entered, but right away they vanished into their bedroom.

I didn't get anything from them. Mom made spaghetti for dinner and then left it on the stove for us to eat. While she cooked, she wouldn't talk about what happened. Just "your father's tired. You and I can talk to him tomorrow."

As if she didn't already know what happened.

"I'm not an idiot!"

"Kaia, let's just have a quiet evening. We all need it."

So, I was pissed off, and I stayed in my room the rest of the night. But the next day, things weren't any better. They both whispered outside on the porch, and whenever I tried to listen they would change topics or talk to me in their fake-happy voices.

Same whenever Nate and Rhys came around.

At last, I said, "I'll just leave. If you two wanna have your secret little conversations, I won't stop you."

Nate and Rhys watched me as I stormed away from the porch.

"Bike ride?" I called to them.

They followed me to the barn. As we went, Mom and Dad didn't say anything. They exchanged looks and watched us go. By the time the three of us were pedaling on the road and heading for those hills, my blood was boiling.

"Obviously, something big happened!" I said, yelling to be heard. The bike hummed as I sped along, working my legs faster than normal.

"Kaia, they'll tell us sometime."

I looked at Nate and laughed loudly. "Yeah, sure."

The wind rushed by as I pushed harder, putting distance between us. I pumped my legs faster, up and down, until they were burning. Breathing hard, I flew down the road. Farther and farther away from Nate and Rhys. I had dreams of riding all the way to that house. Forget everything, I'd go by myself.

Yes. That's what I need to do.

But then I remembered the last time I went. The dark hallway at the back of the house. The creaking boards and the ghostly sitting room. I shook away any thought of doing it again.

Not until it was time. I was just waiting on a plan.

I pushed my bike faster and faster. It whirred across the asphalt, and I turned right, heading toward the hills. Up ahead, a few minutes on, the road turned left and carried through. I pulled off, bumped into the grass, and drifted to a stop. Down by the dead tree, I hopped off, breathing heavily, and left it leaning there. Behind me, Nate and Rhys were in the distance, coming closer. I didn't feel like waiting, so I started walking up the first hill.

Out here, the hills were covered in long grass and wildflowers. They were everywhere, and the whole place smelled wonderful. Today, the sky was half-covered by clouds, but it was still warm. Whenever a breeze came through, I could've even called it perfect.

I didn't mind the towering house in the distance, either. Not anymore. I liked watching it, because I liked to keep an eye on things. Until I was ready to do more.

Step by step, I groaned my way to the hilltop. My legs usually weren't this tired, because I didn't take off racing, but at the top, the familiar view awaited me. More hills stretched out, bigger than this one, until the shadow. After it, they were covered in vast, beautiful forests. Below, New Haven sat peacefully in the heat.

So many flowers grew in these hills. Daisies waving back and forth, dandelions peppering the grass. I took a seat and watched the world shifting. Like I said, it was nice to keep an eye on things from here. And whenever the boys arrived, we'd probably walk up the next couple hills. Gain a better view.

It wasn't long before they showed up. Nate and Rhys didn't speak. I saw them from the corner of my eye but didn't look over. They left their bikes beside mine and trudged their way to me.

"You okay?" Nate asked when they got within earshot.

"Yeah."

He took a seat beside me. Rhys joined him.

Nate studied me. "Are you lying?"

I smirked. "Maybe. I'm just… mad they're hiding stuff from me. *Again.*"

Nate nodded and picked at the grass beside his legs. Last time they hid stuff, he'd been the one to tell me, but not right away. I didn't blame him for it. He was just a kid.

To my surprise, Rhys spoke up next. "What do… do you think happened?"

He was sitting crisscross, rubbing his hands together while avoiding my eyes.

"I have no idea."

"I... I think I do."

Even Nate looked at him in surprise. "What?"

I leaned forward. "What do you think, Rhys?" He had my curiosity, at least. After some of the weird shit I'd heard him say... And he did seem to know more than I thought.

Rhys paused for a moment and swallowed hard. "I think they didn't... find the girl, because they would've called the cops. And stayed there. And them... they must have been in danger. If they left so quickly."

"Maybe not, though," Nate said.

"What if they found something else?" Rhys asked, speaking faster now, gaining confidence. "Something they didn't expect. But they can't check it out yet, because—"

"Let's go," I interrupted him, climbing to my feet. "Let's just go. Right now."

Nate stared up at me. "Uhh..."

"Why not? It's... We can be in and out. So fast."

"Maybe not today..." Nate trailed off. His face had turned pale.

Rhys added, "I'm not scared." He stood up, too.

I watched Nate intently. His eyes were glued on the house. Slowly, he climbed to his feet, legs trembling. Just when I was about to try convincing him again, he spoke.

"Guys... Who's that person?"

I turned to find a dark figure in the distance. They were one hill over from the house, fully sprinting toward us. I couldn't tell, but they seemed incredibly tall. And very fast.

"Oh shit." I looked around at them. "Let's get back to the bikes."

"Yes, please, the bikes." Nate took off down the hill, and without his baseball speed, we were left behind.

"Come on, Rhys," I urged him. "Run! Come on!"

Rhys picked up the pace and jogged beside me. I saw Nate below us, already at the bikes, motioning for us to hurry. I turned back to look, however, and saw the figure had stopped.

He was probably a mile away from us, staring in our direction. I couldn't make out his face or anything about him. It was more like a shadow. But it seemed tall and broad, and I didn't want it to get any closer.

"Who is that?" I asked out loud, squinting.

Rhys stood beside me and didn't say a word.

After a minute, Nate trekked back up to us, grumbling, "What are you doing? Let's go!" When he saw we were watching the figure, he folded his arms and stood there.

I shook my head and pulled out my phone to take a picture. "Why are they watching us? Why are they by the house?"

I held up my phone and noticed Rhys staring at me, terrified and shaking. I took one picture—not that I could see anything clearly—and stuffed it in a pocket.

"I think they're watching me," Nate said. "Ever since me and Mom got attacked on our bike ride. I've seen that person… three or four times now. Rhys, you know." He gulped. "And it's happening more and more."

"Yeah, I remember when you came running in my room from a nightmare." I looked over, smiling, and dropped it. "Sorry. Not the time."

"It's okay," Rhys added. "I can deal with our stalker. If I need to."

Without teasing Nate any more, we made our way home. The three of us didn't talk about the figure we'd seen, because there wasn't much to say. It hadn't chased up. It hadn't made any closer moves. No, it was simply watching.

I felt a weird relief, because I thought the person had been coming after me. The one who escaped the house. But if it was following Nate… I still didn't like the idea of him in danger. Or how the danger seemed to latch onto each one of us.

While Nate took the bikes into the garage, I stood outside, waiting with Rhys. Nate vanished into the red barn through a side door, and I turned to him right away.

"Rhys, you're not scared? Of the house?"

"I…" Before answering, he paused and studied my face. Then he went on. "I've been there. A few times. So I'm not scared anymore."

"You? You've been there?"

"Shh!" He refocused on the barn, where Nate had just emerged. Quietly, without moving his lips, he added, "We need to talk. Without him."

<> <> <>

I decided to go into town soon after. I wanted to check for another letter… and get away from my parents. Even though the sky had filled up with dark clouds, I figured I could make it to the post office and back before it rained.

"Into town?" Mom asked. "Why? It's about to rain."

"I just want… to get a new library book."

"You just got a book yesterday."

"Well, the book wasn't very good!" I stared at her, arms folded, not backing down.

"Well…" She groaned. "Okay. Take my keys. But don't be long. It's gonna be a bad storm. Every summer, you know how it is."

"Thanks, Mom."

I drove into town bitterly. I'd have to start thinking of a new excuse soon. The library wasn't gonna work if I wanted to check daily.

They were always saying "This is gonna the bad one. Storm of the summer." And sure, we got some bad storms in this part of the country, but it was more like one-a-month than one-a-summer. Not the end of the world.

The sky looked like it always did right before a thunderstorm. Walls of clouds moved in from the north, over the hills. The ominous black pushed up against the wispy and fluffy white, like waves crashing and foaming as they came in. Waves in the sky.

Maybe I shouldn't have gone. I could've sat with my family on the porch and watched it.

But I was sure glad I did.

In and out of the post office. Ducking my head. Hoping I wouldn't see anybody I knew. To my shock, there was another letter. I couldn't send back a reply today, but I would keep it overnight... Think about it.

Kaia,

I'm sorry. I'm not pranking you.

I'm entirely sure Allison is alive. To prove you can trust me, I'll tell you what they found. The ones who dared go into the forest.

They found a church. A small one. And inside, there is an old, forgotten door.

It is too late to turn back now. Those unwanted visitors have disturbed it. Everything is moving quickly. Maybe it's for the best. They were growing suspicious of me.

You'll see, this day. You are not alone. Do not assume you are safe.

You will have Allison if you open your mind. Don't be afraid to trust a stranger.

Hurry, Kaia. To home.

Soon you will see who stays and goes.

On the drive home, with the letter sprawled open on my knees, it started to rain. Droplets splashed against my windshield, picking up speed. The landscape outside was smeared and battered. I didn't pay attention, repeating the letter in my head. Over and over. But it didn't make any sense. These were less helpful each time. Less specific.

But they said Allison was alive. And they said I could have her back. I just needed to wait a little longer. I just needed to hold out hope.

As I turned into the driveway and bumped up the gravel toward my house, the rain increased. It was pouring buckets now, and I parked beside the barn, bracing myself for the dash to the back porch.

But then I saw in my rearview mirror something else.

At the edge of the driveway, a car turned in. Started coming toward me.

A police car.

CHAPTER 11
NAOMI WOODS

What started as a trickle of rain running down the side of the house turned into a downpour. By the time Kaia appeared, it was coming down in sheets.

From the safe, dry porch, I watched. The wind lashed through tree branches, and even the oak tree bent. I felt a rush of cold air as the storm rolled in and unleashed. Hear its rhythmic beating on the ground. Raining so hard it came off Cliff's truck in a fine mist and sounded like a wild drumbeat. Puddles filled and overflowed. On every surface, a thousand raindrops splashed and rolled away. Soon, Cliff's soybeans would drown out there. He sat beside me, watching closely, not quite as relaxed.

"Not gonna rain tomorrow," I assured him. "They're fine for a day. You know that. Just relax."

To our left, Cliff's grill sat off the porch, covered in a tarp. The raindrops made thunderous, musical notes as they smacked against it. It was a calming sound, meditative. Cliff was still rigid, but I felt more relaxed than I had in weeks. Until Kaia came running from the driveway. She was holding her hands up, squinting as the rain drove right into her eyes.

"She's back," I noted. "With no library book…"

Nate and Rhys were on the other side of the porch. They'd been outside, playing baseball, and now they were silent, dripping on the dark red wood. Nate scuffed his heel against the porch and pouted as they rocked on the bench swing, but Rhys stared around, wide-eyed. He didn't seem to care about their baseball time cut short. Instead, he hugged himself tightly and cringed every time thunder rumbled in the distance. When he saw Kaia heading toward us, he walked over quietly and stood behind me.

"Hi there," I called out as she closed in.

Kaia jumped over the few stairs and onto the porch. "The sheriff's here."

Cliff stood up. "What?"

"Right behind me. His car."

I was still looking around, trying to register what she'd said, when Cliff sprang into action.

"Nate. Rhys." He opened the kitchen door. "Get inside. Quick."

Nate didn't stand from the bench swing, but Rhys started moving through the kitchen door.

"Nate, go." Cliff used his deeply serious dad voice—a rarity—and said, "Get inside. Take Rhys to the attic."

"What?" Nate grumbled as he slowly rose from the bench swing. "Why?"

"I'm gonna tell the sheriff you're both gone. At a friend's house." His head was on a swivel, commanding Nate, then watching the side of the house and back to Nate. "Do it! Don't argue with me."

"Okay." Nate rolled his eyes as he followed Rhys into the house. "I'll just take my freaking PlayStation up there."

I heard Cliff's rapid breathing as the screen door slapped shut. Through the kitchen window, I watched Nate lead Rhys to the staircase, and then they were gone.

"Why are you freaking out?" Kaia asked. She was standing at the edge of the porch, leaning against the rail.

"Doesn't matter." Cliff paced back and forth, pulling at his beard. "Just have to… act like…"

"In case Sheriff Wheeler is looking into Rhys," I explained, since he wouldn't or couldn't.

At that moment, we all saw him. Crunching across the gravel, then passing through the wet grass. The rain cascaded around his brimmed hat. But he moved slowly. In no hurry. He didn't shield himself from the rain, and when he approached he didn't smile.

"Ben, *relax.*" I stood up beside him, nudging him with my shoulder.

Kaia was still against the railing.

The sheriff approached. I thought I saw his eyes glance upward, toward the house, but maybe he was just looking at the sky. There was no attic window on this side, anyway.

The wooden steps groaned as he climbed them and stood on the porch. Out of the rain now, he didn't shake off his jacket or coat. Our gutters were overflowing, so a waterfall poured down only inches from his shoulder.

"Cliff. Naomi." He nodded at me and then, "Kaia."

The sheriff's voice was joyless. Whatever he'd come here to do, he took no pleasure in it. None of us answered. Nobody knew what to expect.

"I've got…" He cleared his throat and shook away the fog. When he spoke, it was more formal. "We confirmed what Jeremy found." He looked mostly at Cliff while he spoke. "The two bodies were the missing Clarks."

"That's… good news, right?" I asked.

He didn't acknowledge me. His eyes flicked to Kaia, who was shifting nervously.

"And something else," the sheriff went on. "Well… more than one thing."

I let out, "Oh shit," before I could stop myself. "Sorry," I went on. "Is there… someone else dead?"

He nodded. "I'm sure you all know the Turners. Mr. Turner owns the pizza place on Main. Beth Turner…"

"I know her from church," I cut in. "She's been praying for the Clarks for a couple weeks now. Mallory is her sister. Our prayer meetings, you know. Has she… does she know yet? That they found 'em?"

Sheriff Wheeler bowed his head. "She's gone missing, too."

I gasped. Cliff did the same. We exchanged a look, and I couldn't think of anything to say. Nothing seemed right for the moment. When I looked at Kaia, though, she was staring at the sheriff with no emotion. Not even a frown.

"Kaia," I asked, "did you know Beth?"

She nodded real quick. "Little bit."

"It's tragic, of course," the sheriff went on. He was still dripping wet. His stern voice cut through the sound of running rainwater. And what he said next cut through my heart. "But… well, there's something else. Something involving you."

He looked toward Kaia.

She stiffened against the railing.

"We questioned Malaki again. About the small church you two found." He gestured to Cliff. "I had other questions, of course. 'Bout all the… the livestock dying around here. You know. People's dogs… And the Turner's had some livestock die. Terrible mess, too. Your boy found 'em, right?"

Cliff nodded.

I pressed, "But what's this got to do with Kaia?"

Sheriff waved his hand in the air. "Sorry. I'm… all over the place. Apologies." He cleared his throat. "So, Malaki says about that small church building. If we… take him there, he'll show us where Allison's body is."

Kaia didn't flinch. With one hand on the railing, her stone features could've been a statue.

"Malaki will take…" The sheriff exhaled. He frowned at me and Cliff. "Myself, Cliff, and Kaia. He also agreed to take Jeremy."

"She can't go!" I said right away. "Listen, I know —"

"Naomi." Sheriff Wheeler shook his head. "I don't want this, either. But he *specifically* insisted *you* could not go and that Kaia has to. And, look… right now, there's no other way."

"There has to be—"

"It's not up to me." Sheriff Wheeler rubbed a fist into his forehead. "I've got… people above me, too. And they want answers. After what happened last time, and after everything happening since… Malaki's got some push. He's holding it over me. And we've gotta do this, because until we do, he's gonna *keep* holding it."

I gaped at him. This was different than any conflict I'd ever had with the sheriff. He had lost all his ego, all his aggression. He almost seemed as distraught as me. But still, he came here, trying to take *my daughter* back into that hellhole? I couldn't let it—

"This is our only shot. I'm sorry." He turned to Kaia. "What do you think?"

"I'm ready." She crossed her arms and raised her chin. "I can do it. I can do whatever you need."

He nodded. "Good."

"Kaia! You…" I stood up from the chair. My breath was

coming in sharp bursts. "You can't just—"

"Mom, it's okay." Kaia stepped closer to me. She placed both her hands around one of mine. "It's… It'll be safe. Right?" She turned. "Sheriff?"

"We'll have backup following," he explained. "It's safe. They can't get too close, but it's safe. We'll be armed. And it's just Malaki."

"You don't know what's in that house," I hissed. "It's not Malaki I'm afraid of."

The sheriff turned his dead gaze to Cliff. I was ready to interrupt, but Kaia squeezed my hand. I saw something in her eyes I hadn't for a long time. When she mouthed "I'm okay" and forced a smile, she held so much hope.

"I'm trusting you, Cliff," Sheriff Wheeler went on. "This is big time. It's in my blood to protect this town. So I will. Don't cross me." He paused. "If I find out you're hiding anything from me… or you haven't been honest… I'll make your life a living hell."

Cliff glared at him. "I'm not hiding shit, Sheriff."

"Let's hope not." The sheriff studied us all once more. "We're not wasting time. It's happening tomorrow. So, get yourselves ready." There was an unfamiliar pause, and he added, "Please."

Then he left. Without any emotion, he turned and walked back through the rain, slowly, the same way he'd come, as the storm rolled over us. Sheriff Wheeler disappeared around the corner of the house.

As we all stood there, numb, Kaia spoke first. "I can't believe it…"

"Kaia, you know I can't…" My voice cracked and I stopped.

"It's okay, Mom." She leaned over and hugged me tightly. I felt it again. Her radiant hope. "I'm gonna get us some water. And then we can talk about all of this."

She went into the house, and I was alone with Cliff. He pulled at his beard more, pacing back and forth. Watching him, I couldn't help but feel a twinge of anger.

"It's too much, Ben. She can't… Look at me. Please."

He did.

"That place isn't… it's never easy. You know how it changed things. And you're just gonna… let her go through that?"

"She won't be alone, Naomi," he said. "You were, she won't be."

"You're right. I was. And you said you'd never leave me alone again." I huffed and collapsed into a deck chair. "But you have. You left me here, taking care of our family, holding everything together."

"I'll protect her in there."

"Will you?" I stared up at him and felt the tears threatening. "If it's either protect her or save your ass… Will you?"

Cliff sat down next to me, reached for my knee, and pleaded, but I knew it was all a performance. His mind was made up. This was happening. All the men had decided. Jeremy, Cliff, the sheriff. They were gonna take my daughter from me, throw her in that house, and see what happened.

I couldn't do a damn thing to stop it.

"You aren't better than everyone," I cut in. "None of you are. You can't work miracles. You aren't Superman—"

"And neither are you!" I glared at him, and he paused, softened his voice. "This is it, Naomi. I promise. I'll protect her. We'll fix everything. And once Kaia gets that closure… it's over. It's all over. Right?"

I shook my head, turning away so he wouldn't see me cry.

"Everything will be fine. It'll go back to normal. Don't you see?"

"Just go, Cliff," I managed to say. "Just go inside."

CHAPTER 12
NATE WOODS

"I can't believe them," I complained.

Sitting toward the front of the attic, I watched through the circle window. Raindrops were rolling down the glass. From this side of the house, I couldn't see anything important. The window faced the long field out front and the road, and I didn't see any police cars, so there was literally nothing unusual about the sight.

"Why's Dad always doing that?"

I looked back at Rhys in the dark attic. The floors were all wooden — with splinters, too. Nothing up there but old boxes, and everything had an inch of dust. I hated it, the whole place. Smelled like old people.

"That… that pisses me off," I spat.

He raised his eyebrows. I rarely ever cussed — except around Mike Baggs, but nobody knew about that.

"Just bossing me around for no reason! Us, I mean."

Rhys didn't respond.

Maybe I should've brought the PlayStation if he's gonna act like this again. No, it would've been too much work. Not worth it.

I decided to be straight up and just confront him.

Turning fully to face him, I crossed my arms. "Do you just

forget how to talk sometimes or what? You do this like… every other day."

I expected Rhys to look shocked again or maybe even cry a little. But he didn't do either of those things. Instead, he smirked.

"What are you laughing at?"

Rhys shook his head. "How dumb you are."

"I'm not dumb!" I got on my knees, ready to launch across the attic at him.

"Right. Course you're not. Just a regular townie."

I opened my mouth but couldn't think of any response to that.

Something about him unnerved me. There'd been a shift when we came up here. His voice sounded a little sharper and meaner. His face was like stone.

"Whatever, Nate." He moved into the darkest corner, away from me. "Just remember I told you so."

He squatted over in the corner, reaching for the floor. It was dark, so I couldn't tell what he was doing at first. I had the bizarre idea that he was about to poop—on the *attic floor*—but then I heard the sound of wood grinding together.

"What are you doing?"

He looked at me over his shoulder with a wicked grin. "Don't worry about it."

Then he pulled something up from the floor, a cloud of dust exploding around him. As Rhys set a plank of wood to the side, I realized he'd opened a small hiding spot. He coughed and waved a hand through the air as he reached into the hole.

"How'd you know about that?" I scampered across the attic floor. "Rhys? Hey, answer me!"

He pulled out a small bundle and set it beside him. "Chill out."

"What do you mean 'chill out?' Rhys!"

With a frustrated growl, he turned to me. "Listen. Do you *want* to help your sister? Or do you wanna keep being like *everyone else* in this town and ignore it?"

"I… Um. Ignore what? I mean, I wanna help her —"

"Right. So don't *worry* about me. I'm here to help. And this proves it."

He unwrapped the red, knitted blanket and revealed three objects.

There were two pictures. One of them was a poster for a missing dog. I didn't recognize the name Davis or the address on Main Street. But in the picture, there was a man I recognized very well holding the dog. The whole town had been talking about him for weeks. I'd been to his funeral days before.

"That's George. His dog was missing?"

Rhys nodded and silently tapped the next image.

This was a much nicer photo. Older and faded, too. It was a picture of a family, posed together in a fancy room. I saw gigantic candle holders on the walls and maybe even a chandelier in the background. The man sat in a large, antique chair, like a type of king. There was a mom, hand on his shoulder, and a couple kids.

"Rhys… Is that…?"

He blinked.

"Is that you in the picture?"

He looked down at it. Beside the man, there was a boy who looked about our age. He had the same shaggy, unkempt hair, long nose, and toothy smile as Rhys.

"No. And it doesn't matter." He reached for the third object: a small, silver key. Holding it up, he added, "This does. This is how we get inside."

"Get… get inside where?"

He smiled again in an unsettling way. "Where do you think, Nate?"

I gulped. "Right."

"I know where he goes," Rhys said. His eyes got real wide and he gestured around, closing his hands together and then spreading them apart. "I knew it before we saw him earlier, but now I know for sure. He goes up there."

"The one stalking me?"

"Well, actually…" Rhys hesitated. "Yeah, sure. Stalking you. So, *now*, we can go after him. If we want to. Or need to." He leaned back and grinned. "See? You just gotta trust me. We don't have to sit and watch like everybody else, Nate. You just gotta be less of a coward."

"Okay."

I felt unsteady now, but I nodded. Rhys seemed different. I didn't like it. But he was trusting me with these secrets, so I could trust him. For now.

"Okay, Rhys. I can. I will."

He smiled wider than I'd ever seen. "Good. 'Cause it's almost time."

CHAPTER 13
NEW HAVEN (SPORTS BAR AND GRILL)

There was only one bar in New Haven. Main Street Grill was about a block from the baseball field, and for most of the week it was mostly empty. A handful of people drank casually in the middle of the day. The lunch and dinner rush would fill up the booths, and then those folks would trickle out. As far as food options went, it was never the emptiest—that'd be the diner across the road. But it wasn't the busiest, either.

Except for Friday nights.

On this particular Friday night, it seemed like the whole town had forced themselves into Main Street Grill. It was standing room only, and anyone with a table felt blessed. The four bartenders could barely keep up as a whole town drank away the work week. Most of them traveled to Brooksville for work, but there were local farmers and shop owners as well as the local schoolteachers who worked odd jobs in the summer. In a few weeks, they'd show up to school sunburnt and exhausted to do it all again.

So, by eleven, the room was filling up and everyone was screaming over each other. The whole place echoed with laughter, hoots, clanging glasses, and slurred speech. Some people didn't dare show their face at Main Street Grill on a Friday night—the

Banks family, for example, who were always the main topic of conversation. Even Cliff Woods — if he *did* show up — might be sent on his way in a heartbeat.

"You know, I met that fancy lawyer from outta town!" one man shouted as beer dripped from beard. "Met him a year back. Believe it, the Banks ain't gonna have a cent when he's done."

"Yes, he's a real vampire!" the woman on the barstool beside him shouted. "Oh, Lordy. Suck 'em dry."

"Serves them right," the bearded man hollered.

The barkeep — who distanced himself from the unsavory gossip one finds at eleven on a Friday and preferred the light-hearted ramblings of the a.m. — didn't speak. He gestured to the empty glasses in front of them.

"Don't even ask!" the bearded man shouted.

"Keep 'em coming!" the woman replied, and her chins rolled as she laughed. "Next round's on you, Bobby."

"On *me*?" Bobby with a beard frowned. "I got the last three, didn't I?"

"Bobby, you don't know nothing. *I* paid for 'em."

"You did?"

"Sure, I did. Just pay up."

"Alright, alright." Bobby handed over a ten dollar bill to the barkeep. "How many rounds is this?"

"One."

Bobby shrugged and turned back to his date.

"But, Marge... have *you* heard about Sheriff Wheeler?" he asked, raising his eyebrows.

In the dim lighting and booming chaos, his date leaned closer. "No!" Marge said. "What'd you hear?"

"Well, seems he's — "

Before he could finish, a skinny woman wearing heels and a

dress barged between them. She was holding herself up on the shoulders of a much younger man. He opened his mouth to apologize, but the woman was faster.

"Did *I* hear you talking about the Banks family?" she asked in a shrill, hungry voice. "Did *I* hear correctly now?"

"Yes, ma'am," Bobby answered.

"*Well,* now, if you ask me—"

"We didn't," Marge said under her breath.

"—the Banks are gonna spend *twenty grand,* and some fancy lawyer can't fix their problems!" She clicked her tongue disdainfully. "Gonna lose their house, their car… Hell, gonna lose the ass off their pants, but that boy's a murderer, and no Brooksville-smoking, piece of—"

"Easy now, honey," her date said. Even in the neon bar lighting, it was clear he'd started blushing.

"Don't call me honey!" she said. "Makes me feel old. Damn."

He didn't answer this time.

"I didn't *say* it was a good idea," Bobby went on.

The woman in heels leaned closer. "What'd you say? I can't hear you."

"I said—"

"Speak up! Christ."

Bobby cleared his throat. "I know that lawyer's bad news! Don't matter to me. Banks are gonna go broke, leave town. Better for everyone."

"I don't know about that," the barkeep chimed in. "More folks that leave, the less town there is. You know what I mean?"

"Some folks ain't ever gonna leave, and that's why we got a town!" Bobby went on. He was halfway through his tenth beer, and his sentences were getting cloudier. "Like… Sheriff Wheeler."

"What were you saying about him?" Marge thought to herself,

Before this bimbo interrupted, and laughed at her own joke.

"Oh, right. Right!" Bobby clapped his hands. "Oh, listen here. Listen up, hey!"

Not everyone did, but a good amount of people turned toward him. Bobby looked around at their expectant faces and smiled to himself. He felt a surge of real power and sat up straighter.

"Sheriff Wheeler," he started. "Good ole Sheriff. Been here forever, right? Family practically built that police station, right?"

"That man's as solid as they come," someone shouted.

"He is. Or he was." Bobby smirked. "But there's something going down this weekend, you hear. I heard about it from a deputy friend. We got any cops in the house tonight?"

Nobody answered.

"Well, good. 'Cause you all ain't supposed to know this — and me either — but there's a little trip going on. Some folks visiting the old Donnelly house. And you know who's leading it?"

"Sheriff?" Marge asked.

Bobby shook his head with a wicked grin. "Nope. Old Jeremy Adams."

"He ain't even a deputy!"

"How come Jeremy — ?"

"Listen up!" Bobby shouted. "Listen, and I'll tell. Sheriff Wheeler ain't doing so well nowadays. They say he's… his hands is shaking all the time. He's looking 'round, like somebody's watching. They say he's losing it, good folks. Our old sheriff is losing it. Started after the Banks child murdered that pretty life wife — "

Some murmurs in the crowd.

" — and they say the sheriff's dog been killed last week. No, something ain't right with the old cowboy. But he's going up to that house. Him and Jeremy Adams. There's something going down this weekend, folks. Something up there."

"Ain't *nothing* up there!" someone shouted from the back of the dark room. "Hasn't been for decades!"

Everyone else was silent. Whenever the Donnelly house got mentioned, folks had a way of zipping their lips and letting someone else speak first.

"Oh, don't be so sure," Bobby went on. "They still don't know who burnt down the Davis shop or killed the Turner cattle. Don't be so sure, folks. That's all I'm saying. We all know that house got dark energy around it, dark things in the history. So, Sheriff… he's taking some kind of last stand."

"You're just guessing, Bobby!"

Someone else yelled, "Bullshit. Load of bullshit."

The murmurs turned into side conversations, and then the bar was alive again, full of roaring voices and sloshing glasses. But Bobby kept to his story, and after Marge had wobbled home and the bar had dropped a few levels in volume, the barkeep approached him.

"You mean what you say about the sheriff?" he asked. "I was… We were good friends back when I was a deputy. Or trying to be."

Bobby nodded. "I mean it. He's not right in the head, now. He's lost it."

The barkeep shook his head. "That's a real shame. I'm not… Seems like he shouldn't be going up there in such a state. That house… it does things to people."

Bobby chuckled. "Oh, you're one of them superstitious folks?"

"Not superstitious." He paused. "But I've heard enough stories. You always do, working at a place like this. And when someone tells a story on a Friday, that's one thing. But I've heard 'em every day… Mondays, Thursdays… And I'm starting to think… What's the saying? Where there's smoke, there's fire? Well… might be some fire."

"Maybe we could use some fire," Bobby suggested. "Burn that place down."

The barkeep sighed. "Maybe so. But I'm thinking Sheriff's in over his head. And when a man like that loses it… not always a pretty sight. I'd hate to see him caught up in… the fire."

CHAPTER 14
KAIA WOODS

On the day when everything happened, I woke up with a terrible headache.

I hadn't slept well the night before. That was to be expected, I guess, with so much at stake. I grabbed the Ibuprofen off my side table and shook out three. Then I lay down again with a throbbing pain in the back of my head.

The first hour of my day was completely normal. I stayed in bed for a few minutes, sprawled out face down with a pillow pressed against me. The bedsheets were too soft and warm to leave. I wouldn't fall asleep again, but I didn't want to wake up, either. Getting out of bed meant more than usual. I wasn't getting dressed for a trip into town. I wasn't putting on makeup so people on Main Street wouldn't give me nasty side-eyes. When I threw on my most comfortable pair of jeans and a tank top, I specifically thought, *This is what I'll have on when I get her back.*

I put on the quartz necklace I'd been wearing every day since she vanished. And I thought, *This is the last time until it's hers.*

Or not. Maybe Malaki was bluffing. Maybe we'd get a phone call from the sheriff. Any minute, he could cancel the whole thing. But I got dressed anyway and chose shoes I didn't mind getting dirty. I didn't need to look *nice*-nice. I didn't need to be brave. I just needed to keep going.

You won't be alone. It'll be fine.

Or it wouldn't.

I tried not to think about the worst case scenario. Those never happened anyway, right? But yeah… the worst case scenario here would be pretty awful. Life-changing in a whole different way.

It'll be fine. The sheriff and Jeremy have guns.

Maybe Dad, too. But when it came down to it… I didn't actually trust him to protect me. That was the honest truth. After how he reacted to Malaki… No, after my whole life, really… He didn't seem like the kind of dad who could kill somebody to save you.

While getting ready, I couldn't help but think about Mom. She'd be waiting for me downstairs. Anxiety carved into her face. The night before, she'd talked to me for hours.

"All I want to do is protect you," she said. Repeated it multiple times, on the verge of tears, and every time I'd lied. "I wanna protect you from everything," she said. "If I can't, then what am I even doing? Who am I? I just wanna keep you safe. It kills me to think of you getting hurt."

"This is the only way for me, Mom," I pleaded with her. Not lying yet.

"Oh, please, just be okay. I need you, Kaia. This is the hardest thing I've ever done. Letting you go. And I… I trust your dad." She'd gulped. "He can… try. If Malaki hadn't said… I'd come, you know, happily… I'd go with you, and we could…"

She'd been spiraling, so I'd interrupted her. "Mom, it's okay. I love you. And I know how hard it is."

"Can you promise me this is the end?" she had asked. "Tomorrow morning, when that sun comes up, we're done? Whatever happens today, it's over?"

"I promise, Mom. This is it," I lied.

We hugged once, twice, I forgot the count. Each time, she squeezed me until I might pop. Each time, I held her just as close.

"I'm scared," I admitted. I almost felt guilty putting that weight on her. I knew what she wanted, the easy answer, but I didn't have anyone else to talk to. "I'm really scared."

She paused. There was pain in her eyes.

When she spoke, she didn't say, "Then don't go." And I'll love her for that forever.

"We all have to do things we're scared of," Mom said quietly. "We have to go. We have to let go. And we have to keep doing it every day, forever. I'll do it… so you can too. Okay?"

"Okay."

When I came downstairs, there was no sound in the whole house besides the air-conditioner. I went into the kitchen and found Mom at the table. I saw her right leg bouncing, like somebody might bounce a child on their knee. Sitting with an untouched mug of coffee, her eyes locked onto my face, and I knew how she was feeling.

"It's okay, Mom," I assured her while heating up a breakfast sandwich in the microwave. "I'm not gonna take any chances."

"You need to be *careful.*"

"I will." I forced a smile and turned away. The microwave's little green numbers counted down to the end of the world. "I won't leave the group. I won't do anything stupid."

"I know I can't stop you from going…" She looked down at her coffee mug and gripped it with both hands. "But… please, Kaia… If anything happens… This is the hardest thing I've ever done. I *need* you to come back okay."

"I'll come back, Mom. Just like I am. And maybe… maybe she will, too."

<> <> <>

Dad drove his truck. From the passenger's seat, I stared out the open window. Fresh, New Haven air rushed through the cabin, throwing strands of my hair like a tornado. I wore a headband, and it was almost a hundred degrees outside, but for a moment there I felt chills.

Just the two of us, like old times. His blue pickup rumbled toward the hills and then over them. I smelled the fumes at first, until he started driving faster, and then I couldn't smell anything at all. The wind smacked against my face, and I closed my eyes.

"How are you feeling?" He offered, "Ready?"

I nodded. "Ready."

I felt bad about lying to Mom. Truthfully, I would do *anything* to get her back. I would take all the chances, make all the stupid moves. I had no plan. I was gonna wing it. But more than anything, I was going to keep moving. Anytime I felt scared or wanted to turn back, it was an easy choice.

Just think about Allison.

It'd been so long. Where was she at? What would she look like? What had they... done?

Is she alive?

I pushed that thought away. At this point, I trusted the letters a hundred percent. I didn't know who was writing them, but they seemed to know things. They knew about what I'd seen in the house. They understood what happened there, and they predicted I'd get another chance to go inside.

If they said she was alive, then she was. If they said they'd keep me safe, somehow, then they would.

It didn't matter, anyway. Blind faith could be the same as bravery. It would drive me forward. I'd be scared—I already was—but I wouldn't turn back. Until I found her. Even if it cost me everything.

The closer we got, the less real it felt. This was a scene from someone else's life. Somebody different than me. Stronger and older. It couldn't be mine. This couldn't be happening.

But as we continued to ride the hills—my stomach fluttering, up and down, a steep drop—I saw it. Only a mile away. I hadn't been this close since the night I went through the front door. But I'd been alone then. And it had been dark.

Now, it was midday. There was a bright sun overhead, birds in the trees, and as long as we were outside, I didn't worry about anything sneaking up. The forest shivered in a gentle breeze. An intense heat pressed against my skin.

We got closer and closer, and small details jumped out. Sunlight exposed every rotten plank and moldy corner. The Gothic house of my nightmares looked much gentler during the day. Just a forgotten, old man, lined with age, broken windows. Damaged, hiding.

"It's a nice day," Dad said as we climbed the final hill. He winced. "I wish we could stay out here."

"Where exactly are we going?"

"Oh. I forgot you never saw it." He hesitated and pointed to the trees behind the house. "There's a creepy little church back there. And a door."

"Weird."

It was like the anonymous letter had said. A church and a door.

"It was freaking me out. The whole place is just…" He shuddered and went on. "Jeremy didn't seem as scared, but I just keep thinking… What's through that door?"

"You didn't go through?"

He shook his head. "It gave me a horrible feeling."

I stared out the window at those towering pines. Neither of us spoke. There was nothing left to say.

On the overgrown slab of concrete, the police car waited. Outside of it, I saw Sheriff Wheeler himself, still wearing that sort-of-goofy hat. Jeremy was next to him, looking around. And finally Malaki.

He wore handcuffs, and a chain connected his ankles. He stood entirely still, almost lifeless. When Dad pulled up to the left and parked, Malaki glanced over. We made eye contact. With no expression, he dropped his gaze to the cracked ground where weeds broke through.

I put my hand on the door, but Dad said, "Hold on."

"What?" I gestured outside. "They're waiting for us."

"I just…" He exhaled and said in a low voice, "You need to be careful here. Things could… If things go bad, get out. Run. Save yourself if you have to."

I smiled a little. I could tell it caught him off-guard.

"What's funny?" he asked.

"Nothing," I said. "I'll be safe. Don't worry."

We climbed out of his truck, and I thought about what he'd said. Not "I'll protect you" or "everything will be fine," but instead he told me to get away. Save myself.

I was right about Dad. He couldn't protect me, not from this. Maybe nobody could. But I sure as hell wouldn't run away. I had nothing to run to. Everything I wanted was inside this house somewhere.

Sunlight glinted off its broken windows. Dark birds waited on the jagged rooftop, watching us. A thousand flies were buzzing in my stomach.

With a deep breath, I turned toward the woods. Over the

police car and their heads, every tree waved back and forth, moving together. The wind picked up. Inside my chest, a dull drumbeat.

As we approached, Jeremy stuck a pistol into his waistband.

"Just that?" Dad asked him. "That's… small caliber, right?"

"Nine millimeters. That's all I'll need."

Sheriff Wheeler cleared his throat. "Shotgun in the truck?"

"Mmhm. We'll come back if we need it."

The sheriff took a deep breath. "Everyone ready?"

I locked eyes with Jeremy. He seemed to know more than he was letting on. I raised my eyebrows, and he turned away.

So, this is who I'm trusting with my life.

I'd survived the house once. The forest couldn't be much worse.

<> <> <>

Malaki and Sheriff Wheeler were at the front. Jeremy was right behind them, pointing out where to walk. Dad and I were in the back, not speaking.

"It's back there to the right," Jeremy said.

Malaki didn't speak the whole time as we passed the house. It fell behind us and out of mind, but I thought it was weird he didn't talk at all. Not to me, not to anyone. He didn't look back. He didn't laugh. Just a blank sheet of white, unlined paper.

On the ground, there were knotted roots and tangled weeds. It felt like pushing through a barrier with each step. Dark shadows moved in the underbrush and branches reached down to smack us in the face. This forest wanted to keep us out.

Birds chirped overhead, different than usual. It wasn't a song. It was more frantic, like a warning. They flew from branch to branch, high above. And a sharper call, like a vulture, circling too.

The sun streamed through the leaf canopy, painting strange patterns on the mossy ground. It flickered in and out, dancing with the trees.

"So, Malaki. What do you know about this place?" Jeremy asked. He was right behind him but still spoke really loud.

Malaki didn't respond.

Sheriff Wheeler said, "Let's hear it, boy."

Malaki shook his head. "I didn't agree to answer questions."

"I don't give a *shit* what you agreed to." Sheriff Wheeler stopped.

We were deep in the woods now, no buildings in sight. He grabbed Malaki by the shoulders and shook him, chains rattling.

"Listen here!" Sheriff Wheeler yelled. "You'll do what I say exactly." He shook him even harder. Malaki groaned in pain. "And you won't try any funny business. If you forget those rules..." The sheriff put one hand on his holster.

Malaki bowed his head, whimpering.

I spoke up, asking, "Malaki, have you been to this place before?"

He turned to look at me. His eyes were red and puffy, shoulders sagging. There was a bruise on his cheek that hadn't been there two days ago, as well as a thin cut.

"I have."

"So, why is it important?" Jeremy asked, getting in Malaki's face. "What do you know?" And why didn't you want Naomi to come?"

Malaki glared at Jeremy. He clenched his jaw, and I thought he might answer. He rose up a bit, standing taller. "Not always up to me. You would know, right?"

"Listen, asshole!"

"Try me, old man." Malaki glared. And then he spit in his face.

Jeremy drove his knee up into Malaki's crotch. When he doubled over, gasping, Jeremy brought his elbow down. It crashed into Malaki's shoulder, an awful crunch. He cried out and hit the ground.

Jeremy smirked as Malaki lay there in the dirt and leaves, pressing his forehead to the earth. He didn't try to get up.

"Understand yet?" Jeremy laughed.

"It's not what's in the church," Malaki hissed. "It's what's underneath."

"Get up," snapped Jeremy.

He stepped back and so did Sheriff Wheeler. Dad stood by, watching. I knew he was uneasy—tight lips, wrinkled nose—but he never tried to step in.

"I said get up!"

Malaki struggled to his knees. With chained ankles and hands cuffed together, he was having trouble standing up.

"Here." I stepped forward, pushing through Jeremy's shoulder, and extended a hand.

Malaki stared up at me, wide-eyed. Without a word, he grabbed my hand. I pulled, and he climbed to his feet. He didn't dust himself off or thank me. He didn't make eye contact.

I turned around to see Jeremy and Sheriff Wheeler shifting awkwardly. I wondered if they'd forgotten about me, so caught up in their hate.

"You don't have to act like that," I said, staring them down. "He'll show us. I know he will."

Malaki opened his mouth, but he didn't speak. I moved to the back of the group and thought I saw his lips quivering, but then he turned to face the front.

"Well, there you go, asshole." Jeremy clapped him hard on the same shoulder he'd elbowed. "Someone actually likes you.

Imagine that."

We moved on like nothing had happened, crunching twigs and shuffling leaves. But I couldn't stop thinking about it.

Since when had Jeremy been *that* kind of person?

I wanted to ask my dad about it, but he didn't look back at me. He wouldn't have answers, anyway. Probably just as confused.

I felt more disturbed now. Malaki was so quiet. Jeremy turned cruel. And whenever Sheriff Wheeler talked, his voice shook like I'd never heard before. Things were crazy off already.

But either way, our unsteady group marched along.

Ahead of us, I saw the church building. Small and simple. It was a moss-covered cube with a sharp-angled roof. We got closer, and I saw a tiny cross at the top. The tree branches around it reached out like twisted fingers.

Through my shirt, I pressed the clear quartz against my chest.

"Sure you don't want your shotgun?" Sheriff Wheeler asked.

Jeremy nodded. "No point carrying it. We'll be fine, though. Right, boy?"

Malaki nodded.

All of us walked up to the church. There was an open doorway, and inside I could barely make out dark benches. Nobody spoke. Even the birds were silent. The whole forest was holding its breath, waiting for something.

"There's a door inside," Jeremy said, watching Malaki intently. "Is that where you're taking us?"

He nodded again.

"Well. No reason to wait."

We all moved forward into the darkness, air choked with dust. What little sunlight came through the opening died right away. I noticed old books on the pews, some left open, pages falling apart.

"Bibles?" I asked.

Dad turned to look at me. His face had gone pale, and when he opened his mouth no words came out.

"Never mind." I put one arm around his back. "Just keep walking, Dad. We're fine."

He took another shaky step.

"Here's the door," Jeremy said. He turned to Malaki again. "Is it locked?"

Malaki shrugged. "You know as much as me."

Jeremy reached for the handle. The door opened inward, creaking on its hinges, revealing a dark stairway descending into nothingness. They were sharp, steep, but I knew we had to go down.

"There," Malaki said. He gestured to Jeremy. "Ladies first."

Jeremy scowled, but he did go first. Followed by Malaki, Sheriff Wheeler, Dad, and finally myself. The whole way down, I kept imagining the door closing behind us. Locked down here for eternity. But the deeper we went into nothing, the more I forgot. About the forest, the sun, and New Haven. There was only us and the dark.

Sheriff Wheeler had a flashlight, and he clicked it on. I followed the faltering, yellow light. There was a room at the bottom of the stairs with nothing in it. Entirely bare, all the walls and floors. Strange stains marked the room, but I chalked those up to… a long time ago or something. Malaki didn't stop, though. He continued across the room, and the sheriff lit the way.

"This," Malaki said with a wave, "is the tunnel. Stay quiet. There are… things we don't want to wake up."

Where I expected the back wall, there was nothing. The room stretched on, growing colder and narrower. Sheriff Wheeler shone his flashlight that direction, and I heard scampering, like rats, across the tunnel floor.

Just like the stairway, it was too dark to tell, but it seemed to run on straight for a long time. Malaki stared that way for a minute, listening. Then he stepped back.

"It goes from here to the house. And sometimes it's not empty. I guess today is our lucky day."

The deeper we went, the more everything smelled like damp earth and decay. There was definitely a faint odor like cat pee, too. A terrifying silence fell around us. I heard every footstep. Ahead of us, tiny feet scurried into the shadows. Every time the sheriff moved his flashlight, rats went running, spiders crawled on the walls. I felt terribly cold down here, shivering behind the group. When I looked back over my shoulder, I only felt worse, so I tried to keep my eyes straight ahead.

There was nothing behind me. And there could be anything at all hiding there.

"Are you okay?" Dad whispered from my left.

"I'm okay." I paused. "Are you?"

"Yeah… Keep going…"

The air around us felt heavy, and I struggled to keep moving on the uneven floor. The rough, stone walls had a pale glow in Sheriff Wheeler's light. It threw shadows to both sides, twisting on the strange drawings that must have been down here for a century. I wanted to look at the floor — footprints — but it had a slime coating, and beady rat-eyes stared back.

There was nothing to see. More of the same. The people in front of me were shadows walking. A black hole behind. I felt alone. The hallway ran on and on. The house couldn't *possibly* be this far away.

Maybe he's leading us somewhere worse.

What if she's not here?

Jeremy seemed to have the same thought.

"Where *exactly…*" — he lowered his voice. In this dead space, it was deafening — "…are you taking us?"

Malaki answered simply, "To her corpse."

Every time he mentioned Allison, I cringed. At times, I felt bad for him. The way he acted in the interrogation… How Jeremy yelled and abused him… But then I remembered *he* was the bad guy. Jeremy was on my side. Why did everything feel so mixed up right now?

No turning back. I took a deep breath. *Just keep going. Sort it out later.*

"And where's that?" Jeremy went on.

Malaki groaned and didn't respond.

"You're gonna answer me, or I'm gonna slam your head into this goddamn wall. Now choose."

"Okay." Malaki turned. I couldn't see his expression. "You want an answer? The truth? It was an accident. We… we didn't mean to come down this far. It just happened." He added, voice cracking, "It was an ac-accident."

Jeremy's silhouette looked back at me for some reason.

The hallway grew narrower as we went. At first, I didn't notice. Then, without discussion, we were moving in pairs.

"It was an accident," he said again, more quietly. "I'm trying my best now. I am."

The farther we walked, the less certain I felt. Wondering if I'd ever come back from this.

CHAPTER 15
NATE WOODS

"Boys! Get your shoes on. We're going!"

When Mom hollered up the stairs, I was playing MLB on the PlayStation like usual. Rhys stared out the window, and when I'd asked if he wanted to play, he'd refused.

I didn't move at first, although Rhys started putting on his shoes. When Mom came thundering up the stairs, repeating what she'd said, I finally turned off the console.

"Okay, okay," I grumbled.

"Hurry, will you!" she snapped. Then she turned and left, mumbling, "Can't tell *me* to stay put. Hell no. Not when all this —"

"It's time, now," Rhys said quietly.

"What do you mean?" I asked, reaching under the bed and pulling out my Nikes.

"Just get ready. You'll be fine." He took a deep breath, his shoulders rising and falling. "This is gonna be hard for me."

"What is, Rhys?"

"Remember that key from the attic?" he asked. "The one I was hiding up there?"

"Yeah…"

"I've gotta use it, now. I've gotta go back." He closed his eyes.

"Back to hell."

About ten minutes later, we came downstairs. Mom was rushing around, looking for something. I saw her come out of the big bedroom she shared with Dad, holding a gun. She gave me a look, shoved it in her purse, and then walked through the kitchen.

"Let's go."

It took another five minutes before we followed her. I think she would've chewed my head off if she hadn't been so nervous. I didn't know what was going on because I hadn't been paying attention. If I had, maybe I would've hurried. Maybe we would've gotten there sooner.

"What are we doing?" I asked, stepping off the porch and onto the gravel driveway.

Mom was sitting in her little green car with the door open. She had both hands on the wheel and the engine running.

"Going up there," she said. "Following your dad and sister."

"Oh."

I could've sat in the front of Mom's car—I almost never got that chance—but I decided to sit in the back with Rhys. I didn't want him to feel scared, and just the thought of going up there turned me inside-out.

Walking to the car, I looked over and thought, *This kid's terrified. I'll help him out.*

Turned out, I needed it more than him.

Mom drove through the hills, holding her steering wheel so hard her knuckles turned pale. She leaned up in the seat, sticking her head forward. It was the middle of the day, bright outside, so I knew she could see fine, she must've been nervous. And seeing her like that scared me.

The fabric seats in her car were warm from sitting in the sun all morning. They'd been like a heated blanket when we first climbed in. Even though it wasn't twelve yet, it was almost a hundred outside, and I felt sweat trickling down my sides. Rhys didn't offer much comfort. He sat on the left, looking out the window as Mom's green car rolled up and down the hills. There was a nice view of New Haven from up here, but I'd seen it so many times, and I had other things on my mind.

"Can you turn the AC on?" I asked.

"Oh. Sorry." Mom turned the dial, and I felt a steady stream of cold air blow toward us.

"Watch out!" Rhys yelled.

She looked up and screamed, "Shit!" slamming on the brakes. The car screeched to a halt, and the end swung around a bit. Right in front of us — running across the road — were four deer. They all stopped and turned. Their large, black eyes watched us for a minute, then they took off again, heading away from this terrible place, heading somewhere safer and better.

"Oh my God." Mom leaned her head against the steering wheel. She was breathing so hard I could hear it from the back seat. "I... Oh God..."

"It's okay, Miss Naomi." Rhys leaned forward and touched her elbow gently. "We're all okay. Keep going."

"Right. Right, let's keep going." She straightened up and cleared her throat.

My own heart was beating outta my chest. "You okay, Mom?"

More confidently, she answered, "Yeah."

We didn't see any more deer, maybe there weren't any left. Everything had run away. Everybody leaving. Except for us, heading to a place nobody should ever go.

"I'm gonna have to leave you two in the car," Mom said as the engine hummed, going downhill. "So I'll leave it running when we get there." Mom adjusted her grip on the wheel. The engine squealed as she pressed down on the gas, and we blasted up the next hill. "But I didn't want to leave you home alone. We all need to be together."

It sounded like she was trying to convince herself she'd done the right thing. I didn't have an opinion, really. I just thought I'd rather be at home, playing my baseball game. And the closer we got to the end, the more I wanted to be anywhere else.

I pointed out, "But if we're in the car—"

"You'll be safer." She looked at me in the rearview mirror. Her face was scrunched together, and her hands started shaking. "Just lock the doors. You'll be okay. You could always drive, right? Like your uncle taught you?" She shook her head. "Doesn't matter. I'll be back in no time. With your dad and Kaia."

Me and Rhys knew what was going on. Kind of. I'd overheard their conversations after the sheriff left, and I knew they were going up to the house. Without Mom. It had something to do with Allison. The sheriff would go, of course, and probably Jeremy. They mentioned his name. But the part that stood out was they were taking Kaia and not Mom.

So, we didn't know *exactly* what was happening, but it didn't matter. They were all doing something risky. Enough to make me nervous. I would stay here, on the warm seats, and sweat through it—but I *could* probably drive away if I needed to. I'd kinda learned a few months ago from my uncle.

Rhys didn't speak the rest of the way. I glanced over a few times, but he never turned. His eyes were locked on the world rushing below us. He was sweating, too, and for a moment the beads of sweat looked red. Like drops of blood on his skin.

The closer we got, the more I felt like somebody was sitting on my chest. It was harder and harder to breathe. Harder to keep my eyes open. A thick, dark curtain covered the sun.

— Kaia's face is stone hard. The police lights paint her in red and blue. She leans on Mom, who is talking. I see Mom's jaw working. I don't hear any words. She looks so afraid, more than I've ever seen.

Behind them, I can see the house outlined against the dark sky. The moment replays in my head, countless nights, time after time. Dead windows, and sometimes there were faces in them.

Dad runs toward my sister. I can't hear anything they're saying, because I'm in the truck. With Rhys. But everyone is so shaken. They can barely stand. The weight is too much. It presses on me, now. My parents collapse. My sister falls. The house even caves in.

There's nothing left now except us in the truck, colored in red and blue police lights. —

Mom pressed hard on the brakes, jolting the car. I unfroze and pushed away the memory, but the house was right in front of me. Towering over. I still couldn't breathe right. I heard myself wheezing, and I turned to Rhys, but he was staring outside still. Not even looking at the building.

Mom parked right beside Dad's truck. There was a police car, too, but both of them were empty. She reached for the door handle and paused.

"Whatever you do, stay in the car." She turned around and locked eyes with me. "Got it, you two?"

"I will."

"And you?"

Rhys nodded.

As if I had a choice. I didn't think I could move for any reason. My legs felt like I'd run ten miles. My body was glued to the warm seat. Everything outside the car moved from side to side, but inside we were safe. And terrified.

"I love you, boys." Mom opened the door and stepped out,

ducking her head. "I'll be back very soon. I promise."

Before I could respond, she slammed the door and took off. She didn't go toward the main house or the front door but instead turned right. Past the mold-green fountain. Into the trees. They swallowed her, and she was gone.

I focused on my breathing. Deep inhales. Exhale through the nose. I tried not to think about what could happen. I pictured Mom coming back to us, holding hands with Dad, with Kaia right beside them. A calm sunset that night as we all sat on the back porch. Everything would be okay.

"Will you keep a secret, Nate?"

I opened my eyes and saw Rhys staring at me.

"What?" I frowned at him. This didn't seem like the time or place.

"I need…" He hesitated and rubbed his hands together. "I need to go inside the house." He dug in a pocket and pulled out the key he'd shown me the day before.

"What? *Why?*"

"I have to. Right now." He offered a smile. "But you can't tell anybody. It'll ruin everything if you do."

"You can't leave—"

"Nate." He leaned forward and lowered his voice. "They said if I ever came back, I could never go. Said they'd keep me… But I have to. I gotta go back. It's for Kaia, okay?"

I nodded, holding back tears. I didn't want to be alone in this car. Outside this house. I knew I could never leave. I couldn't even open the door. Both arms wrapped around myself, ankles crossed, I was stuck.

"Nate, I gotta do it. I'll be quick. Promise."

And then Rhys opened the door.

"Wish me luck." He took a deep, shaky breath. "I hope I see

you again."

He shut it behind him and ran to the front door of the house, jumping up the steps. I felt my whole body shaking as he approached it, shoved the key in his pocket, and opened the door without it. The mouth of the house swung open, and tiny Rhys stood in front of it, not backing down.

He turned and waved at me. Then he stepped inside, and the door shut behind him.

I couldn't move. I was alone.

CHAPTER 16
KAIA WOODS

Malaki and Sheriff Wheeler — still holding the flashlight — were in the front. Jeremy and Dad squeezed together behind them, and somehow I'd been pushed to the back. I felt more vulnerable than ever back here. *Anything* could sneak up behind me.

I asked, "Jeremy, you said you have a gun, right?"

He chuckled. "You bet. Worried about this idiot?" He shoved Malaki's head.

"No. I'm not. Leave him alone," I huffed. "It's just awful down here."

I was never very brave. I wouldn't even pick the back of the line for a cheap-scare haunted house. But Allison had always been into that creepy stuff, so I did it for her. And I would do this a hundred times over. For her.

I swallowed my fear every minute and didn't look back.

Everything changed a moment later.

For the first time, there were noises ahead. We took a few more steps as if nothing had changed. But the noises grew louder and rhythmic. One dull thud after the other. Like heavy pillows smacking the rough floor.

Dum, dum. Dum, dum.

"Who is that?" the sheriff asked.

The steps echoed around us, but I knew it was coming from the front.

Faster now. *Dum dum.*

We stopped walking. Everyone looked around at each other. The sheriff's unwavering flashlight showed the dark hallway ahead. Slimy walls and rat shadows.

The sound grew closer. It started to slow down. We couldn't see anything yet, but I felt colder now.

I shivered and hugged myself. "Malaki… What is that?"

Jeremy pushed his way to the front, standing beside the sheriff. I saw Sheriff Wheeler hand over the flashlight—a gruff "Hold this"—and pull out his gun.

"Malaki?" I repeated.

He didn't answer. He stared ahead without a sound.

"Damn it," Jeremy fumbled for a minute and almost dropped it. He was reaching at his waist. His hands were shaking. "I can't—"

"Here." Dad stepped forward and took the light.

The three of them were squeezed together. Malaki and I stood behind.

Dum, dum. Dum, dum.

Jeremy drew his gun. All of us were frozen.

The footsteps had slowed down again. There was still noise, but it changed. It was softer and slower. Maybe shuffling feet. Maybe something heavy dragging on the floor.

It was muffled. We still couldn't see.

The three men stepped forward. My dad gripped the flashlight, which shook. Jeremy and Sheriff Wheeler raised their firearms and aimed straight ahead. There was nothing to aim at. The black mouth of the hallway glowed yellow with no teeth.

Malaki took a step closer to me. Our shoulders were nearly touching now. He could have reached out and grabbed me. His breaths were heavy, wheezing. My legs began to shake and my arms were going numb.

In the moment before he spoke, I thought about how strange this was. It couldn't be real. I didn't feel afraid enough. I was shaking, sure, and I had a racehorse for a heartbeat, but I didn't feel gut-sick terror like I had inside the house.

Until he spoke.

"I didn't think it was here," he moaned quietly.

"What'd you say?"

"You have to go deeper," Malaki whispered, leaning over. His chains shook as he reached out, but he didn't touch me. "Stay to the right. Don't go with Jeremy."

"What right?" I tried to keep my voice quiet. I think the others were too focused to hear. "What do you mean?"

"This is it," he whimpered. His breath smelled like the inside of a dead fish. "I'm sorry. I really am. But I'm trying to… fix things. It really was an accident. And it wasn't supposed to be here."

"What wasn't?" His shadow turned to face forward, holding his chin up. "Malaki, *what* are you talking about?"

"I loved her," Malaki whimpered. "I really did. Please save her. I didn't want it to go like this. It wasn't supposed to… You can do it, though. You can easily do it. Please take our place."

Jeremy called back, "Kaia! What is he say — ?"

But he stopped when the thing screamed.

It unleashed a horrible, high-pitched sound. Like a thousand animals dying at once. I forgot about the sky and the trees and even Allison for a moment. My lungs stopped working. I was bending.

Then it charged.

A roar. Heavy footsteps and echoing screams. It launched from the darkness, running on all fours. For a moment, in the yellow light, I saw.

The muscular, thin beast, covered in black hair. Thick, sharp teeth. Eyes like hell.

Gunshots went off. The air erupted and smelled like lead.

"Get back! Get back!"

I nearly tripped. The men started backing up, and the beast reared on its back legs. Dull thuds as their bullets struck. It roared, but it did not fall.

The flashlight shook, and the tunnel was spinning. The dark creature scrambled. Long nails scratched on the floor. I couldn't hear myself scream as the gunshots erupted again. Flashing lights and burning eyes. My head nearly split open.

"Stay to the side," Malaki hissed.

I was too stunned to move.

"*Side,* Kaia. Get over. This is your chance. You're better than me."

"What do you mean?"

Malaki shoved me to the side. I smacked against the wall and dropped with a thud. All of his warnings and apologies clashed in my head.

"What the hell, boy?" Jeremy yelled.

He and Sheriff Wheeler stopped firing. They struggled for a second.

Dad yelled out, clutching at his leg. I saw blood on his hands. "Fuck, Jeremy, you shot *me!*" He dropped the flashlight.

As Jeremy reached for it, Malaki pushed through. I watched from the ground.

"Run!" Malaki screamed, not looking back. And then he threw himself forward.

Jeremy held the flashlight up just long enough to see. Malaki raced ahead, waving his arms. The creature stood up on two legs like a human. Its head — dark and wide with a thick jaw — brushed against the ceiling. With two long arms, it reached out and grabbed his head and feet.

I'll never forget his screams. The way its sharp claws ripped him from both ends. And then it opened its huge jaw — a hundred, thick teeth — and chewed through him.

"Let's go! Quick!"

Everybody turned to run, but I couldn't. I felt tears leaking down my cheeks, but they couldn't be mine.

"Kaia! Come on!" Dad yelled from somewhere. He cursed, grabbing at his bleeding leg.

Then I was on my feet and running with them toward the underground room and the staircase. Jeremy held the flashlight down, so we ran in the dark. Dad was limping, muttering, "My leg, you fucking idiot," and everybody was gasping for air. Malaki's screams were gone. But awful sounds carried on behind us — flesh tearing, juices squeezed.

Something grabbed me from the floor. It tripped my ankle, and I collapsed. My elbow smashed against the ground. I felt white-hot pain shoot up to my shoulder. My head hit next, and I saw stars in the dark tunnel.

I tried to cry out, but it came in groans, not words. The others ran on. Dad. Jeremy. Their steps echoed, going and going.

"Wait…" I could barely breathe. I had no hope of screaming.

I couldn't see anything. I bumped my head into the wall and winced. Everything burned. My elbow throbbed — maybe broken. I might pass out any second.

Not here. Not now. So close.

I almost cried when I heard the horrible, high-pitched scream again, and it was closer.

"No…"

Everything started to twist in my vision. The stars were getting brighter. I wanted to sob, and I wanted to be with her. Was this what it took?

The creature screamed again. Those clawed feet were only seconds away now.

And then little fingers wrapped around my ankle. Something pulled me toward the wall.

I tried to fight, but they said, "Quit! I'm saving you!"

Right away, I knew the voice. I slid across the ground easily — slime — and *through* the wall. But when my head bumped something above me — another blast of pain — I realized it was a small, two-foot gap at the very bottom.

On the other side of the tunnel wall, I gasped for breath. The beast scratched against it, hollering and thrashing. My stone shield didn't give. I moved away, scared he might reach through the gap. Then his movements stopped.

Silence. My heart pounded. A terrible head pain. My elbow could barely move. But I'd survived.

"Kaia…"

CHAPTER 17
BENJAMIN "CLIFF" WOODS

"I can't! I can't go this fast!"

I followed behind Jeremy and the sheriff, limping. With each step, a jolt of pain shot through my leg. They sprinted through the dark, and I was stumbling behind, Kaia somewhere by me. I couldn't focus. I couldn't see. I was pushing through pain with every step, grinding my teeth.

"Come on!" Jeremy snapped. He was still holding the flashlight, pointing ahead. "Hurry, Cliff!"

I was breathing so hard I couldn't talk. Barely thinking. But I kept moving, one step at a time.

Ignore the pain. Ignore the side-stitch.

The darkness was suffocating. Far behind, those awful, squelching sounds made me nauseous.

Malaki. Screaming. Ripped apart. Crying out.

Don't picture it. Don't think. Just move.

"You shot me, damn it!" I yelled. "Jeremy, slow down."

"We can't. Get to the truck… Get my shotgun."

Sheriff Wheeler didn't speak. We didn't slow down. Jeremy led the way, and we emerged into the dark, underground room and left the tunnel. It was instantly a few degrees warmer, and I saw light ahead, peering in from the open door.

"Up, up!" Jeremy yelled. "Let's go. We're taking this thing down."

The sheriff and him leapt up the steps. I hopped the first two, slipped, and barely caught myself. A bolt of pain shot through my forearm. Gritting my teeth, I climbed the rest.

Don't fall. Don't die.

"Sorry, Kaia," I panted. "I'm trying to go fast."

There was no answer. I couldn't think straight. Was I bleeding out?

Wheezing bad, I reached the top of the stairs and ran through the open doorway. My lungs were about to burst. My entire leg stung. Everything went hazy, and all the sunlight only made things blurrier. I thought I might die for a few seconds, but the sensation passed.

I took a seat on one of the old pews and bent over, heaving. When I glanced up, the three of us were alone in the forgotten, filthy church. Jeremy and Sheriff Wheeler exchanged looks. They stared at me and then at the dark doorway.

I watched it, too. That void. Nothing came through. There was no sound.

"Kaia?" I called out.

I hobbled to the door frame and peered down the staircase.

"Kaia?" a little louder.

Jeremy answered softly behind me. "Cliff..."

"Kaia!" I yelled. "Kaia! Oh, fuck, Jeremy. She's not here. She's not... Where is she, Jeremy?"

For the second time in five minutes, I thought I might die. This might kill me. And if it didn't, Naomi would.

"Cliff..."

I turned around. Jeremy and the sheriff were wide-eyed. I

fumbled for any words, choking on all the phrases.

"I've gotta go back down," I said, finally.

"Just wait," Jeremy said. "Hold on now."

"This is it," the sheriff mumbled. "We're done for. We ain't gonna make it."

"Calm down. Both of you." Jeremy groaned and pressed a fist to his forehead. "She's gotta be hiding somewhere. She's gotta be fine. If it got her, it wouldn't be chasing us, and—"

Right on cue. A low, growling sound from the room below. I felt the ground shaking. Before I could react, Jeremy leapt forward, slammed the door, and pulled me away.

"Let's go, Cliff! We gotta get to the truck!"

Sheriff Wheeler was already outside. He'd bolted through the rows of pews as soon as we heard it. But I stood in place for another minute, my injured leg burning and unsteady.

Jeremy gripped my wrist. "Cliff. Now. *Run.*"

His voice didn't sound scared enough. Maybe that's why I didn't move at first. It was urgent, sure. But it wasn't afraid.

I frowned at him. The ground shook more.

"Come *on,*" he begged. "We've gotta kill this thing if you wanna save her."

My feet moved on their own. A few steps, and then a sprint. We dashed out into the warm, soft air. I smelled leaves and dirt and heard the wind again, whispering stories.

The door behind us flew open. It crashed against the wall and splintered. I glanced over my shoulder as we ran away from the church building, saw it standing in the shadows. A massively tall beast. Strangely human and covered in muscle. Gnashing its sharp teeth, it crouched on all fours. But it didn't chase after.

"What the hell is that?" I yelled. "An animal?"

Neither of them answered. By the time we stopped—a football

field away from the church — we were all gasping for air.

"See," Jeremy panted. "See. It wouldn't... be chasing us if it... if it had her."

Again, no fear in his voice. He sounded confident almost.

"But what do I do?" I asked him.

Sheriff Wheeler was standing to the side, leaning against a tree. I heard him sobbing — low, guttural noises, like he tried to hold them back — and when he turned around, there was a wet patch all down the front of his pants.

"We can't." He struggled to speak. "We can't do it. We're done for."

"Shut up, Sheriff." Jeremy reached into his pocket and pulled out his phone. "Come on. Let's get to the truck. I'm gonna call some folks from town. Backup is already on the way. The more, the better. You saw that thing bleeding after we shot it?"

The sheriff mumbled something and shook his head.

"Hey!" Jeremy walked over to him and grabbed him by the collar. "Listen to me! That thing bleeds. I saw it. You saw it. It bleeds, and with my shotgun and the townspeople, we're gonna kill this monster. But you gotta keep it together."

Sheriff Wheeler nodded.

They kept talking on the way back to the truck as we moved through the forest, but I couldn't pay attention. I kept looking over my shoulder at the church building — there was no sound.

Where is she now?

What have I done?

CHAPTER 18
KAIA WOODS

Behind the wall, safe at last, I stared up at my rescuer.

"What are you doing here?!"

"Shh!" Rhys whispered, "I'll explain. Just come with me."

"But… I need to go get—"

"I'll show you where she is."

Those words stopped my heart for a minute.

"O-okay."

Dressed in dark clothes, Rhys helped me stand. I kept my head low at first, but when I stood fully there was no ceiling to avoid.

"How did you get in here?" I asked quietly. "Or down here? Wherever we are."

"I know my way around," he said. "I've been here lots of times. That's why I knew I could help you."

He led me in the pitch blackness. At first, I didn't think I could go on, but the farther we went, the steadier I felt. Of course, my head was still aching. There was a constant, sharp pain in my elbow. I felt dizzy as hell. But it was easy to ignore.

Everything was so dumb. So pointless. All the shit leading to this. It was like a dream. I couldn't even remember all that shit now.

I reached up and felt the clear quartz stone behind my shirt. I pressed it hard into my bare chest until the skin burned.

"It's this way," Rhys said, and he sounded like a little kid again. His hand reached back in the dark and fumbled for mine. "Hold my hand. Please."

"Okay."

"I've been here before, but it's still scary. And I don't wanna get lost from you."

For a few minutes, we kept walking. This side-tunnel — I had no clue if we were actually on the side — was worse than the other. The air down here was cold and damp. Everything smelled like mold and mud. So dark, too. We didn't have a flashlight, so it pressed in hard. Walking along, trying not to let it crush me.

What if she's not here? What if there's nothing?

The floor was slick in spots. I didn't know what it was and I didn't want to. The longer we went, the colder I felt. I began to shiver, and the darkness wasn't so easy to hold off. It started to reach inside me. Not just pressing but crawling in.

There could be anything two feet from my face... A body, a snake, the whole black sea...

"Hold on." I stopped and let go of his hand. "Hold on, Rhys."

"What?" He sounded impatient and nervous. "We can't stop. It's not safe here. Not 'til the end."

"I... Why is this taking so long?"

"It's not exactly quick," he said.

"But how do I... Why should I trust you?"

Rhys groaned. "We don't have *time* for this. You have to."

"No. No, I don't." I swallowed my fear and said, "Tell me what's really going on. And find a light, damn it. I hate this... this dark."

"In a minute," he said, reaching for my hand again. "I'll find a light soon. But you… you don't wanna see what's around us right now."

"What's—?"

"Come on." His small fingers squeezed into mine. "I'll explain. Just keep walking."

So I did. He was right, really. I didn't have a choice now.

"First, we gotta walk faster. I'm serious. You think that monster doesn't know a way around?"

I gulped. "Okay. Okay, let's go. I'll go faster."

"Alright. Good." He went on. "We followed you here. Your mom and Nate and me. But I snuck in through the front door—they're outside, they're fine, don't worry—'cause I had to come help you. I know this place. I've been through the whole thing. And that stalker? He's been coming a lot, so I knew Allison must be here."

"What? The stalker?"

"The person watching us. You haven't seen him as much because he already got you. He has Allison, so he got you. But he's been trying for more. And he's been… following me."

Rhys hesitated. He cleared his throat. "We're almost there now."

He stopped walking and I bumped into him.

"Sorry, Rhys."

He said, "It's okay."

I heard him fidgeting with something, and then a flashlight clicked on. He held it up, and his face was deeply serious. More serious than I've ever seen a twelve-year-old look. It disturbed me.

"There's a door."

He pointed the flashlight ahead. There was a wooden door set in a stone wall. Something green grew on the wall, and an unknown liquid dripped from the ceiling. Worms hung down, too, and spiderwebs and ooze.

"Through there," he said. "But don't look too hard. This place sticks in your nightmares."

Rhys stepped forward and pushed open the door. He went first, and I followed.

"Close the door," he said once we passed through.

I shut it. When I turned around to face him, my stomach dropped.

We were in a huge room, a hundred feet tall. It smelled like rotting wood and decaying meat. The smell was so strong, I clutched a hand to my face and gagged. There were a few fading lightbulbs hanging from the ceiling, just enough to see by. And once I'd looked around, I realized light wasn't a gift here. It was a curse. After seeing, I could never forget.

To our right, there was a stone wall, just as slimy and disgusting as everything else down here. Strange fungus grew on it. Even stranger insects and slugs moved around, so it looked like the whole wall constantly shifted in slime. Chains hung, too, empty and rusted.

But to the left… It was worse than anything.

A wall of cages stacked on each other. They were like small prison cells, stacked three-high, and each row had fifty or more. It covered the whole wall, and it spread into the darkness ahead where the light bulbs stopped. Little whimpers came from some cells. They didn't sound human, but I couldn't find strength to ask.

"This way," Rhys whispered.

I followed him without a word. Passing by, I noticed the cells were made of metal. Everything had a faded, chipped layer of paint. It looked ragged and haunted in here. The smell got worse the deeper we went. The small sounds of pain grew louder. And before I knew it… before I could even imagine…

"Allison!"

She was standing with her back to us. Both arms hung limply at her side, barely more than bones. But she was standing. She could stand.

I pressed my face to the bars and gripped them with both hands.

"It's me! It's Kaia! Allison!"

She turned around.

It was like waking up on a perfect Saturday in October but death is at your door.

She stared back, and I had such intense love running through me it ached. My stomach churned, and I almost doubled over and grabbed it. I couldn't move for a minute. I couldn't think. She was there. She was alive. Those eyes looked back, and it was her, really her.

Only feet away. Breathing. Beautiful. Somehow, someway, still so beautiful.

But the intense love made it worse as I scanned her body and saw the future scars.

I'd never felt that emotion before—watching someone you desperately love being torn apart. I hoped I'd never feel it again.

Allison stared back from behind bars. Her mouth opened, and those lips—her gorgeous smile—were bloodied. She was missing teeth. Her skin was stretched tight over her bones. Allison's face was like a sunken mask. She gaped at me, not saying a word. She kept looking, even as I started to cry.

"Allison, I'm here to save you. Ally? Ally, can you hear me?"

She nodded slowly. Her clothes were torn to shreds. Deep cuts stood out on her chest and midsection. Bruises on her shoulders. When she held up her hands, all ten fingernails were long and jagged. Some of her fingers were crooked. I couldn't see any horrible injuries—no glaring signs of abuse. But her eyes were different than before. They stared back, and they saw through me, and I wanted to hold her so badly it burned.

"Ally, I'm gonna get you out. I'm gonna get you home."

She shook her head. "Leave, please. Don't let them find…" Her face twitched and she closed her mouth tightly. She moaned quietly, closing her eyes.

"I need to get her out," I said, turning to Rhys. "I need to."

He handed me the flashlight and reached for the door, gently shook it, but it didn't open.

"It's locked." He stuck one hand in a pocket and yanked out a small key. "Just a… second…" He messed with the right side of the door, rattling the bars. "What the…"

"What's going on?"

He turned around. "This key doesn't work. I thought… thought it worked on all the doors down here. I'm—"

"So, it's locked? What… what can we do?" I ran my hands around the door, reaching for the edges. There was a lock on the right side. "There's… What can we try? Rhys, what—?"

"I don't…" Rhys covered his mouth with both hands. "I don't know… Oh, no. The key won't… Oh no, he's gonna… they're gonna…"

He started to wail, and then he dropped his voice to a whisper. He was breathing faster now. "Kaia. We have to go. If they find me…" He pulled the flashlight from me. "The key only works on the first door, these aren't—I'm so sorry, we have to go—"

"I'm not leaving," I grumbled. "I'll figure it out."

I kept clutching at the lock. It wouldn't budge. Shaking the door gently but not too loud, I tried to feel around it.

"Damn it, damn it…"

"Please go." Allison knelt down on the ground beside me. She reached through the bars and grabbed my hands. "Kaia.

Honey. I'm fine here. I'll die here."

"No!" I growled. I refused to look over. Her thumbs—her frail, bloodied thumbs—rubbed against my palm. They were so weak. "I can't… I can't leave—"

"Don't come back," she pleaded. "Forget me. Please. Please just go and forget."

I turned to her. I was full-on crying now. So close to her. Touching her. And I couldn't get this fucking cage unlocked and there was no way to fix this. No way to get her out, no way either of us would ever leave.

Holding her hands, I stayed there for a minute that felt like hours. I was sobbing, and she made no sound. I felt Rhys shifting behind me, but I didn't turn back. I stared at her. Through the bars. And it almost crushed me, the way things weren't fair.

"I would take your place," I whispered to her. "Ally, baby. I would… I would do anything. Take me. They can take me. You don't deserve this… You aren't—"

"Shhh." She frowned. "You can't—"

"I would! I want to!"

"Come on, Kaia!" Rhys whispered. "He could find us any minute. I can't let him… We don't—"

Allison dropped my hands and stared at him.

"You know him?" She shuddered. "How… how do you know *him*? Who *are* you?"

"Rhys, get back," I snapped at him. "You're freaking her out." I turned to him, and that's when I saw.

Rhys stumbled and saw my face in the flashlight. "What, Kaia?"

"What… what is that?"

I pointed one shaking finger at the opposite side of the room.

CHAPTER 19
BENJAMIN "CLIFF" WOODS

Heading back to the truck, Jeremy was talking with Sheriff Wheeler the whole time.

"You can do this, Sheriff. One more time. One more day. Just hold it together, man."

"I can't!" he whimpered. "Jeremy… my chest… I… I need an ambulance. I'm having a heart attack."

"You aren't having a goddamn heart attack, Sheriff. We talked about this. It's like that night with your dog. You're having a panic—"

Before he could finish, I heard Naomi yell out, "Ben!"

I looked up from the ground where I'd been kicking sticks and leaves. She was running toward us from the edge of the forest. I held my breath.

Beside me, Jeremy muttered, "Oh, shit, man."

"Ben, I've been looking—" She stopped dead in her tracks. Still thirty feet away, I saw her expression turn from relief to utter horror.

"Naomi, I—"

"Where is she?" Naomi screamed in a way I'd never heard. It cut through my chest. It collapsed my windpipe. "Ben, what have you done?"

Everything changed. She ran at me. Jeremy stepped back. Sheriff Wheeler was already on the ground. I stood there, arms open wide, readying my apologies.

"Ben!" She shoved me in the chest, hard.

I stumbled back. "Hold on—"

And then her fists. She whacked my head, my shoulder, punched my chest. Each blow stung, and I moved away. She shoved hard again, and I fell to the ground.

"Shit, stop! Naomi, stop!"

She backed away, holding her face, sobbing. I sat up, reaching for my leg.

"Damn it, Naomi, I—"

"You fucking liar!" she yelled. She approached again, and I scurried away, thinking she might start kicking me. "You piece of shit. You're a—"

"I didn't—"

"Stop! Stop lyin'!" She hugged herself and those furious eyes burned into my skull. "I *know* you lied 'bout Rhys. You ain't called anybody! And you said… keep her safe… Ben, how *could you?*"

I sat there, not saying a word. Because she was right, and I knew it. And now we all knew it.

"What happened?" she asked, turning to Jeremy.

For a moment, he didn't answer. The sun was beating down, and I was covered in sweat. My leg covered in blood. The sheriff had pissed himself. Nobody knew what to say.

"Please, tell me."

"Well… people are on the way," Jeremy explained. "I called… every emergency vehicle. Local folk. Everybody's bringing their guns. We've got… We'll be fine."

"Where's my baby?" Naomi pressed.

"She—"

And then everything changed again. We heard a howling sound from the church, and my blood turned cold. The sheriff went pale, and Jeremy closed his eyes for a moment. I scrambled to my feet.

I managed to shout, "Naomi, run!"

It shot out from the church building, racing on all fours. The giant wolf head speared between trees, a straight shot for us. Sheriff Wheeler hurried to his feet, but we were all running now. I fell behind, limping. Our footsteps thundering. The beast closing in.

"Faster, fast—!" I tried to yell, but I couldn't breathe.

We were near the edge of the trees. Sheriff Wheeler turned around and fired a few shots. The beast reared on its hind legs, screeching.

Naomi said, "Come on, Sheriff!"

"Just go," he said, gritting his teeth. "I'll hold it off."

"No, you can't—"

Before she could finish, a high-pitched whistle pierced the air. Coming from the house. It was sharp and distant but undeniable. It blew once, twice, three times. On the hottest day of the year, it sent a chill down my spine. As Sheriff Wheeler aimed his gun, the beast paused in its tracks.

It turned toward the house, sniffing. And then sped away in that direction.

Nobody spoke for a minute. The four of us grouped together. I felt sweat dripping from my elbows and sat down again, hands on my bleeding leg. It was hard to tell with all the trees in the way, but the beast went toward the back of the house and then vanished around the corner.

A cool breeze swept across my face. I groaned and lay down on the ground.

"Where the *hell* is my daughter?" Naomi asked again. She crouched beside me, grabbing my collar.

"She's safe," I said, still catching my breath. "She's—"

"*Where?*"

Jeremy cut in. "She's hiding. We got caught under the church. There's a tunnel, and the… Malaki gave himself up. But she's hiding somewhere. I know she's safe. I'm certain. That thing… it wanted us, not her."

"Safe where?" Naomi asked. "Where do we go? How can I get her?"

Jeremy didn't answer. I couldn't. And Naomi's face grew more and more infuriated as the seconds ticked by.

Sheriff Wheeler said out of nowhere, "The whistle."

All heads turned in his direction.

The sheriff was pale and his shoulders slumped. He held his gun loosely and stared at the trigger. Jeremy reached out an arm for support, but the sheriff didn't move an inch.

"Who blew that whistle?" he asked.

Jeremy said, "Sheriff, I'm not sure, but at least—"

"Who, Jeremy? We searched that house. Searched the whole hills. How… Why haven't…?" He bowed his head.

"Sheriff, it's okay," I offered.

He shook his head. "I've failed. I've failed you all."

Minutes later, the emergency vehicles arrived and an army of pickup trucks. Jeremy took command and started telling everyone where to park, what the plan was. Naomi and I sat together, not speaking. Sheriff Wheeler was nearby, picking blades of grass like a child.

"Jeremy wants to go in, I bet. Wants to take an army down there."

Naomi didn't answer.

"I'm sorry, Naomi. But it'll just be—"

"Don't talk, Ben." She hugged herself tightly and closed her eyes. "Don't talk. I don't wanna hear a single… No more of your fucking lies."

CHAPTER 20
KAIA WOODS

Behind Rhys, halfway across the massive room of metal cages, there was a woman standing there. I saw her silhouette, and when Rhys turned with the flashlight, she was clearer and more familiar than ever.

She was completely still with thin, dark hair hanging around her like a curtain. Just like last time, she wore a linen dress with a high neck. I couldn't see her arms in the long, sheer fabric flowing down.

"What, Kaia?" Rhys turned back to me.

"Shine the light over there!" I hissed.

He did so, staring hard at the spot.

"Keep it there," I said and hurried over.

She was staring at the ground when I approached.

"You," I said. I stopped a good distance from her. "Do you remember me?"

She raised her head a few inches. I couldn't see her eyes, but the woman had sharp cheekbones and skin so pale it almost glowed. She had freckles around her nose, and lips the color of the sky.

"I told you help would come," she said.

"Have you… Did you write those letters?"

"I can't." She stared at me blankly. "They would never allow it. What did they say?"

"I thought you… Never mind. I need my friend, because someone wanted me to come here, and I'm *not* leaving. We can't get—"

"Shhh. Listen. Get out. You don't belong in the cellar."

"And neither does she!" I snapped. "So, if you want me gone, you have to let me take her. I'm not leaving."

"Your friend… she will never be the same," the woman said. I saw a tear roll down her lips and fall away. "She's seen us—all of us—and she might not remember, but she'll never be the same."

"*Please,*" I begged. "I don't care. I love her. I'm taking her home, or I'm staying here, and I'll die with her. You don't scare me. None of this shit scares me. What… what really scares me is losing her. I won't let that happen."

She raised her head and looked at me with penetrating, pale eyes.

"I won't leave," I said firmly. "I'd switch places with her if I could. Anything for her."

She didn't answer at first. She continued to watch me, and I thought I saw her frown.

"Say something!"

Her lips parted, and she spoke softly. "If you do this, you will never escape the pull."

"I don't care!"

"They will be watching you. Following you. They may be already."

"That's fine, I just need—"

"Listen. Listen to me." She extended a closed hand. "If you take this, you will have to take her place. One day."

"I'll do it. I'll do anything. Just… help me."

I reached out just as she opened her fist.

A small, silver key fell out and landed on my palm.

It stung when I first grabbed it, but the feeling faded.

"Thank you," I said quickly, turning away. "Thank you, thank you."

"I am sorry." She bowed her head. "I will keep the others away until you can leave. But now… your days are numbered."

I ran back to the cage. Rhys stared at me with wide eyes and shook his head. He tried to ask, "What the hell was that?" but I blocked him out. With fumbling hands, I unlocked the door. It swung outward — with a thousand creaks — and then she was in my arms.

"Come on," I said, wrapping both arms around her. "Come on, Ally. We gotta go quick."

Rhys led the way and held the flashlight. The whole way back — through the side-tunnel and across the slime floor, ignoring everything around us, wobbling toward the end — I held her hand and wrapped my fingers between hers.

"Where did you get that key?" Rhys hissed as we moved quickly and carefully.

"From the woman. Didn't… did you see her?"

"I didn't see anybody," he snapped. "Kaia… are you okay?"

"Yeah, I'm…" I looked at Allison, clinging to my arm. "I'm more than okay."

"What did she… say to you?"

I hesitated before answering. "She… gave me the key and said she'd keep us safe 'til we get out."

"And?"

"Nothing else," I lied. "That's it."

It was later in the day when we finally emerged. Late afternoon or evening. We climbed the stairs together leading to the church and left it all behind. At the top, she stumbled, and her legs gave out. I carried her from that point on. Between the dusty pews and through the open doorway. She wore a wedding dress. She was half of my soul.

The air was full of wedding bells and a beautiful choir. Crowds of people in the distance, wearing their finest wedding-day clothes — waiting for us, it seemed. Rhys hurried toward them as I brought her into the sunlight. I knelt down in the grass and caught my breath. Everything ached. My arms and legs had nothing left. I had nothing left.

But I had her.

Allison reached down and felt the grass. She grabbed a handful of earth and held it to her face. I reached under my shirt and pulled the necklace off in one motion.

"This is for you," I said, outside the church.

There was a crowd of people clapping — I imagined — and her new wedding dress shimmered in the light. She had a white veil, and I brushed it aside.

Allison stared up. She looked confused.

"This is my first breath," I said, holding out the clear quartz necklace. "This is waking up. I've been waiting for so long, Ally. So long. And I know it now. I love you."

She leaned forward, and I draped the stone around her neck.

"Kaia… It feels like…" She closed her eyes. She didn't smile. "I'm waking up."

"We'll go anywhere," I said. "Anywhere you want. I'll be happy anywhere. I'm not gonna lose you again. I'm never gonna…" I stopped as my voice broke into glass shards.

Allison exhaled. The wedding party rushed around us.

"Anywhere but here."

CHAPTER 21
NAOMI WOODS

Before they came out of the church building, I was pacing back-and-forth. Cliff was on the ground, still. Somebody was tending to his leg. I guess he'd been shot during all the chaos, a ricochet bullet.

And I guess I hit him. He had a bruise on his cheek. But I couldn't find any part of me that felt bad. I couldn't feel anything except worry. A crushing anxiety, pain in my chest. The sun was blowing up the world, and I paced around, waiting for it.

Sheriff Wheeler was sitting against a tree. Nobody tended to him because he didn't have any physical injuries. I walked over there at one point and sat beside him.

"Naomi…"

"What is it?" I asked.

"You ever…" His face was twisted in a strange way. His bottom lip quivered. "You ever think about this place in twenty years? Thirty years? After we all… we're all dead. You think this place is ever gonna exist?"

"I think it'll all be fine, Sheriff," I lied to him. "Take it easy, okay?"

"But it feels…" He took a hundred shaky breaths in a moment.

"Feels like my chest's gonna cave in."

"It won't, Sheriff. It's all gonna be fine."

He nodded. "But you promise?"

"I promise."

I'd never seen him like that, and I didn't think it changed anything, but it did make me wonder.

This house owns us. All of us.

Staring at our scene — the sniveling sheriff, my hunched-over husband, and Jeremy Adams preparing for a war — I only had one thought. New Haven stretched out below us. A fleet of cars rolled through the hills. There were long shadows in the grass and a cold voice settled in the space between my ears.

We all have debts here. Our time is running out.

I wanted to run inside, crash through the front door, but I knew we weren't in charge. We never had been. In these hills, with this house, we never had a choice.

When they came out of the church — my baby, her baby, and Rhys — there was a whole group of us standing around. Mostly cops — so many of them, most had come from Brooksville — but plenty of people from town showed up, too. Hauling shotguns out of their pickups. I guess Jeremy had called the whole phone book. He was mustering an army.

I stuck right beside Kaia and Allison as soon as they came out. Once I saw their faces, I knew I couldn't leave. Cliff was there for a moment, and then he sat with Nate. The cops had Rhys off to the side, questioning him. I wasn't sure I'd ever seen a little kid look so afraid. While they were pointing and shouting, he shrunk back against the tree bark and shriveled up.

"Thank you for letting me go," Kaia said at one point.

"I knew I could trust you to be okay in there," I lied.

They brushed past my daughter and took Allison away for

a minute. The paramedics. I saw Kaia tense up, and I rubbed her back.

The paramedics had Allison by a Brooksville ambulance with the back doors wide open. Her parents showed up. Both a little heavyset, dressed up nice, and sweating out months of pain. When their eyes met, Allison's face changed. Her mouth opened up real wide and tears started pouring like I'd never seen. They hugged and kissed, and Kaia watched from beside me.

"Do you think she knows?" Kaia asked.

"Knows what, honey?"

"That…" She paused. "That they stopped looking for her."

"No, I don't think she does. And I don't think she ever should."

—I wondered briefly about Malaki's parents. What they were doing right now. When they would find out.

After a few minutes, her parents stepped aside. Allison was sitting perfectly still while the paramedics poked and felt her, took her vitals, stammering to each other. They were rushing around like ants.

The whole scene on the hill was so intense—cops and paramedics nearly trampling each other. Way too many white men, all clustered together, and a chunk of them were just sticking their fat noses in our business. That's how it was in small towns. Anytime something happened, a whole bunch of mosquitoes started running around and taking bites.

But this was family business. Our family and Allison's. It had nothing to do with the New Haven gnats.

"I haven't seen her mom since our graduation party," Kaia said quietly. She was staring at Allison through the bundle of paramedics and family. "She looks… so much older."

"Everyone does," I said. "Her, Allison… us."

Kaia laughed. It wasn't forced. It wasn't unsteady. She

genuinely laughed.

"I guess it *hasn't* been the best summer of my life."

I couldn't help but grin. Then I saw the expressions on her parents as they waited. Biting their fingernails, rubbing their foreheads. They looked in agony until the paramedics moved aside—throwing up their hands—and Allison reached weakly for her parents. They closed in, and I couldn't see any faces.

"The paras…" I shook my head. "They've never seen nothing like her. Nobody goes in there and comes out alive."

Kaia smirked. "I've done it twice. You've done it once."

"But nobody's in there as long as her."

Her smile faded. "She looks okay, though."

"I think her body will be okay. But her mind…"

There was a silence I didn't know how to break. I looked around and saw Sheriff Wheeler. He was now sitting near the second ambulance. He had a blanket over his shoulders and a dozen people around him. But he was staring at the ground and shaking.

"I heard that…" I cleared my throat. "Malaki's dead?"

Kaia nodded. "He gave himself up. To that…"

"Monster," I said. "I saw it, too. I've seen it before."

"And you never told me?"

I dropped my eyes to the ground. Another pause. "I never thought…" I took a deep breath and met her gaze. "There are lots of things I haven't told you, Kaia. But I'll tell you everything now. As soon as… we can process this. Soon. I'll tell you everything I saw in there. Soon."

She huffed. "I'm not really mad about it. I guess… we all find out different, right? But I still can't believe Malaki did that. I wasn't… He just ran, and he told me to stay… He helped me do it. Find her. Somehow, he helped me."

"And Rhys?"

"I don't even know, Mom. I'm not… sure about all that." She crossed her arms and watched. "I'm just happy she's back. I'm happy it's all over."

Allison waved her down. I saw her motioning and felt Kaia tense.

"I'm gonna ride with her to the hospital," she said. "I already talked to her. Is that…"

She stopped before asking.

"Do it," I said. "You should. And when you get back—after we can process all this—when you and the boys can really listen—we'll talk about everything."

"Okay, Mom." She leaned over and hugged me. She smelled like dirt and sweat. "I'll call you when I can."

And she took off, running toward the ambulance.

As soon as she went, Nate came over. He pointed back at Sheriff Wheeler and asked, "What's wrong with him, Mom?"

I didn't answer at first. The ambulance doors were closing behind Kaia. I saw Allison's parents walk over to their car as the Brooksville logo shrank. Kaia and Allison rode the hills again, this time heading home. I thought I'd be afraid for her to go. When the time came, though, I was just happy she could.

"What'd you say, honey?" I asked Nate.

He nodded toward the sheriff. "He's… like, mumbling and stuff. He kept saying, 'Find him. Have to find him. He's in there.' I don't know. It's weird."

"I think he's just in shock, baby. He was really scared. And he… He'll be okay."

"Jeremy said he's probably done," Nate went on. I assumed he'd really come over just to tell me this. "After all that. Said the sheriff's probably gonna retire."

"Sheriff Wheeler? There's no way. He'd die before he…" I looked down at him. "Hold on. Jeremy said that?"

"Yeah. He did."

When I looked away from him, I saw Rhys staring at me. He was backed up against a tree. The deputies had left him alone and were congregating a few feet away. Behind their backs, Rhys raised his eyebrows at me.

I cocked my head. Nate turned around and saw him staring.

"What do you think about him, Nate?"

Nate sighed and shifted to face me. I saw Rhys watching us intently.

Can he read lips? I wondered. There was so much I didn't know about the boy and so many questions that I'd been ignoring. They were starting to burn.

"I think he's a good person," Nate said.

"Do you trust him?" I asked.

"I think so. But…"

"But what?"

Nate shook his head. "Nothing. It's not important."

He saved Kaia, I thought. *He's only helped us. Only brought good things.*

"I think we need to figure out where he came from," Nate said, his voice shifting. "As soon as we can."

"Yeah… I think you're right." I shook away those thoughts. "Don't worry, honey. Me and your dad will figure it out."

About an hour later, I was driving Cliff and the boys home. My husband was still alive, and he didn't have a blanket on his shoulders, but he'd been really quiet ever since Kaia and Allison came out. I didn't bother trying to break the silence.

"I told the cops I got lucky," Rhys admitted as we left the house behind. "But I lied to them."

"Then what really happened?" Nate asked.

In the rearview mirror, I saw them exchange a look.

"That house has lots of power. Always interested me. So, I've snuck in there lots of times before. When I was younger, too. I knew how to get to Allison, but I couldn't do it by myself."

"I think we need to talk about that, Rhys." I cleared my throat. "Not now. But… soon."

He nodded. He stared into my eyes and never blinked.

"And I've got things I need to tell you, too." I paused and turned to Cliff. "Boys, when Kaia gets back…"

Cliff raised his eyebrows but didn't speak.

"I need to tell you all," I went on, "what happened to me in there. What's inside."

Rhys didn't react, but Nate looked shocked. Behind him, I saw the house shrinking into the distance. The sun was setting now, lowering behind it. A shot of orange was spreading into our blue sky.

When we left it behind that day, I told myself, *I won't make the same mistake as last time.*

Last time, when I thought it was over.

Last time, when I didn't tell the children what I knew.

This time—next time—I was going to be prepared.

CHAPTER 22
KAIA WOODS

A week after - Halfway through July

I'm coming now, I texted her. *Be there in an hour.*

I was in town. I'd driven the boys and dropped them off so I could take Mom's car to visit Allison. Smith, I took to his house. He'd been hanging out with Nate and Rhys a lot over the last week. Despite his cast, they got into all sorts of stuff. The three of them seemed like best friends.

They were always talking about school coming up soon. My parents were planning a shopping trip to Brooksville before then—these days, it took them forever to do anything. Always bickering or not talking at all.

They'd agreed on one thing: letting Rhys stick around, I guess. So, he'd joined the baseball team. And those three were always messing around at our house. Yelling in the backyard as they hit baseballs or yelling downstairs as they watched TV.

With the boys always rowdy and the deafening silence between my parents, there was never a calm moment at home.

But with her, it was like all the puzzle pieces fit together.

Whenever I got the chance, I took off like a bullet and left New Haven. It was a familiar drive by now: crawling down Main

Street, hitting the speed limit sign, pressing on the gas. An hour of asphalt and yellow lines separated us.

I listened to music whenever she couldn't call. I thought about her lips.

Over my visits, she'd been revealing what happened. Little by little. Allison couldn't talk for long, and she couldn't remember much at first, but it came back. Bits and pieces. I listened to her, mostly. I didn't have anything to add. I would lay beside her on the white bed with plastic sheets, holding her hand. And we cried together. Laughed together. We remembered how things used to be and thought about how they'd turn out.

"It's so hard," she said. "It's so hard to wake up."

"It's okay, Ally. I'm here for you. Hundred percent. We're gonna get through it."

I kissed her tears and held her for as long as they'd let me. Then I'd drive home in the darkness and listen to the same fifteen songs I had before. When I came near New Haven and started to recognize the farmhouses, I could barely stand it.

—A dense sick in my stomach. A closed hand around my throat.

"I need you so much closer than this," I told her in the hospital bed. "So much closer."

"I'm not going anywhere." She reached around me and squeezed my sides. She was getting her strength back now. One day at a time.

July sixteenth was the last day I really thought about Malaki. Right after I dropped my brothers off at the baseball field— "Dad will be here to get you, not me, remember!" —I turned right onto Main Street and saw Malaki's dad walking into the sports bar. He looked over, and I swear he saw me through the window.

Why'd you do that, Malaki? Why'd you save me and her after you tried to kill us both?

Some things still didn't make sense. What my dad said about the monster there — the way it turned back after a whistle — disturbed me. Or why Malaki had given himself up. How Rhys could do what he did. He told us all his parents were dead. I didn't know if I believed him, but he said he'd been with an abusive uncle and ran away from Brooksville.

Good enough for us, I guess. He stayed, and he enrolled in the local middle school with Nate.

There was Sheriff Wheeler, too. He wasn't doing very well. Rumors were he'd retire soon. Leave the sheriff's department. If he ever made it out of the hospital, anyway.

But it didn't matter much to me. Mom was gonna tell us later that week about what happened. Whenever I didn't go visit Allison. I'd been up in Brooksville every day since I got her out, but I promised her, this weekend, I'd stay home. We'd all talk. We'd hear everything she had to say.

"I want you to be ready, Kaia," she told me. "We've gotta be careful and we've gotta watch out for the signs."

"Mom, it's okay. We're okay now."

She never looked okay. But she lowered her head and moved on.

"There has to be a next time," she told me. "There always is."

"Okay, Mom. But let's not worry right now. Let's finish snapping these beans. Got strawberries to wash, too."

I should've known she was right.

It happened as I drove to see Allison. I stopped at the vintage store on the edge of town to buy the Baja hoodie she'd looked at months ago. Inside jokes were a pretty strong medicine, and I wanted to do stuff for her now. I wanted to do everything for her.

When I came outside, though, holding the hoodie in my arms, two things happened. First, a wave of humidity and heat smacked me. It felt like stepping into a sauna. Next, I looked at my mom's green Malibu and got deja vu.

Stuck between the windshield wiper and the glass, there was an envelope.

I rushed over and pulled it out. Once I'd jammed my keys into the ignition and twisted, I cranked on the AC and opened the dirty, yellow paper.

Kaia,

Your bravery is astounding. I admire your courage, dedication, and love.

Do not think, however, it was by chance.

Never has someone impressed me like you. Not in all these years. I'm sorry for this next step. It pains me. And those close to me. You have left us no choice.

Find solace in her — your Allison — because what comes next will take everything you have to offer. You have debts to pay. And you will.

S.H.

ACKNOWLEDGEMENTS

Two down, one to go.

If *The Misery House* was the beginning of this journey, I'm finally on steady ground with *The Silent Forest*. I had so many ideas for this book. My planning page was overflowing, and some of it got bumped to Book 3. I can't wait to show you everything in store. But this novel wouldn't exist without the help of some rather incredible people.

My dad is always my first reader, and he always gives incredible feedback. Afterward, I got some help from fellow authors, such as Evan Myers who writes exciting thrillers and is also an English teacher and dear friend. Next, Theresa Jacobs gave some plot development tips, and Jordon Greene helped in a plethora of ways, including formatting this book.

Aspire Book Covers created the perfect cover for this book and they are already working on the cover for Book 3. I couldn't be happier with the outcome. Marni Macrae worked with me to professionally edit the book and improved it many times over. Without her, this book wouldn't have been the same.

I had family and friends who served as beta-readers and

inspiration. I mentioned my mom, my grandma, and my wife in the dedication, but all of them gave this book life without knowing it and inspired me to write about one family, sticking together, in the face of everything. They embody the tenacity, hopefulness, and values that I admire and look up to.

While I hope this book entertained you and the tunnel underground sticks with you, the next one is going to take things up a notch. I've shown you the town, the forest, and everything there is to see. So now, next time, we're going inside the house itself, and we aren't coming back.

This is far from the end.

Thank you to everybody who has made this possible, to everybody who continues to help, and finally to everybody who opened this book and gave it a chance. Without all of you, none of this would be possible. There will be more soon.

ABOUT DAVID KUMMER

David Kummer is a young author who grew up in Madison, a small, southern Indiana rivertown. He grew up in a large household with many siblings and studied English and Education at Hanover College. David is now a high-school English teacher, happily married, and living in New Albany, where he is constantly influenced by the city around him. When not writing, he enjoys listening to indie rock and watching sports, but mostly spending time with family and friends.

VISIT DAVID ONLINE AT

www.DavidKummer.com